Hunger
and
Thirst

Daniela Kuper

Hunger
and
Thirst

St. Martin's Press   New York

www.stmartins.com

Library of Congress Cataloging-in-Publication Data

Kuper, Daniela.
    Hunger and thirst : a novel / Daniela Kuper.—1st ed.
        p.   cm.
    ISBN 0-312-20885-5
    EAN 978-0312-20885-1
    1. Jews—Illinois—Chicago—Fiction.   2. Jewish families—Fiction.
3. Chicago (Ill.)—Fiction.   4. Jewish girls—Fiction.   5. Girls—Fiction.
I. Title.

PS3611.U637H86   2004
813'.6—dc22

                                                                    2004044139

First Edition: September 2004

10   9   8   7   6   5   4   3   2   1

For my mom, Annie

Acknowledgments

Thanks to Michele (Davis) Piel, who knew her way around the old neighborhood, and to Valerie Grant, Linda Erman, and Laura Goodman for their patient editing and encouragement. Thanks to the Ucross Foundation (especially Sharon Dynak), Djerassi Foundation, Natalie Goldberg, Roger Jordan, Ginny Jordan, Marcia Chapman, Mary Cheney Gould, and the Nada Hermitage at the Carmelite Monastery for sanctuary and support. And to my children, Judah Kuper and Sahra Kuper, for believing in me.

Hunger
and
Thirst

One

Today

THE MOTHER RETURNED THIRTY years later like any visitor with a Sunday to kill, ringing the bell, offering up chocolate, gauging the depth of her reception.

The daughter, thinking it was Amway or religion, half shut the door when she noticed that preposterous yellow diamond, a brain caged in platinum. The smear of lipstick on a tooth, the blood-shined fingernails, the garnet watch with the silver safety chain, the same watch her father bought after one of his lousy nights.

The black wig had hardened into pagette points, the long neck pulsed. Irwina was alive, her crystal necklace throwing off the green in her outfit, the blue in her skin, the head tilted down and to the right like this time she'd listen as long as it took.

She carried an expensive-looking carpetbag, a diminutive spin-off from scrappier times and, for her age, she carried herself well.

The mother's arms reached for her, Joan pulled back. This was too much.

She wanted to refuse the chocolates, the mother with no moles, no nothing to mark her but a familiar smell. Lemons and gardenias. The confidence and lack of it in her Hush Puppies, those confused shoes, that mortared soul, the waist blowing into a sea foam skirt with legs that could still make a postcard out of any beach.

But a child's heart, unskilled at anything else, waits. Wants to skip the reunion embrace, the useless talk, rip off the mother's careful linen blouse, the full slip modestly showing through and see down to birth scars. Run her hands over keloid, start over from there.

Two

1941

"GET YOUR FINE SHOES on Winnie I'm taking my girls to the Aragon." Joe. Joe and Bessie wanted Irwina to meet a man maybe even marry up that night, and Joe said hey, if she couldn't find anyone at the Aragon Ballroom there was no end to the places. Arcadia. Dreamland. Green Mill Gardens. Savoy. Trianon. White City. He had his eyes squeezed closed and was counting off dance halls.

Bessie said, "So how come you rattle off places like you own them and I never been?"

"You been, Moose."

"Not to the Savoy I haven't."

"You been, you forget."

"I wouldn't forget the Savoy."

He thrummed her leg. It wasn't so much talk with them as tendon the way her sister poached Joe's eggs at four in the morning before he went to the *Trib*. You want a little egg, she'd say? Every morning and at night a hot dinner. Irwina felt a scrape of loneliness.

"Midway Gardens, Paradise, it's time Winna. Stop reading *Life* kiddo and live, live, live! You been cooped up with Ma so long you're gonna forget how to act in the world," Joe said.

She and Ma in the same two-bedroom, Rose and Bess gone for years, oldest and youngest sisters tucked away and Ma, well Ma would be Ma whether Irwina lived with her or not, "So go on," Joe said, "get the hell out and take a shot." He lit up a Lucky. "Tonight's your night. I'm tasting it."

"He's right for once," Bess smoothed the hairs on her sister's arm like when they were kids. Ma did it too, the stroking to bring her back like staring out windows was a crime.

"So you're here, you two. Your mission is nag till I go, is that it?" She folded the corner of the article she was pretending to read, threw the magazine at the window seat.

"Thatta a girl," Bessie said.

"Gal in your situation can't wait for some momzer gets himself lost climbs three flights slobbers his goodwill all over you," said Joe. "You gotta act babe, you gotta act now."

"Don't put so much pressure," Bessie said.

"You gotta get your mug on the street."

Maybe she had lived with Ma too long. Ma, who never looked past a decent brisket and called America Land of Stinkin' Deals. She gave birth to Rose while Pa was in the same hospital dying. Aneurysm they said, out of the blue they said, and nobody told her till the baby was sucking. She said what kind country gives a new body, takes the tired body held me at night? Who's gonna hold me? She nursed Rose and cried to the relatives crammed into her tiny living room putting back rounds of schnapps.

Three girls, no money. Ma took in boarders, people with doubtful professions and jittery social skills. Irwina could feel the strange things they did behind doors. She watched them eat Ma's food. No matter what they said Ma stood there, a rock holding up a meat platter. They had to share everything with these people. Soap. All the clothes they wore had been somebody else's longer. Their hemlines had concentric creases, age rings marking another kid's growth spurts.

Ma said *sha*. Be quiet in the head or somebody'd hear and they'd be out picking poor-people things from the pile behind Elkin's Drug. Speak when spoken, don't ogle the riches. The sisters got so good at silence they could hold conversations with their eyebrows.

But Irwina never could take her eyes off unworthy hands fingering real pearls, the fat diamond popping off the man's tie while he stared at Bessie's chest and pulled gristle from his mouth, setting it carefully on Ma's white tablecloth.

She wanted what the boarders had. She wanted it so bad if she squinted and concentrated she could make the room go black and lift the pearls off the lady's neck and make them come to her. Ma stroked her arm, a whisper dusty from deep in her throat. "You don't stare like that. They go, where we gonna find more people?"

Ma was tearing chicken from the bone, dropping it into boiling vegetable water, calling steam to her like Sabbath light. Irwina couldn't take it. She wanted new things, things without the memory of somebody else's body. She spoke to Ma in Yiddish to change her mood. "One dress Ma to dance in, then I don't stare." She felt the cold floor through her socks as she cleared each plate of meat back into the roasting pan.

Ma wiped her forehead with the inside of her shoulder. A chicken back. A chicken neck. A parsnip so the food would look original. She shook her head.

"Please, *Mamalah,* one dress that wasn't Bessie's and you'll see I'll take such care it'll last a life."

"Nothing lasts."

"But Bessie and Rose—" And the wooden spoon came down *Wap! Pam!* so fast she never felt pain. The red mark on her cheek would last days.

Ma put the spoon down, wiped her hands on a towel, turned the stock to a simmer, covered it, faced her daughter who hadn't moved. "Get your coat on, we gonna walk," Ma said.

They found a place on a bench in the Hyde Park sun, pigeons tap-dancing for food.

"Listen good to me, Winala. You talk dresses we got strangers at our table, in our beds, eating our meat. You think it goes from that to dresses? You know what it means, work?"

Irwina placed her hand casually to cover the red mark and her embarrassment at this loud public Yiddish.

"Pa dies from their heavy presses. Why? So they get ironed suits. He irons their suits perfect then he dies."

"I thought it was an aneurysm."

"He was a David, a scholar, whole Talmud he knew from his heart." Ma touched her arm. "You listening? Presses killed him, I'm telling you."

Irwina was watching women, making them perfect. This one needed a higher brassiere, a better line, posture. This one had a skirt made her look like a matron. Too much girdle, not enough heel. Cleaver hair. Helmet hair. If only she could tell them, how their lives would change.

"Winna?"

"What."

"You don't listening."

Her cheek hurt like hell.

"Pa had a minute he had a holy book. I told him make a living, books don't feed. I make fun of him. One page he reads day after day. Same page. David, I says, turn already. He says this page is good. Why leave it?"

Irwina felt for crumbs in her pocket, scattered them to the birds. "That's nice."

"Nice? Nothing got more spirit than an unpractical man. In the shtetl we had a problem, we talked. Who I'm gonna talk to here? You? I talk to him."

"You talk to Pa?" Ma had no pictures. Irwina couldn't even give him a face.

"I'm lying in that bed thinking how a roast can go one more day and Pa says to me 'Sara? You weren't so clever when I was alive.'"

"Pa talks back?" Never had her mother spoken of unseen things, things that couldn't be counted and shelved.

"Three girls I raise on nothing. Two take what I got, one wants dresses." Ma gave the pigeons a dirty look. "You speak dresses no more."

So that's where this was going.

"Swear me this."

"Okay. Okay."

"Swear me."

"I swear."

"You got his brain."

"What?"

"I'm talking to you not them. Why? Pa's dreams went with you. Bessie's a doer, Rose kvetches, but you got the brain." Ma gave her a juiceless, chicken hand. Irwina would never let herself get like that. A woman in black walked by. Simple, well-fitted, nice cut. She wanted to follow her, see if the rest of her life looked like that.

"What I say?" Ma said.

"I should run from presses."

"I let Pa read the same page he'd be here with me. Dresses is presses is dresses. Say."

"Let go me Ma, you're hurting."

"Say."

"You putting a curse on me? It doesn't even make sense."

"Curses don't make sense. Repeat!"

"Ma, please."

Ma dug into her arm. "For you the price is big. You speak dresses no more."

And she did not, but what she couldn't say out loud grew big inside her.

Dresses. Shoes. Feathers in hats. Pearls on necks. Silk stockings that demanded white gloves before she slipped them up her thin legs. Perfume. Real perfume, not toilet stuff. Perfume from Paris. Men from Paris. Unseen partners in suits with perfume from Paris and oh it wasn't just the things. They were all right, but it was where things could *take* a girl, how they made her visible. A girl dressed nice, people saw. People listened! Who listened to Rose with her dirty bra strap hanging out her blouse? Rose was

worse than invisible. It was Irwina who could find the creamy
center of a room. And hold it. And keep it there.

Presses is dresses is presses. Ma said it so often it became a hiss in
Irwina's ear canal. She couldn't shop at Fields without hearing
Ma's curse between the shorty coats. She kept her mouth shut
and ironed hand-me-downs like they were organdy, forcing pleats
and darts, changing buttons and when that didn't work she ripped
dresses to pieces and re-sewed them, pushing the old Singer till it
burned.

"Big shot. You always gotta make something outta nothing,"
Rose said. "They're Bess's rags and everybody knows it. They
can smell it on you."

"Nobody has money who should," Irwina said. "What's in
your hand?"

"Nothing." Rose pulled back.

"What're you hiding? Gimme!"

In Rose's fist, Irwina's cultured pearl earring broken from its
clasp.

"Thief!"

Rose popped it in her mouth, swallowed.

The Crash, when people's clothes got thicker, heavier, darker, sad-
der as though the clothes themselves could be made to protect
them. Clothes were not clothes anymore, they had become shelter.
Irwina got her first real job at Formfit Brassiere Company, re-
lieved, buoyed, infused with faith from working near the closeness
of cotton to skin. And she had ideas. Why must the strap of a
brassiere cut into flesh leaving red marks to match those left by the
girdle? She'd had enough of red marks. Where was it written that
a fanny must be made to shrink and submit? A woman's body gave

off enough signals to wake the sexless. This, up! This, in! Tighten! Pull! Lift! Separate! What was the use of cashmere if the foundation underneath crumbled or, worse, surrendered. There was no money, no food, but there were hips and waistlines and the soft promise of bellies to silence the appetite. Enhance! Play! Tease! Offer! The right garment could sing through a horsehair coat.

Formfit ate her ideas like honey. She sketched, she gestured. She dressed nice, designers listened with pencils behind their ears, running back to offices without a thanks. Though her name was never mentioned and her pay envelope grew no fatter, Irwina didn't care. Under dresses, women were wearing her ideas. On an intimate level, the world looked better. Sometimes the manager asked her to model the bras and had the artists sketch as she showed them what was wrong. A thicker bra back, more hooks, more comfort, better lines, longer garters, yes, but with a flap of silk to cover the metal clasp. So simple, so right. Cantilevered support? Her idea. She'd slip in the backroom, take off her clothes and Formit made the dough. Ma thought she took dictation but Bessie knew, and Joe.

He said, "Tonight Winna, the Aragon. You got it somebody oughta see it besides a couple ass backroom bra scribes."

It was a minute before World War II. The Dick Jergens Orchestra was playing with dreamy vocalist Stan Vann. "You'd Be So Nice to Come Home To," "When the Lights Go On Again," and the regularly requested "Boogie Woogie Bugle Boy."

Men in uniform were holding women like it was the last good thing they'd touch, and for a lot of them it would be. Joe pushed Irwina into a ballroom that smelled like people's inside things and what they longed for. Bess and Joe had been there, but Irwina? Such a place? Never.

Joe said, "Eighty thousand feet of orgiastic dance pleasure." Bessie slapped him. He smiled. "Aw Moosie, it cost 'em over a mill with that freshwater cooling system? So no wonder."

"Cooling system," Bessie said.

"Typical night you got, let's see, you got about eight thousand bodies. Say. Winna. Those odds even you oughta find a guy."

She wasn't listening. Irwina was lost in minarets of silver and huge granite walls covered with ancient arabesques of gold. Moorish carvings and scrollwork like Old Spain. She wanted to wear the walls, drape the palm trees. Palm trees! And above that ANOTHER FLOOR with uniformed matrons looking for underage women sneaking booze or smokes. They had tuxedoed floorwalkers to prevent close dancing, but nobody listened that night. And above that, SKY. Flesh clouds, stars that blurred from the wet in her eyes.

The floor was so crowded with couples it looked like one uniform, and while she was dancing Irwina was saying no to every man whose eyes caught on the dip in her waist or the real leather strap over her ankle. No no no no until one by one they left her for the White Blouse Betties who had that special something, and Irwina didn't care to know what it was. The band got more brilliant as the night moved along. Women were sly eyeing the horn man as he dumped spit from his instrument and Irwina could smell people's wet coming out for each other, hear the ocean that would sit between these men and women, see gray battles these men couldn't imagine, battles that would fold into one big war where a man didn't care anymore and he'd pull out a photo of White Blouse Betty, risk a match to see her like she was tonight.

He was in the corner, smoking, only decent suit in the place, hair like she had to touch it. He was coming toward her, the only live thing in the place, this man, coming for her, tossing his cigarette on the floor, stomping it like part of a dance, grinding it into burled walnut, leaving a mark so years later when nobody heard of the Aragon or even believed it existed, a janitor would curse the mark, the only imperfection in his nightly cleaning ritual.

In a woman's life there is only one first dance.

Irwina didn't see the small no of Joe's head or Bessie's arm coming up on its own to hold her sister back. What she saw was good wool, a decent job, and his hands, the dry sure of them.

"Name's Buddy Trout. Dance with me doll."

Woman didn't have to think to answer.

They had the fit from the get-go. Hips and neck, feet and parts knowing how to be with each other. She filled her body with his scent, a natural lavender and mace from his pores to hers. She memorized how his hair made a point to the right center of his neck, the extra tag of skin, how his hair lay over his stiff collar. This was Unseen Partner. She dreamed him and brought him to her, this man whose hands held her just shy of pain.

"I'm gonna know you," he said.

She willed her hips into sophistication.

"Whatta you like most about this place?" Buddy talked to her hair and she became visible.

"The palm trees," she whispered.

"You seen the bathroom? Real French boudoir, maybe you like that better."

She'd touched the palm trees, they felt like honest-to-god bark with coconuts hanging from them. All she'd seen was Illinois, South Haven and the water show at the Wisconsin Dells. No, she was sure. Palm trees.

"Coconuts, huh." Buddy pulled her tight to him, his arm reaching around her waist. "I'm the one can give you coconuts."

At the break she stood out front with Bessie and Joe, Bessie fanning herself with a clutch bag that did her no good against the muggies.

"Air so wet a guy could fish." Joe took his jacket off. His summershirt was soaked. It stuck to his undershirt and showed every hair on his chest. His beard was showing too, even though Bessie made him shave right before. She made him shave every ten minutes, but his beard never left and his thumbs were permanently inked from working at the *Trib*. They both stared at Irwina, not knowing what to say.

"Here, Winnie, hava Schlitz." Joe handed her a sweaty cold one, but Bessie grabbed it and guzzled. "Say something to her Joe, you know, like we talked in there. Tell her."

"Gimme my beer Moose. You need water. I'll get you water, but here, gimme that thing back, I'm dying."

Bessie waved him off. "Talk to her. You know what I'm saying." She raised and lowered her eyebrows, held the beer out of reach.

"Man those women in there I'm telling you, poker hot and ready to rock." Joe wiggled his hips, fluttered his lashes.

"A regular Miss Boop," Irwina laughed.

Bessie finished off the beer. "Where'd you pick up the ooh-la-la stuff? I'm throwing out your girlie magazines." She kissed him. "Every *Argosy,* Buster Keaton."

"Aw jeez shoptalk, Moosie. You know guys shoot off, specially the night guys." Joe winked at Irwina.

Bessie tossed the bottle one handed into a trashcan. "Okay so I'll tell her. Winna, see, we, me and Joe, we got a feeling about that man you was dancing with, don't we Joe? And it ain't a good feeling."

"I danced with a lot a men."

"That last one."

"So. What."

"So Joe hates the looks of him."

"Moose!"

"Well, honey, I don't much like it either. He's . . . smooth."

"You said be less picky."

"Not that less picky."

Joe popped another beer and lit a Lucky.

Irwina reapplied her lipstick, speaking into her compact. "If it's meant to be, you know how Ma says things are right, they're *basherte.* Maybe this is my big fat *basherte.*"

"Yeah but that don't mean it don't hurt," Bessie said.

"Let her be," Joe said. "We'll see what's what."

"One dance you don't get a man's life history," Irwina said.

Joe laughed. "Sure you do."

Bessie jabbed him. "Talk."

"You're makin' a federal case a this," Joe said. "Oh okay. Awright look. Winnie. Men. Some men they got other things on their mind. Well no, that's not right. Okay. Men. Men got other things on their mind, it's just some men, some men have more of the one and less of the other."

"Good Joseph." Bessie sighed out his name.

"I dance with a guy once you peg his soul? What is with you two? I come here to get you off my back you nag me worse than home."

Joe searched the street for words, looked to the stars touching the Chicago skyline, not so nice as Aragon sky but decent. Pretty soon they forgot they were waiting for any particular words and the band was calling them with "These Foolish Things" and Bessie shrieked, "*Yank in the R.A.F.* with Tyrone Power and Betty Grable" and all that was written in the great Akashic and in the small scratch pad of what if, taking into account the probable edge of free will over determinism, would simply come to pass.

A week went by. Bess brought Ma Bibb lettuce and the *Jewish News*. She sat on the old couch picking tufts of horsehair from a hole in the arm, making nice talk with Irwina, circling her like a B-1 bomber.

"You look tired Bess. The baby still getting you up at night?" She'd been trying to wean him.

"You're the one's out every night," Bessie said.

"Ma talked to you?"

"I got eyes."

"Yeah. And."

"I'm saying. Can't I say?"

Bessie had worked the couch stuffing into a snake, which the baby gummed and spit out on the floor. He pawed Bessie's blouse till she undid two buttons and flopped out a half-hearted breast.

"You still have milk?"

"You should give this guy up temporarily, I'm saying."

"Still with the guy, you don't even know him."

"I know plenty. You love this man?" Bessie didn't wait for an answer. "Love stinks. Love makes a woman a moron."

"Last week you were selling it cheap."

"With the right guy." The baby patted Bessie's breast like he concurred.

"You and Ma."

"Truth's truth. What's his name anyway?"

"Buddy Trout."

"A fish. Jew?"

"Would that make you feel better?"

"No. How's Ma?"

"She got her eyes tested at Weiss. I gave her cab money she took three streetcars."

"What'd they say?"

"Cataracts."

"I coulda told her."

The baby was sweating. Bessie pulled off his sweater, him sucking the whole time.

"You look good Win, lousy sign."

"He's got money."

"You been to Fort Knox? You touched it?"

"I have three gardenias in the fridge."

"Whoo boy."

"Enough, you little *momzer*." Irwina pulled the baby off Bessie with a loud pop. His mouth was still working. Bess's nipple let out a few sympathy drops. "You want real milk? Auntie Win'll give you a whole glass you'll die of ecstasy."

Bessie opened a window. The fresh air screamed with kids playing and made the apartment seem older, dustier. Fall was in those screams, everything those kids had to get out before school corked them.

"You met his parents?" Bessie said.

"It's been a week. I haven't even seen his socks."

An image sharp as hunger. Buddy's face over her naked hip. Afterward, decent Italian. They'd open a dress shop together, plans were firmed on napkins. Irwina knew where they could get a three-way mirror that made life look better than itself. Buddy knew where to get the classics.

"They're gonna come doll," Buddy said. "West Roger's Park, hell, Highland Park. We call it Buddy's Frock Shop, we get your Chanels, your coats with silk linings. I know this guy who puts in their initials. Purses with their goddamned initials! Even Field's don't do that. Buddy's Frock Shop'll bring 'em home."

She licked her finger, wiped tomato sauce off his mouth. He traced the migration of women with his cigar. The skinny waiter mistook this for a request and stared into their full wine glasses confused.

"Don't go nowhere." Buddy emptied his in two gulps. "Get the good stuff it'll do the work for you. I learned from Pa." Buddy sniffed at his ash, relit it with his silver lighter.

"Aren't you just so nervous?"

"Me? Naw."

"I mean it takes a lot of dough," she said.

"My dough, your gorgeous brain, doll we're travelin'."

She had sixty-five dollars and owed more than that. Buddy said he could put his hands on ten grand. She never asked how. Ten grand. Ten grand. Say it enough it wasn't money anymore.

Bessie wasn't impressed. "He got family?"

"His parents are dead and he's got a brother, Nate, an architect in California. The father was in the dress business."

"He tips waitresses?"

"Of course he tips. He tips big."

"He looks at them when he tips?"

"In the face?"

"This is important."

"I don't know. Yeah. Yeah, he looks."

"That sailor with the dry-cleaning business, what happened to him?"

"You hated him."

Irwina rubbed her mouth over the baby's hot cheek. He laughed. Where had this baby come from? How did her sister get a child like this? Blond hair, flaming cheeks like he fell from Hans Christian Anderson. What could she tell Bessie so she'd understand?

"Buddy's got a great walk. Look at me." Irwina set the baby on Ma's faded carpet. He tried to pick up the pattern.

"Look at me one minute." She lifted her chin, threw back her shoulders and walked the walk of a king with a full shopping cart between his legs.

"You been alone too long. Woman over thirty-five can't think so good. It's the egg situation."

"Oh my god."

"Joe was, how old was I? Fifteen? Sixteen? I seen him I knew. Rose? Same with her Louie. Our brains were tick tick tick. See? It's the eggs. Is this daddy for me? Eggs talkin'. You dropped too many eggs, what you got left can't pass an IQ test."

A house no father, where was it written that the older sister had to grow chin hair and hold the family like a man? Her sister's face worked through its worries. Irwina slept with the Buddy's Frock Shop napkin under her mattress. Nobody would understand how he touched her, their unbearable love.

Silence.

The family sat in Bessie's living room listening to lox curing. Irwina turned on a lamp. Ma turned it off.

"Wait a little," Ma said, "it's not time yet."

"It's dark, Ma," Irwina said.

"Too early for the electric."

Silence.

Say something! Somebody say something!

Habits left from hiding. They were the Ann Frank family. Potato eaters. Gristle pickers with no need for social. She was ashamed. The entire family annoyed her. The baby annoyed her. Lou with his belly rising and falling like he breathed through it. Rose with her doomed look. Joe's thick fingers. Their shop would have skin colors and natural light. She had to get out of this place. Even with the lamps on it was dark from the crabby ancestor portraits hanging high enough to kill a neck. Rose's gray bra strap hanging down. Bessie with her legs around the chair like a man. Ma opening and closing her purse, no idea what she was doing. Joe's filthy fingers. Lou with that belly. How did they make love with that thing between them like a baby, like a—like a stale bialy? SAY SOMETHING!

Rose broke off a piece of banana and shoved it in the baby's mouth.

"So what's a guy like you do for fun?" Joe said.

Every face on Buddy.

He told her before they came, he said if this was gonna be some kind of test he'd flunk it before the first question. He wasn't a test kinda guy. He was real life, and if her family couldn't see this, well, they'd learn.

"Last week he took me to the Orpheum." Irwina smiled. "Didn't you honey."

Buddy slid his hands over his knees a few times.

"What she say?" Rose asked Bessie.

"Opium." The sisters stared, horrified.

Joe rubbed his stubble. "Say. You got any interest in the horses? Wanna go to Sportsmen's Park, put aways a few bucks with me sometime?"

Irwina tried to catch Buddy's eye. What was the matter with everybody? She put her hand on his knee. Took the hand back. This silence was making her sleepy. She needed his words to wake her. Fit. Zoot. Jake. Doll.

"So. That was some show at the Aragon, huh? Helluva thing they put on. You go dancin' much?" Joe said.

"Why, you wanna take me dancing with you?" Buddy said.

The baby put the mushed banana in his ear. With one elegant movement, Ma scooped it out and started singing. *"Oyfn pripit-shik, brenta fayerl. Un in shtub is heys."*

"I think we should eat," Irwina said.

"Ma's singing," said Rose.

"I know Ma's singing Rose. I can hear Ma's singing."

"Un der rebbe lernt kleyne kinderlech." Ma sang like a curse.

"Chick chicky manna," the baby wailed.

"We eatin' in the dining room or what?" Buddy with his double-wide lapels, same tailor as Capone. "You got a nice table goin here, walnut if I'm not mistaken."

"We eat in the kitchen," Joe said.

"Got that when we were married. From Joe's boss," Bessie said.

"Table like that you oughta eat on it." Buddy looked at Irwina, who looked at Bessie, who looked at Joe, who said, "Dining room's for funerals and guests. Kitchen's family."

"And it's easier with the baby and everything," Bessie said.

Ma, singing her head off.

Irwina took out the linen napkins she'd ironed in preparation. "Dining room would work," she said to Bessie. "Dining room table's a little higher, maybe the baby would—"

"Man can't bend his knees?" Ma said.

Joe pulled Bessie aside.

"Joe? What am I gonna say?"

"Nothing kiddo, nothing. Your sister's happy the guy don't have to win a ribbon. Keep your mouth shut, make me a promise."

The sisters composed platters of cold chicken, potato salad, coleslaw, sliced new pickle and rye bread while the baby yanked at Bessie's dress, a look of mournful intent in his eyes. Bessie didn't have a bone in her body that could say no.

"It's not going so bad." Irwina carved radish rosettes with a small paring knife, working it in concentric circles without cutting off any chunks. She'd dunk them in ice water so they'd open like petals.

"Here gimme the salad they're starving out there," Rose said. "Will you give me the damn potato salad?"

"It takes a minute for the radishes to bloom and it'll be perfect."

"It doesn't need to be perfect. It needs to be potato salad."

"You know the difference between your Buddy and my Joe?" Bessie licked mayo off her fingers and settled with the baby in the kitchen window seat, a place the sisters fought over. Ma liked it too. She said it was the only place a person could see somebody else's life for a change. Irwina slipped in next to Bess and gave the baby her finger to suck. He smelled sweet and sour. "I'll tell you the difference. Joe does what he says, Buddy says what he does."

"And this is brilliance?" An ache like something was trying to rip the walls of Irwina's stomach.

"Joe's not much on the outside, but if I have to throw up—"

Irwina made a fart sound on the baby's neck, sending him into fits of laughter. "Your mama is so refined. We know the throw-up story."

"—he holds my head all night over the toilet never complains. Some men they don't know the inside of a diaper. He gives me every penny no funny business, lets me stick my feet between his legs when they're freezing."

"Ma, what're you doing with my napkins?" Irwina said.

"Sit. Sit. I'm getting tea," Ma sang.

"I ironed those. Bess what's she doing with the napkins?"

"Ma, what're you doing with the napkins?" Bessie said.

"She's getting tea," said Rose.

Ma put the napkins in a drawer and counted out paper. *"Roshinkes Mit mandeln,"* she sang.

"What's she doing?" Irwina said.

"Ma."

"I spent all morning ironing those things, tell her to stop. I can't believe she's doing this. One small attempt to dress up the family—"

"Stop Ma."

"Man says when you're married Winnala you don't visit me so much. Once a month he says, I'm lucky."

"Married? Who's talking married?" Irwina said.

"Man says—"

"Stop calling him that. It's Buddy."

"—distance is good for family. I tell him distance is good for runners and telephone calls. Nothin' else."

"You said that?" Bessie laughed.

"Mr. Valentino. He can eat like we eat," Ma said.

Lox. Smoked sable. Tomato and red onion slices. Black olives. Green olives. Half-sour pickles. The family stuffed and grabbed. Buddy Trout had fine manners: Cut, put the fork down, change hands, chew. Irwina made herself eat the same way, the two of them, one movie.

He took her to the good places: the Oriental, the Apollo, the Orpheum with its two dozen ushers. At the Chez Paree, they had a photo taken at long table with women on one side, men on the other. She had an orchid corsage. At the South Side Trianon they danced to the music of Sammy Kaye.

"This night's a tribute to democracy," Buddy said, which confused her because except for the trombone there wasn't a Negro in the place.

He said every woman should get to know the lounges at Marshall Field's and personally showed her how she could send telegrams, cablegrams, get hotel reservations, theater tickets, railroad timetables. In her new life, she told herself, there would be a great need for cablegrams. Buddy taught her the proper way to sit at a writing table and accompanied her, the only man at a women's fashion show. When the models walked past them at eye level down the carpeted runway, he whispered, "Best show in Chicago, doll, cooking classes too. I found a storefront for us, Roger's Park, east over by the lake. Morse Avenue. They got a deli that draws, and they're not asking much." He moved her hair back, kissed her light on the ear. "You only knew how I much I loved you. And no more worrying about dough. They all remember Pa. He was in the business. You say Trout doors fly open."

"Where was his store?"

"Jew Town. Maxwell. What, you think they built him a nice building on Michigan? Mansion on the Gold Coast? A cart and a rack but fine things, not shlock. I want that for us, baby, real wool, classical music comin' out their ears and only the names. Balmain. Jacques Fath. Dior. Stuff Hattie Carnegie would touch."

Irwina refolded her legs, fanned herself with the program. He had check marks on his, the half-pencil sweating in her hand.

"A few ready-to-wears, sure, but gimme the Frenchies gimme. Schiaparelli. Vionnet—"

He was using her words. Chanel. Patou. Schiaparelli. Vionnet. Sex on her tongue. She'd been studying the fashion pages since she was fourteen but out loud? *Wap! Pam!*

"Me and you uptown upscale shee-shee, whaddya say? Woman with your flair could do it sleeping."

That night, they danced the Aragon to sleep. Only one other couple on the floor and a band so tired they were begging.

"You scared?" he asked. "Tell me the truth."

"Yeah."

"What of? Being alone in a dance hall with me?"

"The names you say like you been lookin' in my dream."

He dropped her back at Ma's. She made black tea with one dip and two sugars and watched the neighbor sleep, man on the third floor slept with his lights on. What was he afraid of? What was she afraid of? People she loved dying. Ma, Bessie, Joe, Rose, Louie, the baby. Buddy's face when his lips shrank and he was so sure she'd dance with him. How did Pa dance? Did Ma dance with him? Did he hum the Ukraine? Pump his hands hard enough to make water?

She sipped the warm tea. Added another sugar.

This is what she was afraid of. That he'd take the heat of his chest and leave her with this family. Courting made her ill, all those gardenias dying in the fridge, all the plans. She wanted REAL LIFE TO HAPPEN. She wasn't afraid of being alone with him, just alone with dreams feeding on her head till she popped.

Irwina woke up to Ma and a neat stack of linens on her bed.

"What's this?"

"The wedding." Ma spit over her left shoulder.

"There is no wedding, we're dating."

"Spit now," Ma said, "later thank me."

Irwina stroked the embroidered bedspread, Ma's careful stitches. How? When? She read the newspaper with a magnifying glass. The white tablecloth hand-cut and edged in smoke-colored thread, two pink percale sheets with matching pillowcases, and the napkins Irwina had ironed for Buddy's visit. The stack was tied with a thick white ribbon. It smelled like Ma. When did she do this? Who did she steal from? She thought she knew every simple thought in this Ma's head. Irwina threw her arms around the woman who said little, knew everything and wouldn't live to see her daughter's wedding. To hold her was to hold something fierce laced under sweater.

Three

Late 1950s–Early 1960s

If we have retained an element of dream in our memories,
if we have gone beyond merely assembling exact recollections, bit by bit the house that was lost in the mists of time
will appear from out the shadow.

—Gaston Bachelard, *The Poetics of Space*

FREEDOM, JOAN, ONLY KNOCKED once. A Saturday away
from sighs, regrets, and salmon-colored underwear? From the
mouth-breathing, science fair cousins who spent weekends plan-
ning weeks? From the dead but somehow *there* Uncle Lou who
got crushed in the elevator accident taking all men with names
down with him? TV needed fixing, Auntie Rose called the TV
man. She had a stove man, a toilet man, a furnace man and an
electric man even if they told her it's Bob, ma'am, the name's Bob.
If that door opened Joan would smell the familiar slept-in flannel,
chicken no skin, potatoes no skin. Skin was Auntie Rose's enemy
and eating was the hard-boiled business of staying alive. Iceberg
lettuce cut to a blade dribbled with orange dressing. For birth-
days she provided store-bought vanilla cupcakes with blue candle
wax melted in. Joan would chew till food became a ball of matter
to hide in a napkin. She'd have to sleep with the mother-in-law,
Lou's mother from the old country, in parallel beds of dark ma-
hogany posters holding twin slabs and feather pillows with spines.
And the grandmother snored. It was the only human noise in
that apartment. Joan would make words out of the fits and starts

of those snores. Auntie Rose's. A dry, dreamless place where knowledge was attacked and books lay open resting from battle. A stillborn place where everybody moved like some old fate pushed them around. Lousy way to spend a Saturday, but Sunday was worse. On Sundays Auntie Rose cleaned out the cousins. It was the only time she ever moved fast, a high color to her cheeks, humming as she held the orange rubber bag under the bathroom faucet. And there would be one of the cousins belly down, fresh caught, a cry stuck in her cheeks. Auntie Rose slam-dunked the Ivory soap in the enema bag, ploop! Everything good and clean now. Joan would get caught looking and Auntie Rose would chase her down that hallway, years of women curses slowing her down, sighs cutting her speed to zilch.

She listened at the door. Nothing. FREEDOM. Joan went back to the apartment and called the Slater twins, who came to get her with fists full of candy money and the doorbell double-ringing, yelling because freedom was sweet and yelling made it so.

"IS IT YOU?" Joan screamed down the stairs.

Mr. Dubrow in 2A stomped on his floor, making the chandelier quiver.

"GET DOWN HERE WE GOT BIKES. GET YOUR BIKE," the twins yelled.

"Shaddupa you mout." The Italian on the three who never had a woman over and played tennis with his mother.

"I'M COMING!"

"OKAY!"

"CLAMP IT!" Mr. Dubrow, captain of the hallways, out of work again.

"YOU COMING DOWN? BRING MONEY FOR CANDY. WE GOT MONEY. BRING ALL YOU GOT."

"HOW MUCH YOU WANT?"

"ALL YOU GOT, STUPID. GET YOUR STUPID BUTT DOWN HERE."

Joan saddled her Schwinn and they rode screaming *ahhhh-heeeeeeeee* because it was warm and school was almost over and they had money. The twins screamed because Joan screamed, and Joan screamed because last Wednesday, when it was morning but still dark, Christopher Nobel, halfway through his paper route, tossed pebbles at her bedroom window and the memory of him down there with his arms out, the *Trib* bag slung over his shoulder under the moon made her want to scream and peddle standing.

Joan wasn't used to being seen. She wasn't a stunning double like the Slater twins or brilliantly dull like Auntie Rose's daughters, but Chris was waiting. For her. She listened for her parent's breathing and when she heard Irwina and Buddy give off the sleep rhythm, before she could chicken, she bypassed the hall entry with its paper mailbox names too long to fit and stepped out her window, one impossible leap down to the brick pillar. Her ankles took it hard, but she was up, she was standing.

Chris gave his below-the-belt okay sign. Boy praise. Not a light in the courtyard. Another five-foot drop inside the iron gate, and she had to get it right or the thing'd spear her gut. Chris was looking up at her. God she loved how he didn't wear hand-knit Jewboy vests and put stuff in his hair to make it shine and wore ankle boots instead of Spaldings. She loved his Catholic. He waved. The wind did a movie thing to her hair, the sky broke. Veronica the Pearl Diver. She jumped. A landing like she'd done it a million times. He whacked a newspaper in half over his knee, rubber-banded it, and flung it in his bag without looking.

"You always wear giraffe pajamas?" he said.

And there it was.

She hadn't given it a thought.

Red repeating giraffes on waffle cotton, bottoms above her ankles.

She prayed for Mama's posture to take over and save her. Chin thrust, legs wide, hands anchored on hips she said, "You got a problem with giraffes?"

He smiled. Saint Jerome's rang the six o'clock bell.

"I don't have to stay here, you know. I could leave here, you know."

"Wanna learn to do it?" Slap bang *Trib* over his knee while she tried looking *assured* freezing her ass off watching his dab'll-do-ya hair, that one piece hanging down his forehead, the dirty adhesive holding his glasses together. He set his kickstand down firmly, dismounted and kissed her.

"You're peddling like a maniac," the twins yelled.

"What?"

"Slow down you're gonna kill us. Get off the street." They motioned hysterically to the sidewalk.

"Screw sidewalks." All that stop-start business. Joan hung a right up Ashland toward Morse Avenue, ten inches between the traffic and them. Kill or be killed. Chris tasted like a pencil, clean and smoked. His soft lips opened to other places. Now when she did math homework—

"Joan what are you *doing*?" A car honked her. Girls peddling while standing, against wind, traffic, against— The twins said things she couldn't hear, motioning frantically. Joan pulled over.

"Jesus. Finally. Edie forgot her bike key, we gotta go home," Ruthie said.

"Back home? We can't go back we just escaped. We'll lose the day," Joan said.

"I gotta or somebody'll have to stand outside and watch bikes and it's not me," said Edie.

Unacceptable, not going to Caswells together, not sitting on the floor together arguing candy.

"Okay but do it fast," Joan said.

"If you don't get Mom talking," Ruthie said. "She went to the Art Institute and fell in love with Van Gogh. Tell her you like her Van Goghs then run."

Mr. Dubrow banged his jobless fury on the radiator pipes while the girls slammed around Joan's apartment.

"Wait." Joan never opened her mother's drawers but FREE-DOM, she hesitated. An alarm would go off, a silent alarm bringing a cop, a social worker, a smock, she'd do new math in a cell.

"What are you doing?" Edie yelled. "What's she doing in there?"

"Wasting energy," Ruthie said.

The drawer smelled like gardenias, and Mama's underwear was a tangle of fish. Under a pile of gartered things, mad money. Buddy didn't know it existed. Mama once showed it to her, called it her secret escape hatch, bills wadded thick as a man's fist. If she was ever in desperate need, Mama said.

Joan stripped off a buck.

The Slater apartment oozed small noises.

"What's that sound?" Joan said.

"What. The pigeons?" said Edie.

"Your dad's got pigeons?"

"Pigeons, mice, squirrels, birds—"

Joan saw a family of gray fur huddled in the Corningware.

"They look dead," she said.

"They act dead so he feeds them with an eye dropper. They got him wrapped."

"You ever see a dead squirrel?" Ruthie said.

"On the road?"

"Not car dead, dead dead. Animals get dead they drag the body to a private place and take care of each other."

Being at the Slaters made going home harder.

"Where'd your dad get 'em?"

"He's got a reputation—" said Ruthie.

"—but the pigeons still stink," said Edie.

Ruthie pushed her sister. "Get the key."

The house was filled with Mrs. Slater's statues, including Joan's favorite, the elephant god Ganesh. On the refrigerator was the blue baby Krishna held up by Mizner's Funeral Home magnets. Mirrored tapestries hung above a Charles Russell oil painting of the Old West. Mr. Slater was from Nebraska and loved anything western. His family's furniture was bumpkin massive in the tiny apartment. His great-grandmother's table from the 1800s had pot-sized burn marks waxed by time and was fifteen feet long and cut three rooms in half. It was always piled with birdcages, hamster cages, fishbowls, boxes of animal food, plant food, Mr. Slater's books that fell where his last thought ended, pipes that smelled like rotting vanilla.

Mrs. Slater served red lentil, green dhal, saffron rice and they ate with their hands, except for Mr. Slater, who cut his steak and vegetables before he took a bite. Mrs. Slater was always checking Joan out, which meant feeding her and pumping the twins for information. They never said a word, just kicked Joan gently, rhythmically under the table to make her feel at home. Alone in the twins' room the three girls lay three to a bed, three to an Archie comic, staring at each page till they were done falling into it.

"Mom still wants to live in India. India reeks of sandalwood and jasmine."

Joan never smelled those smells so she settled on sugar pines and Good Humor toasted almond bars.

"Dad says Nebraska smells like pie or pig shit, depending which way the wind blows."

"She's taking us to India. We've only seen pictures—"

"—she takes out her red album when she's had wine."

Van Goghs by the blue baby Krishna, above the sink, taped over real pictures in frames. Van Goghs like Mrs. Slater kidnapped the artist and made him be wallpaper. In the kitchen, a poster of a moaning skull. "I like your Van Goghs," Joan said.

"That one is not a Van Gogh, dear; it is an Edvard Munch." Mrs. Slater gave her the eyes. Chandra Devi Slater, youngest member of a powerful clan known as the women-in-the-building, and she didn't miss much. She'd never rat on a kid, but she'd make them eat vindaloo and hear how she met Keith. Her eyes had light. Mama's eyes were fires with slow roads between.

"Really? The twins said to say that, but I don't mind. What about his work do you like? Tell me." Mrs. Slater had eyes that made Joan want to confess Perry Mason sins so the woman could do something with all her compassion. Once she modeled a sari like orange spun sugar. "I used to be a firefly," she said. "*Zip zap,* you know." She scratched at her wool skirt. Keith liked her to dress American. American itched.

"Oh. I'd have to say uh the colors," Joan said.

"He paints America," Mrs. Slater said.

"Fella's Dutch," Mr. Slater shouted from the den. He had hearing powers. It helped him when mice cried.

"He is forever missing points. You're out? Where is Rose?"

"Not home."

"Do your parents—"

"Yes," the twins said.

"She's gonna talk," Edie said.

"Mom, don't talk."

"In my house—"

"MOM."

"—we lit incense on the puja and looked for offerings. We would walk miles and find nothing worthy. Lakshmi, she was the oldest, she could find great things. Our stones were stones but hers—"

"I think the girls want to go," Keith yelled.

"What else did she find?" Joan said.

"Once, a mushroom so huge she laid it at the feet of Ganesh and waited for god's reward. Do you know Ganesha?"

"The elephant," monotoned the twins.

"My mother got pregnant and blamed this on my sister's mushroom."

Joan must have had a look on her face. Mrs. Slater laughed and hugged her. Such a laugh Joan could climb in, pull it over her head and wouldn't need shelter. People had been giving her things lately, inviting her for dinner, offering to braid her hair, take her to movies. Mrs. Slater held her so long the hug turned sad, a storm everyone could see coming but her. Joan shivered. She let Mrs. Slater take her hand, lead her to the couch, tell her the same story. Joan collected stories and knew more about the women-in-the-building than they knew about each other. But nobody asked.

Mrs. Slater was a Brahmin, Keith a visiting engineer in Kolhapur, and she didn't understand a word he was saying about water filtration systems or sewage processing that make human waste drinkable or garbage that could be compressed into highways, but would he like a little chapati? "Great bowls of dhal I put before him."

Joan could have recited with her. The lime tamarind chutneys, the glutinous rice balls fried honey brown and how three times he made her bring more.

Keith said, "Each time you tell this I'm eating more. I've become a big starving galumph."

"He could identify any bird by its song. One note, that's all he needed." Mrs. Slater patted Joan's hand.

"Mom!" The twins were by the front door.

Apparently Mr. Slater also rolled his curried cauliflower up in kulcha like a burrito, but this didn't prevent Mrs. Slater from staring at his thick hands, fingers yellow from turmeric.

"Aw god, Mom, we're—"

Gone. Outta there.

The twins riding on either side of Joan, bodyguards, piston bodies, pastel streamers past Jew streets of clean-living don't-want-no-trouble people stacked in apartments built around gardens long ago given up to thorn bushes, brown grass, dry fountains of angels. Angels? Fountain water? Who needed this? Only Joan's mother had a fountain of angels that peed blue water day and night.

Girls skimming neighborhoods like fat on broth. Pole, Czech, German, Litvak, each block so loyal they were riding through a series of private rooms. Blocks of Irish Catholic presided over by St. Jerome's, the kiss the pencil ringing every fifteen minutes with longer attributes on the hour. The girls hummed the tuneless bell tune as they cut through alleys.

"You know you want him," Edie said.

"Who," Ruthie said.

"Mud."

"Like I want tetanus," said Ruthie.

"He wants you-oo." Edie smooched the air, riding no-hands so she could hug herself.

"Shut it, fink face. So boys. Is that what we're doing?" Ruthie said.

"Beats my Aunt Rose," said Joan.

They argued three abreast when the street emptied. Mouske- teers, musketeers falling in single file when they heard cars, keep- ing things going, money on a Saturday, sun on thighs, Bermuda shorts with buckles in the back.

"I say we get candy, go to the Granada, see a movie, maybe they'll be there," Edie yelled.

"They're not," Joan said.

They almost smashed into Sazonsky's Sausage truck coming around the corner.

"What a salami," Edie said.

Mr. Sazonsky was laying on the horn. The girls honked back. He was harmless, they knew his story. Only hidden stories could get you. Sazonsky's wife died, and his daughter came to school in white stretch pants stained with menstrual blood as if one thing caused the other. Nobody talked to her, all that bleeding and sor- row. Sazonsky shook his fists and the girls could see his white smiling sausage hat.

Morse Avenue was all a neighborhood needed pressed into three blocks of one-story and basement stores run by old men with accents and fish breath and slacks pulled above their waists. Every day the same stores selling the same things, predictable as relatives. Mr. Leonard sold children's clothing and girls change from a hole in the dressing room. His sign read: Leonard's Chil- dren sWear and he was too cheap to fix it. Horton's Shoes, smooth Mr. Horton with his Brillcream voice let them X-ray their feet blue while the mothers bought Buster Browns instead of the French-heeled Capezios they begged for. Dutch Mill Candies, Geroulis's Shoe Repair, Top Hat Liquors, Ashkenaz (Graab ah teecket! Wait in line!) where waitresses called men doll baby and the good sandwiches were named after comedians. Shecky Green was turkey and lettuce on rye. Joey Bishop, tongue and tomato. Froiken's Knishery with metal trays of hot potato knishes, latkes on the counter, kishke by the inch. Davidson's Bakery, where Thursday was Whipped Cream Day, and Kerrs, where everyone knew the secret: a stick of butter in each burger so it didn't matter about the meat. Rocky's, where the entire Rocky family—dark, tired—worked the counter. Meyer's Cigar Store had big-bellied men clogging the doorway. DeMars, the Greek restaurant on the corner that burned down every two years and changed names but kept the Mars on the end. Morry's Store for Men. The kosher butcher with live chickens in the window. Want this one? Whack Splat Chicken while you wait. Bernice's Beauty Heaven, with a picture window so you could watch women looking horrible getting beautiful. And Buddy's Frock Shop. Joan's store. Here is where it happened. Here it all happened. Her mother's love, her father's love. Hosiery boxes, beige and thin, with tissue curtaining the silk. Her father's dough-re-mi, his spit-silver cash register, his money with the men facing up, the men united.

Mama was in the window, fussing. Possibly this was her best window yet. She painted an indication of a steamship backdrop and had the models in navy and white with champagne and streamers. Dressers were coming down from Michigan Avenue to steal her ideas. Joan would see them outside with their spiral notebooks, breathing on and off the glass. Buddy said cruisewear? For women who never seen a rowboat?

What's so wrong with lifting the denominator, Mama said.

Next you got women in tennis sweaters asking for kreplach. Won't happen. Things are changing. Rome's blazing and you don't smell the smoke.

This neighborhood needs a good goose, Mama said.

Yeah but you gotta go stick the mighty oak up its ass.

"Faster," Joan yelled.

If Mama saw her she'd have to go back to Auntie Rose's. The stolen dollar swelled in her pocket and she didn't look back till their bikes were locked to the parking meter at Caswell's.

They pooled money, careful to set aside enough for a movie.

Six steps down to where Mrs. Caswell sold plastic-coated book covers in flat shiny sheets, tempera paints and it was the only place to get peacock-blue ink cartridges. Twenty feet of Affy Tapples, Dots, wax lips, wax fingernails, Lik-em Ade, buttons on long rolls of adding-machine paper, Slo Pokes, Malted Milk Balls, Junior Mints, Ju Jus, Raisinettes, Charleston Chews, Red Hots, Dots.

They were regulars, but Mrs. Caswell never talked to them. She never talked to anybody. Possibly she lost her voice from years of nonuse. Like Clarabell. Kids made her go to the back for Sputnik bubblegum, then yelled *Fire!* but she never ran, and her lips never came apart.

It was floor to ceiling wooden boxes of anything you could stick on a cake. Gazebos of spun sugar, candied penguins, brides and grooms with different hair. The boys asked for cake toppers so Mrs. Caswell would stand on the stool and they could look up her dress, see where her stockings ended. They'd do anything for a glimpse of the dark world.

"Hey, Mrs. Caswell," the girls said.

She counted out their Grape Fizzies, Pink Owls, jaw breakers, one by one, dropping them on a scale that barely moved, writing the numbers on separate brown paper sacks in red ink. What a life.

The girls sat on the curb picking Pez out of each other's dispensers with their teeth, Edie working a scab, seeing if the pink underneath skin was ready, Joan studying a fly on her shoe that seemed delighted with its front legs. She dug in her bag for more candy, and they discussed what movies were at the Granada, 400, Adelphi and would the boys be playing ball or seeing *Sink the Bismarck*. The fly moved to her other shoe.

"You can't find boys unless you don't want to find boys, then they're all over your face," Ruthie said.

Edie said Ruthie oughta shut her trap, Joan could find whatever she wanted. "Right Joanie?"

Edie believed. Joan pulled out an aqua gumball, closed her eyes and rubbed it elaborately between her palms.

"What's that supposed to be?" Ruthie said.

"Shhh," said Edie, "she's plotting."

"Turning her hands blue is what."

"See anything?" Edie asked.

Joan checked for the fly. Same place. She could sit on that curb all day with the twins, chewing, nothing behind her eyes, nothing on her mind, Saturday sex in the air. She rested. The adults in her life were a distant pageant, their mistaken urgency pulled from her by sugar and time. She could see the boy's baseball game, how the sun made Chris squint and he pitched a spitball gone bad.

"F R E E D O M = S E X." Edie screamed.

"Don't get excited," Ruthie said.

Edie said the boys would want to kiss them. Well not Gock, Gock only wanted to play second for the Sox.

"Loyola Field," Joan said, "that's where I see 'em. We'll sit in the bleachers and— Wait, they're losing."

"You can see that?" Edie said.

"They lost. Shit they just lost the game."

"They'll be in crummy moods," Edie said.

"You believe this stuff?" Ruthie popped a malt ball. "What's the score Houdini?"

"They're, okay, they're on bikes. We'll catch 'em at the beach."

"You're lying," Ruthie said.

"Got a better idea?" Joan said.

"What're they doing now?" Edie said. "Who's riding front?"

"Yeah look in your blue hands and see what they ate for breakfast."

"They're on bikes is all I know."

"Who's in front? Mud? Is he?"

The fly landed on a smooth gray rock. Joan got a funny feeling. "Hey Good Humor man's out, and I say we get toasted coconuts, go to the beach make it look like an accident." Joan brushed off the back of her Bermudas, pocketed the rock.

"Why'd you take that?" Ruthie said.

"Dunno."

The boys were foul. They blocked the girls with their straddled bikes. Everybody straddled, kickstands up, uncertain which way things would go. Last week they all saw *West Side Story* together and the boys were happy just to smell them. Now they were spitting grass and talking like the Jets.

"Jesus what did *you* eat for breakfast?" said Edie.

"Vomit," said Mud.

"You girls are dead meat," said Gock. "Right Mud?"

"Hello to you too." Joan looked at Chris, who pulled his cap low.

Three against three but Mud had teeth rigged like a factory and his night brace yanked back his mouth with g-force.

"Looks like a horse bit slung on a Kotex," Joan whispered, "you're supposed to wear them at home. Alone. In the dark. What an asshole."

"What's that?" Mud said.

"Hey, girlies, you want real action in the alley?" Gock said.

"Oh, like you're real," Edie said. "Maybe you're George Chakaris. Maybe you even know who George Chakaris is."

"Quit pushing Eeed," Ruthie said.

"Spaz," Edie said.

"Ha ha make me pee my pants laughing. We got plans for queers like you," Mud said. "You heard. P-L-A-N-S with a capital P. Who you looking at?"

"The Great Wall of Metal," Edie said.

"Edie!" said Ruthie.

"Think fast." Mud was off his bike, on Edie, pulling her arm behind her back.

"Doesn't hurt, Spaz Brain."

"Yeah?" Mud said.

He pulled higher, tears came to her eyes.

"Hey man, go easy Action Man," Chris said.

That's it. That's who they were, stuck inside *West Side Story* with no Puerto Ricans.

"You say something?" Mud turned to Chris.

"We got better stuff," Chris said. "Cool it."

"He wants you to leave me alone, you stupid piglet. Pick on girls, you oughta go pick your noses." Edie's tears spilled.

"This is unlegal. They'll arrest you," Joan said, "fart brain."

"Won't."

"Will."

"Let's split," Chris said. "Let's scream. Laya patch. Haulass—"

Gock laughed and only stopped when Chris socked him. In the best of times, Gock was a nervous giggler. Joan tried to pull Edie away from Mud, but he shook her off.

"Heh heh you want me to do something, Mud man? I could mess 'em up bad, you know I could." Gock, jumping like a sidewalk on fire. These were the same boys who, last week, put on clean shirts, saved seats, and waited until Tony was dead to put their stumpy arms around them.

"Hurt yet?" Mud smiled.

"Aw fuck let's do something for real for once," Gock said.

"Like leave." Chris tried to miss Joan's eyes, but she caught him anyway. He shrugged, reshaped the brim of his cap.

"How'd you get a name like Mud?" Joan said.

"Melamud. I teach dumb kids like you, so do like I say." The more Ruthie struggled, the tighter Mud clenched. Chris made a move, stopped himself. Joan slipped Ruthie the rock she'd stuck in her pocket.

"My dad's a prizefighter," Ruthie said.

"Your dad's a birdbrain. Ooh I'm scared, I'm running. Ain't that a pip." Mud swallowed, his bony Adam's apple sneaking up for air.

"You shoulda bought boy insurance. Happy Harry Insurance a nickel a pop, then I'da protected you," Gock said.

"Macaroon." Ruthie licked her lips, let them glisten. She could slow down to nothing when she was mad, and now she locked her bike, remembered to turn the combination so it wouldn't spring open, walked slowly toward Mud, her eyes soft. She seemed to grow breasts for the occasion.

"A teacher and you teach what. Torture?" Ruthie rubbed her hand up and down his handlebar in a motion so slow even Gock moaned. She was famous for her unbreakable boy trances, but this? Where did she get this? The boys stared at her hand. Up down, up down.

Chris said, "Look away man, brick wall man, block out your mind."

Let him try for her tongue in this lifetime, Joan thought.

"Stop looking at her, man, you're going soft." Chris put a hand on Mud's shoulder, which had no effect because Ruthie was straddling the front wheel of his bike, rubbing the handlebars, her wet lips inches away.

"C'mon, she's dead meat with cooties on top, right man?" Gock was dancing but Ruthie owned him. Mud was her baby boy. Allied Van Lines could drive a semi through him and he'd be smiling. Ruthie flipped the rock. It plunked him on the side of the head. An obedient trickle of blood followed.

"I love you, Ruth," Mud said.

"Aw god, for crisakes wake up! Let's go to my house, we got groceries," Chris said.

"Don't go saying stuff like that, that's— Hey! The Trout's getting away," Gock said.

Joan was leading them the hell out, boys closing in, catching up, boy sweat in the alley, pencil boys, loser boys, twins peddling home, Joan ducking into the Frock Shop, the Trout piece of safe pie. Joan kept the door from jingling, knew precisely where the balance point was between door and bell. Nobody heard her. Buddy said the shop would be hers someday. She slipped behind the better dresses.

". . . and something before you say no." He was laying out a three-piece red suit for Mrs. Bonfigleo, who loosened her clutch on her purse. "Marie. May I call you Marie?"

Mrs. Bonfigllio felt the material in spite of her financial situation. Cheap. Buddy didn't let her feel too long. He said all women had situations, it was simply a matter of applying the ointment. The right ointment they don't have no more situations, he said. He had ointments for guilt, love, inferiority complexes. His latest ointment was buying clothes off a man in a truck and dragging them in by the bag.

Body bags, mama sniffed. Housecoats, dusters with hems suddenly rising like the seamstress had a revelation on the machine then remembered she had to make a buck.

Those hems, Mama said.

Whose got eyes like that? Who sees? Buddy said.

I see, Mama said.

But I sell, said Buddy, I dress 'em for what they do. Power of positive thinking.

What's positive about a duster? It tells a woman, dust.

Your stuff don't sell, Winna. It plain ass don't move.

Mrs. Bonfigleo's hangnail caught on the material. She tucked her thumb inside her fist.

"Marie. You are Italian am I right, Marie?" Buddy said.

"Sicilian."

"Sicilian. Can a Sicilian pass up the red of a Maranzano? The blush of maraschino?"

"Cherries ain't Italian."

Mama looked up. She was stringing price tags in her gray Chanel suit with the pink silk blouse and freshwater pearls. She had on her wig because it was time for her hair appointment with Bernice.

"And anyway, where'll I wear such a thing? I came for hosiery," Mrs. Bonfigleo said.

"It's not what you think," Buddy said. "Guilt free. Don't take food off the kid plate I say. Eighteen bucks takes it home."

"What's wrong with it?"

"Everything," Mama said under her breath. She put an unmarked tag back in the green glass bowl, smoothed the front of her blouse.

"Say something positive to the lady," Buddy said.

"It's probably fireproof. If you're standing near an inferno—"

Buddy cut her off. "Where couldn't you wear a suit like this is the question. Graduations. Family affairs."

"Not my family."

"Why waste luxury on family?"

"I thought you said it was cheap."

"At the Frock Shop deluxe and cheap hold hands."

Mama made a disgusted sound. Joan wanted it the old way, the way they used to do it. Mama out front, Buddy parting the velvet curtains to the backroom, a room for family only. He'd stop at the cash register to scoop out money, dive into his CB radio—yessir, Charlie Delta Romeo's got a fox in the henhouse—span— Lubbock—rainfall—men reading each other, ten-fouring all over the place—then the backroom would go silent, meaning Buddy had the earphones on and was chewing his unlit cigar stub. Mama didn't want him stinking up the woolens.

Still, it felt good being unseen, knowing how things worked, the cash register waiting for Mama's long fingers to triple keystone, impale receipts through the middle, straight pins with colored heads like teensy summer hats in a silver dish, lavender sachets in every sweater, handwritten labels in shoes so on hot days, the ink rubbed off and the women's feet spelling Buddy's Frock Shop backward.

Mrs. Bonfiglio took a dressing room, her everyday skirt dropping to the floor.

"Can we see you Mrs. B.? Can you come out and show yourself?" Buddy opened Mama's three-way mirror, the mirror that never failed. In the mirror Mrs. Bonfigleo would look dangerous and Sicilian. Outside, a cut-rate Maranzano.

"Anybody else get a turn in that thing?" It was Lil, one of the women-in-the-building, a group of women who knew Mama was different, knew it took a powerful magic to lift her from their agreed-upon world of chicken backs and mandatory Saturday night intercourse. What was it that transported Mama so far from them? Who did she think she was? Princess Grace? Ingmar Bergman? Underneath, they told themselves, Irwina Trout was just like them. Scratch her you'd find chicken fat and regret.

Joan pulled a cocktail dress around her for cover.

The first thing Mama bought for the apartment before the couch, before dishware, was a fountain that spewed blue water through fish mouths and the urinary tracts of angels. Then Buddy bought a hi-fi that took up a wall. Then Mama bought Limoges and wallpapered the bedroom in 14K-gold flecks. They fought with beauty.

Lil put on the accent when she meant business: Vee got a liquor-spewing fountain in the building, girls.

Mrs. Dubrow, a former teacher with thirty-years under her blazer: I heard she dies it blue.

Lil: Husband sips in daylight, yah, and that's the truth.

Fran, whose unmarried status was made lower by the faith she put in Married Johnny: Is it better to sip at night?

Mrs. Slater who watched *I've Got a Secret* to learn English: I had a fountain in India and servants who—

Lil: We heard.

These were the women-in-the-building, and they had an unspoken code any dummy could read: walk head down, eyes covered on the shady side and don't go looking for trouble. Trouble would get no directional assistance from them. Lil's hands were fattened red and swollen above and below the wedding ring. Every Friday night she made Sabbath to compete with Leo's dead mother whose Sabbaths were so flawless, God begged for leftovers.

Lil: Used to beg, now he don't show up. Busy listening to angel's piss at the Trout's.

The women-in-the-building had bodies that told the world they
never measured up, while Irwina Trout had a once-a-month maid.
Colored girl, Lil said, well pardon me boys, but another woman
touching the Danish modern? Her horsehair? Her chenille?

The women-in-the-building didn't gossip, they shook rugs over
back porches, beating them with brooms till they smoked. They
changed cucumbers into dill pickles, drowning them in foot-tall
jars bristling with dill stalks and murky vinegar water. They worked
and never stopped working and had a go away–come closer rela-
tionship with pain, longing for it as the thermometer of their existence, fending it off with saltwater and curses.

And by the way, Lil said, she lets a colored woman touch her
chattel, who's to say, as god is my witness, because god stands by
the women-in-the-building (those fat-footed clots of dirty milk-
weed, Buddy called them), the colored woman don't also, on occasion I'm sayin', dust off the husband?

Mrs. Dubrow said Jesus watched over the wee people and a
fountain of fish regurgitating schnapps in one's living room was
nothing if not an invitation for the devil to spit spit you never
heard it from me, said Lil.

When Mama stopped for coffee-and at Ashkenaz, she got linen
instead of paper, while the women-in-the-building bent with
gratitude over calves' liver and onions. When she-whose-shit-did-
not-emit-an-odor sliced the crusts off her bread, each perfect bite
kicked them in the ass, reminding them of all they'd die without.

They saw Mama switch from decent cigarettes to pastel Nat
Shermans tipped in gold. Each pack she smoked made their living
rooms crummier. And every Friday she got the best of the monger, speaking with hand and head gestures only, never looking at
the fishman so the fishman never looked at her. Mama did her fish
business eyes on the glass case full of whitefish, pike, salmon. The
fishman presented catch after catch, and she'd shake her head and
make him search for bigger, more recently dead fish. Nobody's

back was straighter, nobody's fish fresher than Mama's, not even the monger's wife. (Smelts you bring me? Smelts?) The fishman couldn't say no to Mama, and this was causing trouble at home. His wife, who put up with his smell all these years, came to expect the belly of the lox, the collar of salmon, chub smoked that day under the bridge by the Wilmette boys. What could he tell his dear wife? The good fish slipped home with Mama? He couldn't argue with a woman who had no voice?

Her salmon's red, her nova's boneless, Lil said, how come she gets boneless we get gristle? Her $2.95's same as our $2.95, so how does she pay the monger?

Do you need a map? Fran said.

Lil said, I lean on his cooler, smash my breasts against fish glass, my nipples spread to smiles, and what does he give me? Day-old. A monger cutting nova outside the home spells trouble. For her he cuts so thin I'm afraid for his fingers.

The women-in-the-building detested Mama as much as they needed her. She wore a different dress every day, shoes and ciga-rettes to match. She was their bone spur, their magazine. Who else told them shoulder pads were a mistake? Who painted their eyebrows on so realistically? Who loaned them her own personal jewelry and sprayed Chanel on their necks and threw in nylon stockings for free and let them pay off a dress a buck a week? And who in this damn godforsaken world gave one shit how they looked from the rear? Buddy's Frock Shop was their right and Mama their ritual.

When they shopped they bathed, spritzing between and under, fastening nylons to garters dangling like cow tits. And when they bought they took home their prize and closed the door to their bedroom more gently than a child sick with fever. They pulled shades, made strong coffee, arranged their catch on the bed, lay-ing out a dress with the nylons sticking in shoes, hat on top, sweater over the shoulders. On their bed was the person they wanted to be.

They took off everything except brassieres and girdles, soft and giving as their bellies stretched from child. When they looked in the mirror they did not see rubbery white flesh fighting to get out, they saw Mama's hand-rolled seams. And they turned. Slow, eyes low as a virgin, bedroom mirror their only witness. They pulled against the passing of time to make their backs go straight. They pinched cheeks, withdrew bellies, unpinned hair, fluffed bosoms, tipped the bottle, and drank what was left of their beauty.

"This suit," Buddy told Mrs. Bonfiglio, "suits you. Sheds pounds like a molting bird. I'll open the mirror you'll see for yourself."

"Now's too soon," Mama whispered. She made them earn the mirror, wait for it like their husbands once made them wait for the big prize.

"Too much red," the woman said.

"Darling. You can't measure red."

"I want cheaper." Lil was fingering one of Mama's Mr. Mort's.

"Cheaper we got," Buddy said.

Mama stepped in. "But for the High Holidays? First sixteen rows solid mink you're going to dump a well-made gabardine? Perhaps you should try Goldblatts."

Lil wanted to see in the mirror. Mama was standing in front of it.

"You'll wear it with a brooch," Mama said.

"What brooch?" Lil said.

"You know the one, from his dead mother. You must pin it to something worthy Lillian. Look, this is no heirloom but to hold the place, you know, for later."

Mama unfastened her ruby hummingbird and pinned it on Lil's wobbly breast. She swapped a cloth belt for a green alligator, gave her a hat with tiny sequins and a spread peacock feather. Lil closed her eyes as Mama slid down the veil.

"Like a bride," Mama whispered, so nobody could argue.

Who else treated them like this?

"A brooch? Don't seem enough."

Mama was unfastening her garnet watch, the watch Buddy gave her after a drunk. She could still do it, sell up one building down the other, sell them a black that was blue and a brown so sweet they drank it like Turkish coffee. She knew who could manage cobalt, whose husband would expire, who wore the fat coat of menopause, whose daughter would get ditched, how a life could be permanently altered by a pink angora sweater with reversible collar.

"Ah, Lillian, I definitely see you dancing in that," Mama said.

"A funeral march they should bury me in it. Your watch don't fit."

"Don't worry dear, the safety chain will keep it— Oh Lil Lil Lil."

"Don't wear it out."

"I see you at your daughter's wedding, a sensible wedding, and you're the *ballabusta* in a suit that carries you from the Yom Kippur to Sharon's big day."

"I should steal light from the young? Gimme a look in your mirror."

"You do layaway?" Marie had her bag open. Once they opened the bag . . .

"Certainly," Mama said. But Buddy was writing the full ticket. No layaway on the everydays.

Lil stepped into Mama's mirror. She was short, lumpy, she tilted to the left. You could hear Lil coming like a bent metronome. In Russia somebody carved her right leg with the backhand of a scythe. Her father said limbs are work and work is life and you got three days to get back to the field. Onion and cabbage don't wait.

"What do I look like?" Lil said.

"Keep looking, darling," Mama said. "Tell me what you see."

"Starina Constantine, our village." Lil twirled unevenly, closed her eyes to see better. "I got legs. I got a body. I'm eating . . . I'm eating fresh lamb with beets yanked from dirt this minute."

"Delicious," Mama whispered.

"Delicious," Lil repeated. "Starina, it means 'what's old,' But I'm young, I'm—"

"What else."

"Oh I don't say no more."

"Say."

"I can't."

"Say or it'll disappear."

Joan could barely hear them. Something about a wet purse when her Leon was near, and Mama was going for a box behind the counter. She kept jewelry hidden in identical white boxes and always grabbed the right one.

"Here," Mama said. "We use a gold bracelet to set it off."

"Do I look decent?" Lil said.

"You stand out."

"Yeah? I don't wanna make a scene."

Mama chose her words. "In this you can dance."

Lil ate it. "I miss the dance. Leo was a waltzer, you know."

Mama put her arm around Lil's waist, as far as she could get it, lifted her other arm gently and they danced through the store. Things were looking good. A woman was feeling the cruisewear, another was heaping gowns in her skinny daughter's arms.

Mrs. Bonfigleo was still staring inside her purse like money might jump in. Mama and Lil danced over to the sweaters and finished with a bow. A young woman drank coffee from bone china and scanned *Vogue* in the conversation area, two soft chairs that never let go. The women still bought from her, wanted to be her. When they bought, they *were* Mama and believed the Morse Avenue men were looking at them with aching hearts, craving them worse than halvah. Women walked in with worries, walked out like they had a date with Xavier Cougat.

"You going to the prom, Grace?" Mama took the dress pile from the skinny girl, lifting them high so the hems didn't drag.

The mother said, "Nobody asked her so I says, Grace, I says, you get a nice group of girls together, show them you don't care. Try the pink one, goes with your hair."

Mama pulled the woman aside. "May I be frank? Put her in that they'll serve her with onions and a side of Philadelphia. I want you to . . . just consider black."

"Black? She already don't have a date."

"Something effortlessly chic about it though, like she's not trying. Or white. A clear white that— Wait. Wait wait wait I've got the dress! I know the dress! She'll be the different one, your Grace."

Mama was coming for her. Seeme? See? Me? Her business face. No.

"We don't want different," the mother yelled. "Different's no good."

"Every girl in layette pink and luncheonette blue and you want Grace like them? When she can enter that gymnasium on royal feet?"

"Royal feet?"

Mama was running, the woman was having a heart attack trying to keep up with her. When Mama knew she ran, and she was right.

"Where is it?" She shoved clothes *sttt sttt* along the aluminum rack. "Where's my dress?" Her face was a loss. "I used to know where things were. Buddy?"

"In back."

"I don't think Grace needs anything," the woman puffed.

"Patience. You'll see. Relax, have coffee. Grace will model."

A soft Japanese silk, a silk usually reserved for linings. Mama got it from a hungry designer out of F.I.T. Cocoa and sugar milk demanding pearls. The drama was in the back where it plunged to the waist. Liquid brown. If skinny Grace wore it to the prom, boys would stare at the naked curve of her spine and forget their lives. The dress was wrinkled. Mama lugged out the steamer and hissed at it, urging the wrinkles out.

"Sorry for your trouble," the woman said. Grace was at the door.

"Show you something else," Buddy said, "more realistic."

"Here. Done. Please. Believe me. This is for Grace alone. They made it for her. Just *shhh* one minute let me show you." Mama held the dress to the girl's face. It softened and warmed her.

"A few extra just in case." Buddy added his pile to the dressing room.

An elderly woman in a burnt orange Devore, a zippered sweet potato.

"Beautiful like the sun." Buddy gave Mama a warning look as she climbed in the cruisewear window, stripped a navy bolero off Celia, draped it over the woman, hiding her potato parts, toning the orange, snapping her into place.

Buddy shook his head. CB sounds from the back mixed with Mama's shorthand. Alpha, georgette, empire, French dart, Romeo, Kilo.

Grace who was not Grace anymore. A pale that took generations of in-breeding and her incredible, unblemished back. Body and bone she was done with all that. Grace of the blond edible clouds. Magnificent, milk-chocolate Grace. Her neck, Joan wanted to kiss it. Layers of chiffon lifted and resettled themselves. Boys would stumble. Boys would fall. The next day Grace would sit at a different lunch table, girls with necklaces and single-serving bags of chips. Her phone would ring. Boys' lips would swell. They would step on their own names.

Who's calling please? Hello? Hello?

Beow.

Tesh.

Mawg.

They'd hang up and call again, their names wet and anguished till somebody wiped them from the line.

"Grace." The mother unbuttoned her coat. "Go try on the others."

Joan slipped back outside to watch Mama change the window. Boys couldn't touch here. They were a smelly passing wind, cursing and shooting the bird. She stretched, yawned, good as a Gardol shield. This was *her* fourteen feet, including sidewalk and Mama in the window saying silent things to Buddy.

Joan acted like they were asking her opinion, nodded a little. There, like that. Yeah. More left. Stop. That's good.

A tired-looking woman with two kids at the end of each hand was looking at Mama's window like she couldn't leave. Her kids were scarred with candy and the woman pulled their arms to make them stay.

Here, in this spot, the world came to its senses.

Buddy knew what to grab, Mama knew where to put it.

Mama saw her and stopped working, threw her arms out and twirled like a *Price Is Right* lady. Ta-tah! Buddy picked up a crate of grass, complained with no sound. Mama pointed, lifted a model, and grass grew under her naked feet. Together they unwound a banner held by two old flag stands. RAVINIA PLAYS CARMEN. Buddy made a face, but the window was becoming what Mama called her hunk of good life. Buddy hooked up the record player behind a miniature lemon tree and Mama lifted a model's head like notes were coming down from the sky. The models wore pale summer dresses and sweaters tied over their shoulders. In the grass was an open basket with an indication of picnic. A wine bottle sticking out, the same stale, glazed French bread she kept in the back, a piece of tablecloth.

Come. Come in, Mama mouthed. Joan she stood a little longer so people could see. Envy me this, suckers. See us as a family that hangs quilt-batting clouds.

Mrs. Bonfigleo was buying. Lil was buying. The shop was swimming with goodwill, women fingering garments like there was nothing else in the world. The pink lights under the accessory counter picked up the hard shine of costume jewelry. Mama steamed something, Carmen shrieked, Buddy pulled a baby lime tree out of plastic and set it in a clay pot. He plunked a lime into a model's hand. When Carmen finished, Mama moved the needle and started at the beginning.

"Your Ma's wearing the clown shoes again."

"I want to make a younger window next, something teenagesque," Mama said.

"We don't sell to kids. That's Leonard's job."

"If we pushed a little—"

"The mother's got the dough. You got big-dough items, and the guilt button ain't that big. They don't spend like this on kids."

"They're wearing baby dolls and those full skirts. I could soak the crinolines in sugar water—I read that somewhere—they get stiff and—"

"Bugs eat 'em."

"—that'll make their waists even tinier, and then with the bobby sox and the loafers. Joan. Why aren't you at Rose's?"

"Nobody home."

"What do you mean? Where's she got to go? You're sweaty. Where were you?"

"Riding around with the twins."

"We don't sell that kinda jazz," Buddy said, "Leonard is still driving a Biscayne. Stick to the big names, mix 'em up with housecoats, and we say on top."

"It would be adorable. Joan? Mrs. Auerbach needs . . ." They were busy. All was forgotten. Joan knew when to open the mirror, knew every drawer and the proper way to fit a girdle, though few women would undress in front of a girl.

"You look so young, Mrs. Auerbach," Joan said. Three panels, one at a time so the woman thinks of who she wanted to be.

"You think so? Let me see that mirror."

"You look like before you had kids."

Mama gave Joan a look, but she knew the routine. Another panel, slow, slow. There was order again in two rooms separated by one dark velvet curtain. An inside, an outside. Front room for customers, back for family.

Joan picked up the dressing room, and Buddy counted the dough-re-mi, rubber-banding ones, fives, and tens so all the men faced heaven. His ham radio was on, the scratch talk of men against the blaze of Carmen, and Mama fiddling with the steamer that never changed levels even though she lugged it out daily to flush wrinkles from the just-shipped. Mama steamed slow, shoulder to hem, like she could taste it.

Things were working again. In winter the window got damp inside and icefalls trickled to the bottom and froze into waves. Mama looked skinny in the ankle with her old oxford shoes that made way for her bunion. Buddy hated her in flat shoes. In spikes he called her doll. The quiet in the opening of boxes, saving of tissue paper, knowing when to empty the register into the plastic zippered Harris Trust and Savings bag, Joan stamping the backs of checks, Buddy proofing them against receipts. He put the clammy money bag under his shirt for later when he went to the bank. He knew which teller wouldn't make a fuss when she had to count change and who wouldn't charge for a bounced check and who could put a word in with that Isherwood sonofabitch if they needed more credit. Buddy topped a Styrofoam cup with Sanka-tinted vodka, and Mama didn't argue. She was moving her hips, dragging the steamer around for a partner.

Joan had been coming here since she was a baby. She had memories of dresses as animals to be petted and fed. She remembered stories about Mama and Buddy going to Paris, coming back with the three porcelain models that she named. Only Celia stuck. Celia became family. When she was little, Joan would talk to Celia, make like she climbed in bed with her and Celia said wise things to her. Let them untie their own knots. Or: You know they love you. Or: They're human; they do what they can. Celia could say any slop and it worked.

The plaster floor of the window was now solid grass. Buddy hit the stars with different colored gel lights and Mama propped up a woodsy background and it was Highland Park at night with train sounds and expensive cricket air. Ravinia! Lovers on the lawn! Cheese!

A man stopped to see what Joan was looking at.

"That's good. Open the basket a little more to the front," Joan said.

"She can't hear a word you're saying," the man said, but Mama blew her a kiss and moved the basket. On these fourteen feet, nobody alive could touch them.

Four

SPANKY AND OUR GANG were making sepia sounds on TV when the rain came, taking with it summer dirt and bugs clinging to window screens. The sky was a premature dark and the pavement smoked with relief. Bus drivers rocked to the motion of jumbo windshield wipers.

Buddy said, "I got an idea. We'll open some windows, see, let the rain in, but don't tell your ma or she'll give me hell."

Joan put her nose to one of the wet screens. He was in a good mood, which meant the world could tumble either way. The outside smelled like, what was that smell? Overnight camp. Lanyards, bug juice in aluminum pitchers, puffy food, fish scat in moss, Marietta the counselor dragging her feet, leaving two neat rows of pine needles behind her.

"City needs this rain." Buddy turned off the lights and the TV and let the rain come.

"Gimme your hand kid."

Rain down the sills waking the smell of 20 Mule Team Borax. Rain beading on the lamp stand and the floor where the rug didn't reach. Rain letting in the siren colors of summer.

"Let's open more, whaddya say? Let's open every goddamned window in the goddamned place."

"It's enough, Dad."

"Enough's never enough."

Lightening two three four five thunder. The catalpas sagged in the lush moisture, people were running with newspapers over their heads. Buddy stood on the couch and opened the tops of windows, then he went for the sliding terrace door. The kitchen window he had to smack hard. In the bathroom, the frosted glass refused to give. Had it ever been open?

"Don't break it. You're gonna break it, Daddy, like that."

"You sound like her."

"I just don't want trouble, Dad."

"We're havin' a good time she's worryin' about trouble. Where's your sense of fun? Enjoy."

But if glass shattered and rain filled the apartment, well, what was she worrying? She could take off her shoes and they'd plop around.

He was banging in time to the thunder. "Take this so I get a better grip." He handed her a bottle of bath oil. "I give it to her she don't use it anyways."

"She uses it." His banging drowned her out. *Bam bam* a fighter busting jaws sending the big boys screaming to Mommy.

"Sonofabitch don't give." He was sweating.

She held the bath oil to the light. Clear. Joan used it sometimes, floating in oil pools as big as the water. She'd poke her leg up through, watch oil slide down, pretend oily water was a blanket holding her up.

"Take this. Here, here, take the Airwick."

She put the jar with the electric green tongue on the toilet lid. Airwick was so old it didn't smell mediciney. He took off his shoe, hit the window hard.

"Khrushchev," she said.

"You know about him? Who teaches you that?"

"Miss Sheck."

"Shanghai Sheck? I'm gonna pay her a visit one a these times."

"Nobody visits, Dad; they have Parent Night."

"We'll see." He banged and banged, but the window refused him.

Lightening behind the frosted pane showed the metal honey-comb pattern inside the glass, small octagons repeating the floor tiles. Buddy's shoe made gray smudges on the wood when he missed, then he landed one, and the window shuddered and islands of paint fell into the tub.

"*Ahhh,* now it comes. I want you to see something. Over there, see? Our big payola."

Some apartments she wasn't used to seeing.

"Between them, look over to the left, follow my finger. Oh hell with your shoes. Get in here with me." He put his arm around her.

"This here, Monkey, is what you call your Winnetka view."

She still couldn't see anything.

"Your old man knows what he's talkin' about. Hey I got an idea. What if we start a club me and you? Call it Hocus Pocus? Sure."

His big daddy hand in hers. Was that it? That fifty-cent piece of lake?

The rain was slowing. She hoped somebody in the building was watching them in the tub like this, in love like this.

The world could tumble either way. Hands in prayer under his cheek, Buddy could be any well-dressed man who made a decision and chose to sleep on the sidewalk. Churchers stepped around him and Joan was glad she had mule hands because she needed strength to pull her father from their eyes. She'd never seen actual neighbors' eyes on him, but Mama said and Joan could feel eyes through the slats of blinds, eyes through half-turned backs. Mrs. Dubrow upstairs, watching, tearing sorrel for her pig's feet soup that made the hallway smell like animal sacrifice. Fran, who either did or did not spend the night with Married Johnny and was warming her empty spot with coffee. Mrs. Slater, who never made trouble but patted Joan, fed her like a small mammal Keith was healing. Only Mama slept. Mama had enough vodka Sundays.

Buddy's eyes fluttered, he mumbled something.

"Rest a minute, Dad. Take it easy, rest."

Even though it seemed like he didn't remember her, he did. A part of him knew she was helping. She was sure. She scooped under his arms and let the sidewalk take his weight, his feet vibrating over rough pavement. All his Italian shoes were clawed in the back.

He never questioned leaving at night, waking in his bed. Only once did he stare at her like a wild stranger. Who was she? The hell? And he struck her, but he didn't mean to, didn't know it was her. Later he gave her a box of sputnik gumballs and tucked her in with stories that played like movies on the wall beside her bed.

He showed her his letterbox, he contributed to causes he himself doubted. They sent him thank-you cards and he kept every one. He wrote to famous men, he was on the E's: Einstein. Eisenhower. Eichman. Her father had things to say. He sent them a few bucks and a piece of his mind and watched the news for evidence of his words. Sometimes people answered him, sometimes his letters came back without explanation. He saved everything equally.

"Somewheres in here there's a letter for you. I'll give it to you someday. It's got everything you wanna know. Beautiful. But you're not ready. I let you know when."

They started a club Mama couldn't belong, gave it a secret handshake a secret motto. "I say, Hocus Pocus! You say, Kadocus!" A mission: magic.

The club met once a week, they did some trick, he told her bedtime stories that touched his life knowledge. He gave her a clear lightbulb with black-and-white flags that chased each other, moved by a light source only they could see.

"Invisible forces at work," Buddy said.

She put the bulb in its own cigar box in the corner of her closet and saw dots of light trying to break out.

"Don't surprise me a bit," he said, "more you believe me, more magic's around."

There was the Chinese Penny Eater, a colored wooden tray half the size of a ruler. Stick a penny in the slot, open and close, the penny was gone. Open, the penny came back.

"Now here's the question see, where's a penny go when you don't see it? Think, Monkey."

She wasn't supposed to bust his magic. It killed mystery and she lost his attention. They talked about the lovely painted Chinese Princess on the Penny Eater, her robe of white feathers, admiring herself in a golden mirror.

"Perhaps the pennies went in the mirror, Daddy."

Children played around the princess. A crooked tree grew between them. In the distance there was a mountain with a ring of cloud around its tip.

"You tell me," he said. "I give you one more try, then I break the thing open so you see inside. You gotta see how things work."

"Don't break it, Dad. I know."

"You know tell me."

She'd seen the parallel lavender ribbons, the X ribbon that sucked out the penny and fed it through. But then he'd be gone.

"Not gonna say?" That's how his magic ended. He could only stand so much mystery before fiddling with the underwires. "Hocus pocus?"

"Kadocus."

"Don't bust it, Dad. It's inside the thingie."

But he was hitting it with a hammer, confirming the hypothesis, splintering the princess. Korea, a splinter said.

"Don't worry, kid. I got more."

He asked her to tell him things, tell him about her life and she loved this. She told him about Chris, not the kiss but how she thought he was cute. He was holding her hand, his hand felt cool like the blood ran out of it.

His face changed. "Only a hand?"

"Yup."

"You holdin' anything back from me?"

"Nope," said Veronica the Pearl Diver.

He pushed for information, she pushed it down to empty shafts she didn't know she had.

The club had a secret emblem he copied from Dean's milk carton, a bird on a mailbox. The club bought her a Winky Dink kit with a plastic sheet she could stretch over the TV and color Huntley and Brinkley's faces. And a sixteen-inch robot that made gnashing sounds when it hit the wall. She hid everything from Mama without thinking why.

"Something you'll learn about me, I'm a gizmo guy."

Disappearing lemon ink. Setting fire to black pills making them ooze snakes. Giving Auntie Rose a coughing fit from the exploding cigarette in her Viceroys.

"Every man's got a blind spot, blind spot's the ticket kid, world's greatest magicians know it by heart. Stay in that spot you get away with murder."

She practiced on the Slater twins, taking pencils from their peripheral, but they caught her every time, looked at her like she was crazy. He brought dried sea horses back to life in jelly glasses and took in stray dogs that Mama sent back to the pound.

"You make me the villain," she said. "You read the lease, they'll kick us out and you know that yet you do this to me. I don't understand."

"Kid needs a dog, nothin' to understand. Right kid? Thank your ma."

The Hocus Pocus Club met once a week, and Joan counted the days. How would she know things if not for Buddy? He gave her a hard copy of *Gulliver's Travels* with this inscription:

```
To Joan, the one and only
captain of her good ship Destiny.
    —Dad '59
```

Rope magic, scarf magic, intertwining metal hoops with no breaks that fell apart and joined. Grape juice and a pill that turned it clear then purple then clear again. Wonder Bread transformed into dough balls. Clamshells, exploding flowers, he took off his thumb and stuck it back on. Put the lit end of a cigar in his mouth, puffed backward and swallowed. Gone. He let her check to make sure. He had the answers, he'd give her the letter when she was ready. When they took walks, money fell from the sky. If she stooped to pick it up, he gave her a reminder kick in the butt.

"Things ain't like they seem kid. I gotta toughen you up, make you a little soldier."

She'd find herself looking at girls whose eyeglasses fit snug in marshmallow cases and wonder what he was training her for.

"The mission of our club is comfort." Buddy rubbed her back.

"I thought magic."

"Tell you a little story."

Buddy trained for fights down at the South Side gym with Negroes and ex-cons. Then he moved on. Buddy versus Archie Moore. Buddy versus the invincible Sugar Ray. Buddy goes nine rounds with Roland Lastarza. "Only white guy in the place so any boy tries to beat you up tell 'em the old man was champ."

"Every kid says that."

He took a few swipes at her Ginny doll cabinet. "But you got the McCoy."

Mama laughed, smoothed back Joan's hair, secured it with a plastic barrette.

"It's true, Mama. He one time almost killed a guy."

"Did he. Well that's nice."

"No I'm serious."

"Your father once wrestled my purse from a thief, I'll never forget it. Make coffee after this Winna, he said, we'll need it. He was so brave."

"Did the guy have a gun?"

"A gun?"

"Or knife?"

"I don't think so, honey. He was a boy."

"Oh."

"But it was dark."

"That's okay."

"He might of, a knife, yes I believe . . . You know the penknives they have in their pants sometimes?"

"Oh."

"Listen to me. Your father didn't know what the kid had. He was brave. It was brave what he did, going after that kid in the moonlight."

"What about the war?"

"The war?"

"He fought in."

"Oh. Well. I believe he had flat feet. 4F. They didn't let him in, but he gave lots of blood."

"But his pal in the foxhole? Benny Doosenberg, he told me the guy's name."

"Bernard Ducenberg fixes our car. He's our mechanic."

"But his neck scar?"

"Oh, Pie, you have absolutely no mechanism for telling truth from not truth. Someone says sandwiches fly you'd sit there waiting for your lunch to take off."

Mama was a liar. Buddy was Champ.

He'd let her watch him shave using *zaydeh*'s bone-handled straight razor, sharpening it on the leather strap that had no leather left, foaming up with an old boar brush, dragging the blade down his face, letting her paint foam on him.

"You wanna feel my scar kid?" Buddy said.

She pressed her fingers against raised skin. He had a white stick that stopped all bleeding, glycerin and rosewater to blow up then soothe, gentian violet for when the thrush bird flew in the mouth. His other razor blades were Wilkinson Swords.

"A queen give 'em to me."

There was the package with the price, but he looked so happy with himself clapping his hands, slapping his cheeks. "Bracer, kid, keeps a man standing.

"How many days did you go with no water or food?"

"Oh many. Many many many."

"And your feet stunk, and you thought of me even though I wasn't born?"

"That's it, Monkey."

Buddy rinsed the blade under steamy water, and she memorized his hands, the blue-black mole on his third finger, the eczema under his wedding ring.

"Mama says you have flat feet. She says you didn't fight in any war."

He kept rinsing, turning the blade over slowly. "Your ma knows all, kid. Believe what you believe. "I'd like to meet that Chris Nobel pal of yours sometime."

He showed her how motion made light and gave her Japanese silk day-of-the-week underpants. Friday had a red heart with Friday embroidered in black. Mama used Yiddish, their rage language, and silk was replaced by white cotton Carter's. Joan kept Thursday. Thursday was yellow with gray lace, and when she moved a certain way, silk hit her right between the childhood.

Five

WHEN BUDDY AND MAMA worked late, Joan had to sleep
at Auntie Rose's in the bed next to Grandma Yetta, a woman
from a country that changed boundaries and names so many
times she just called it old land. Yetta spoke little English. Rose
and the mouth-breathing cousins worked around her. Yetta was
used to it, talking quietly to herself.

Who are you, Yetta?

Old.

Where are you from?

Old land.

Joan slept in the bed next to Yetta's. The place smelled like
Clearasil, Polident and old throat. Rose decorated the grandma's
room with old science projects, and she didn't seem to mind.
"From Bread to Protection" with a signed photo of Jonas Salk
took up most of her dresser top. Salk said one must walk away
from a problem in order to see the answer. Joan wanted to walk
out of this bedroom. It was impossible to sleep with Yetta snoring. She slid off her pajamas, touched her swollen breasts, moved
her body against the rough sheet, slid her finger between her legs,
lifted her pelvis to the moon and still couldn't sleep.

"I won't stay there anymore," she told Buddy.

"Can't blame you. Rose had it tough, no husband, two girls, you should cut her some slack."

"But she likes giving the cousins enemas, Dad."

"Got a thing for clean. It's how she holds on."

"She touches me I'm kicking her."

Buddy laughed. "I'll get you a babysitter next time, Melnick's kid, art student. You'll like her."

He let Irwina close the shop and took her on his private rounds. Buddy was master of a three-block radius with a stride that took them to the lucky places. She learned where to place an honest bet, who was holding Cuban cigars, where the day-old doughnuts hadn't gone hard. They stopped at the newspaper stand on the corner run by a man with fingerless gloves. Pauvich's pet shop, Witz Cleaning and Storage, and Manny, who worked at the old Pratt Hotel—Buddy knew them all and could predict their behavior.

"Watch. Manny'll act like it's his goddamned hotel. Guy gets three bucks an hour thinks he's the father of goldfish. You wanna see him go nuts? We'll drop a few pennies in the fountain. Hates it. Thinks it's gonna kill his fish. We'll have some fun, then I'll teach you the Woolworth's lesson."

Which was: People make mistakes and other people get rich. People get busy, they talk, things slip through and that's when your average Joe makes a killing.

"But Woolworth's?"

"Doubt my word?"

"No I'm just saying is all."

"Diamond checker don't always do his job. You didn't know that."

"What's a diamond checker?" She pictured a guy in a lemon cab outfit, diamonds dangling from his cap.

"You're gonna find the diamond that slipped through one, I promise and you're set for life kid, but you gotta keep your eyes open watch the old man."

He had to take his pills first. They were organized in a plastic box under Sleep, Quick, and Spells. Spells were his break from life when he came back mad because where he went they didn't treat him nice. Epilepsy. Petit mal, but Joan wasn't allowed to say or someone would take his car and leave him what? Religion, Mama said. One spell he hit a school bus, but nobody was hurt. His last spell she was in the car with him driving down Edens Expressway. Buddy was driving, then he wasn't. He was looking at her. She pushed his foot down on the pedal and grabbed the wheel. Cars sped by. She could hear their different radios. Buddy came back, pushed her against the door. What was she tryin' to do? Start an accident? Mama didn't believe it happened.

"We take you with a grain dear," she said.

Today Buddy felt rich. They ate at Rocky's instead of Woolworth's. He ordered himself a steak, baked potato, blueberry pie à la carte. She wasn't hungry.

"Give the kid a vanilla malt," and he told Rocky how to make it, and to make sure she got the tumbler.

"You're the man." Rocky looked tired.

No windows in the diner, just good stale air and newspapers soft from too many readings. A man spun his stool twice after he got up. Bricks of hamburger were thawing on the clouded metal counter, potato peels browned on the floor. Rocky had no secrets. He suffered the right amount and rested his belly on the counter. It seemed designed that way, to give his belly a break. The menu was laminated, hand written, unchanging. There were free lifesavers and mint-flavored toothpicks by the register.

"Who could hate a city like this?" Buddy said.

"Know what you mean." Rocky scraped the grill with a large spatula, sending fragments into unseen places.

At Woolworth's, the jewelry girl had lousy teeth and a thin cardigan. Joan could trace her bra ridges.

"World could pass through those teeth the woman wouldn't know," Buddy whispered. "Cakewalk."

The shop girl wiped the jewelry counter with her hand, licking her fingertips, stamping out imaginary crumbs.

"Any woman tries that hard for beauty and misses cracks up my heart."

She showed them tray after tray of rings set in blue velvet. Buddy adjusted the light to get a closer look. "You mind? I'm teaching my one and only."

He insisted she pick.

"This one?" A yellow diamond like Mama's with endless corridors that heaved on her finger and flopped to one side.

"Nice," he said.

"I'll save it for Mama."

He didn't speak till they were outside. "You did it kid!"

"I did?"

"Genuine diamond set marry-me style, enough to take care of a woman for life. How's it feel? Keep it, she don't need no trinket encouragement. And don't forget who loves you. Nobody in your life'll love you like me. Hurry up and take your time. I got things on the agenda."

She was flying. People were staring. She rolled the diamond to the inside of her hand so only the band showed.

"Never hide the goods baby. Tell Daddy what you're going to buy with it."

She told him dresses, records, animals.

More.

Ice skates, hair stuff.

Bigger.

Houses. Boats. A vacation. Another house. A house for Yetta, a house for Bessie and Joe. Record albums.

"Hocus Pocus?" He held out his hand.

She slapped him the magic.

"Details," he said.

A red-and-white house with room for Buddy full of relaxation with a double bed and heated pillows the pale green color of the ice cream at The Peking House.

"Green tea," he said. More.

She gave it to him, let him see her windows, see her curtains lifted by train sounds, front door solid as a courthouse. She told him and she told him and she told him and she told him and when he looked bored, she added a swimming pool.

Then she saw someone living in the house with her. All the times she'd rubbed gumballs in her hand and pretended for the Slater twins and here was a husband with red hair, freckled arms. And she lay next to him, and he made her breathing slow. He had something on his head, a visor the old jewelers wore. He pulled the eyepiece down, made a face at her.

"What you seein', Monkey?"

She did not tell this. He could hear her mind. She made the husband go.

"Who else lives in your big house?"

"Nobody."

"Not Mama?"

"Well Mama."

"You have a family?"

"I don't, no, I don't think so."

"Really."

"Dad we could get a boat and sail it like Pippi to an island and see animals that aren't scared of people."

"I'm just the guy walkin' and you're rich as spit."

"I'll take you with."

"What about your husband? And babies? Do you know about babies? Seems like you know everything. May I see the ring please?"

It got stuck at the top joint of his pinky. They were passing St. Jerome's. The church doors were open, someone was washing the floor. Somehow she never thought about churches and temples getting dirty. The man was on his knees with a brush and Buddy was down on the pavement.

"This is the other part of our lesson."

"What're you doing?"

"Relaxin'."

She'd seen him relaxed on too many sidewalks.

"I think you should get up. People will—"

"Aw they got their own problems. This baby business is, well you know everything."

"I know! I know!"

"She knows. Knows everything this one."

"Dad, they told us in health."

"Not like I'm gonna tell you."

He was on his back letting his knees part, his blowsy trousers. He had her ring, he was moaning. The janitor watched. There was a woman in the pew. Joan hated this watching and was comforted by it. If she stepped back, she could see the problem. It worked for Jonas.

"Where you goin'? Get back here. Only take a minute."

"Get up, Dad."

"Here's the thing about babies see, they try makin' a big deal about it but the simple truth? A woman stops what she's doing, dishes, whatever, feels a crampy down here." He put his hand over her stomach. "Like she's in menstruation."

Men-stroo-a-shun. He made it sound clean, British.

"How do you think it goes?"

"Dad."

"You know everything so tell me."

"Let's talk about it at home."

He was on his back on the sidewalk, moaning. Did other fathers do this? They should show a father movie, Miss Sheck talking over the narrator. *And it is the duty of the father.*

The janitor and the fur lady were coming.

"Or maybe you'd rather go to Rosie's."

No guest room for Buddy.

"Birth's easy it's men got it hard. Provide, protect, defend— you got your war, your make a buck. Women? Blood, milk and cramps. You think anyone else'll get down on their knees for you? Your mama labored two days—"

"I know, we should get going."

"Knows everything my kid. You better know how things break or they break you. Look inside baby, learn the clockwork."

People crossing the street or blinking, he was reaching between his legs, she saw something take air caught between her eyelashes. He was holding up her ring, leaf parts sticking to him.

"Paste, Joan, paste. You gotta understand, or they'll play you for a chump." He hit the ring on pavement. Again. A gash in the diamond, yellow powder blowing to nothing.

The woman in the rat-fur jacket was standing over Buddy. She was made of small bones, gray wire, hacked-at hair, chapped hands, a face that was easy to look at.

"Fitt, this ain't your concern."

"Sure it is. I spend time watching you."

"That's all you got."

She shook Joan's hand and slipped her a small box.

"Joan? This is Sofia Fitt. Keep away from her, she ain't nobody's family."

In her bed that night and certain of their breathing, she took out the box. Schiller's Jewelers stamped in gold. Under a slab of cotton—

Dear Joan,
To honor your twelfth year. And don't worry, they had to come out anyway. Wear carefully.
Yours,
Sofia Fitt

Two teeth hanging from a string, half white, half yellow, and packed with fillings. People gave her things. Why? The teeth made her think of Buddy promising to take her to the Wisconsin Dells. She'd seen commercials of bathing beauties on water skis in a triangle on each other's shoulders, Tommy Bartlett hanging from kite wings, dropping from the sky. When they finally get there, Mama won't leave the Rabbit Ears Motel, and Buddy takes her picture on an Indian's lap, an Indian who tells her he's Lebanese and says that's how Danny Thomas made his money, pretending to be a Jew but really he was Lebanese. The Indian says this. Meanwhile, she's watching the sky for Tommy, but the wind changes or something and Tommy never shows. She and Buddy watch a dog jump a cliff while a man with a Tennessee accent sings "Indian Love Song."

The teeth were real and in her hand. Yesterday she'd have dumped them, shown them to the twins for a laugh, but today she'd been rich and poor and watched her father give birth. She slipped them over her neck.

Six

THE WOMEN-IN-THE-BUILDING PLAYED KALOOKI at a different apartment every Friday. It was stick to the cold cuts and if you wanted to get rid of a few leftovers, nobody's complaining. The decent card players could read a hand by the grease stains on the back while peeling the mood off a husband's shirt or a daughter's nylons flung over a shower rack. Each apartment had its forward smell, furry as any mohair and each woman tried to hold back her secrets with Air Wick and company bedspreads. In Fran's studio there was the occasional cockroach, and the lack of air was visible. It grabbed and squeezed Irwina's lungs and she could feel Fran waiting for Married Johnny to take her for spaghetti and table wine. At Lil's she got the density of onions, busfilm windows, the reliability of radiator heat, the viscosity of Mother Russia. At Mrs. Dubrow's that Jesus ham smell and the depressed husband who had a fantastic new job every month. Chandra Devi Slater's looked like a Punjabi zoo, and her Chex Mix tasted like curry. Irwina could feel herself longing for the servant-filled home of Mrs. Slater's Brahmin youth. Her sisters' apartments, Bessie and Rose's, she shut her eyes to.

Tonight the game was hers. Tonight they'd come to her.

Irwina hid anything that could whisper and covered a large china platter with tin foil the way the women-in-the-building covered sectionals and lamp shades with plastic. Absurd, covering cheap and ugly with cheaper and uglier, but she did it, made sure the Hebrew National had the plastic off and the skin on. Lil loved to peel. Unwrapped the corned beef and arranged it in pinwheel fashion alternating with the salami, roast beef, and her famous radish rosettes. Plunged a butter knife into a tub of Philadelphia and, though she heard it cry for embellishment, tried to call it a night.

It was the Kaiser rolls that broke her.

They looked like dumb dough hassocks and she found herself removing the crust of a Davidson's butter white, and what about those heart and spade cookie cutters? Such an impression with two colors of caviar for accent. She made a delicate but still humble egg salad with the onion chopped extra fine and pressed out thirty-one heart and spade tea sandwiches, staggering them on bone china. Why? Because Buddy turned four sales in ten minutes.

Chop chop they'd remember this spread, remember her. The seller. The one who felt the heat of a dress wanting a woman. The one who never called it wrong. The shop had Buddy's name, but they built it on her knack and today, for the first time, he'd outsold her. She could see his bloated-with-victory face, that emaciated woman, the horrible cocktail dress, five pounds of Tricel and not a bosom to bear it. The irregulars had finally outnumbered the good clothing. Things she couldn't name were slipping from her.

The breakfront needed something. What?

Sex. Chilled champagne. Her Limoges filled with gold-tipped Nat Shermans. The till had been off for weeks. Nickel and dime stuff, but now it was a hundred here a hundred there and Buddy wouldn't talk about it. She plugged in the angel fountain and four cherubs obediently peed blue water. Four sales, ten minutes. There was time. She needed flowers.

"Joan? I'm going to the Greek."

Nick the Greek with the nice arms. "Of course, of course, of course. We got tulips and cal lilies and gloxinia from the truck, Mrs. T. I give you the bucket price."

The apartment was a Broadway of flowers. She put out her Spode creamer with real cream and filled the French cow with skim for Lil and Bessie, who were watching the arteries. Milk was so blah nothing. A few drops of McCormick's blue and milk grew up. Irwina filled the crystal candy bowl with Frangos, laid a white tablecloth over the card table, put the extra caviar in a bowl on rock salt, and did a pickle-olive lazy Susan.

She plucked another Sherman, lit it with a foot-long fireplace match, poured herself a champagne, and why not put out the Polaroid Land Camera? Maybe take a few shots between hands? A spread to remember and Buddy was a gizmo man, after all. They had the only colored television for miles. John Cameron Swayzee on the six o'clock news was so real she couldn't undress in front of him. Keep the TV on low to plump the background, Piaf on the hi-fi later.

Irwina refilled her glass. She didn't need any three-way mirror to give her a body, she had what she had. Small high breasts, impeccable waist, flat stomach and legs for dancing. She pulled Edith and put on a 45, "Walkin' to New Orleans." What was that dance the *American Bandstand* kids did? The stroll.

She closed her eyes and fleshed out Unseen Partner, who was not her husband after all but a dark-skinned man who never pulled on her, never took his eyes off her, needed no instruction, dipped his back leg and teased with his right like he couldn't decide where he wanted to be, New Orleans thick with perfumed ladies as his front leg gave in to the dance and his body shuddered loose, making her body—

"What are you doing?" Joan said. "Ohmygod the apartment. Isn't it kalooki night?"

"Don't second-guess me I'm doing something different, you know, gotta change, gotta keep with it. Come dance with me baby."

"I don't think— The women won't—"

"Dance with me, Pie."

Irwina lifted her arms and Joan saw ribs poking out of her mother's red angora sweater like one of Mrs. Dubrow's stews stretched to last, cooked till the bones turned elegant from heat. She saw too much. Her mother moved not like a mother. The living room was a party with no people.

"I still have it, don't I, baby? Move these hips better than any *Bandstand* kid. Let the music do things to you." Mama opened her arms.

Dick Clark had his smiling arms around Little Richard, whose skinny mustache outlined his lip like black lipstick. The camera turned to the dancers, Dick's arm fell off the singer, and he brushed that arm. Irwina wished she didn't see things.

"When are they coming? You gotta get ready."

"You're like an old woman."

"I think you should take some of it down."

"Like what."

"The camera and . . . and like some of the flowers, and we could freeze these sandwiches, they'll freeze nicely, and put out regular rolls."

"I see. And why would I do that? "

Because they'd hate her, Joan knew the talk. Because Buddy would hate it. Once Mama drank too much champagne at a wedding and danced with everybody's husband and Buddy had to carry her off the dance floor.

"Come here to me," her mother said.

Those open arms. The pull was sweet fields to fall into those open Mama arms but her eyes were closed, those arms never reached for her like this.

"I need to show you something," Joan said.

"What?"

Nothing. She didn't have a thing to show, and Mama was holding someone, pressing against his chest, lifting her arm to cup his neck, sticking out her pinkie finger lady style. Joan could almost see the way he looked. The music stopped, and the quiet was worse than the dancing.

Joan touched her mother's arm.

"Oh god what time is it? Honey, time's getting away from me I've got things . . ." and she was down the hall, in the bedroom, shutting the door.

"You want me to dance with you? I'll dance with you." Joan wiggled her hips and spun like crazy, saw the invisible partner following her mother down the hall, making jokes so she'd notice him plink into thin air, a spiral of tiny man-colored squares, then one note, then gone.

Buddy would be home, he'd make her go to temple while the women-in-the-building played cards. She had to go in place of Mama, sit next to him in her coat and be Mama. She wanted to hear the Buddy Hackett jokes and dirt, see Lil shuffle like Vegas. She needed a plan, needed to hide under the table, safe with the legs.

"I love you, Mama," Joan said.

A committee of feet on the hall stairs. The women-in-the-building showed up together, afraid of what the others might say behind their backs. Mama sprayed the air with final perfume mist and threw open the door.

"Come! Come in!"

They stood dripping in the hallway. It was pouring out, and now it was raining in the hall. They refused to enter with their umbrellas and rain bonnets and double-tied scarves.

"Who died?" Mrs. Dubrow said.

Lil sneezed.

"Seriously," Mrs. Dubrow said.

"Friday flowers from the Greek," Mama explained, "really. It was a bargain."

"A bargain huh. Looks like Lincoln Park. Looks like the Botanical Garden."

"Looks like a Mafia funeral."

"I like it," Fran said, trying to push through. "Smells good."

"You set a table?" Lil looked down at herself. "I didn't dress."

"That's mahooey, I just fussed a little. Please, come in." Mama held her arms out for their coats, but they were unbudged. Lil had galoshes in the shape of her shoes, wet shadow feet. Water plooped off Mrs. Slater's rain bonnet. Rose and Bessie waited uncertain behind them, Bessie's umbrella pointing toward Lil's rump, ready.

Lil to Mrs. Dubrow. "I'm telling you six angels pissing is too much for one heart."

Mrs. Slater stepped in. "But this reminds me of Kolhapur, and we had the fountains for sound and to carry bad air away. It's lovely."

"You didn't wear no raincoat," Lil said.

"It's just across the courtyard."

"We all came from the courtyard, but that don't stop the rain," Lil said.

"Are you just going to argue in my hall all night? Girls. You want to play cards in the hall?" Mama said. "This is ridiculous. It's just . . . will you please?"

"Can't you turn down the shrieking?" Mrs. Dubrow said.

"You didn't wear a raincoat or nothin'? It's wet out," Lil said. "Don't Keith believe in raincoats?"

"I am fine. I am a furnace." Mrs. Slater looked like she might cry.

"She looks beautiful," Fran said. "I'm going in. It's pretty Irwina, what you did for us. People should be more appreciative."

"Oh yeah? Which people?"

"People in general."

Mrs. Dubrow and Lil swapped looks and Lil said, "Anyone's got a Murphy apartment folds into a wall don't know nothin' from nothin'."

Bessie nudged Lil aside with her umbrella. Rose, Mrs. Slater and Fran followed and Mama took their coats to the bedroom.

Mrs. Dubrow and Lil shook themselves like dogs. The sandwiches looked fake and festive, the canasta tablecloth on the breakfront with the kings and jacks at mad angles. Joan hurt for Mama.

Lil. "And since when do we play fancy? And where's her rubber mat? Her newspaper? We supposed to take our shoes off? Don't she care about the Bigelow? Gimme the dough, I'll burn it for her."

"When I have the game, I put together a lovely pound cake and call it quits." Mrs. Dubrow.

"'Cause you know when to quit." Lil.

"I think that's absolutely crucial, don't you? Some people, however, don't come with a stop button." Mrs. Dubrow.

From the bedroom, Mrs. Slater. ". . . and I told Keith we needed a fountain, and he said he will think about it. Where did you get yours?"

Mama. "Oh it's been so long who remembers?"

"Is that caviar? My heavens." Mrs. Dubrow. "And champagne? Perhaps we should all go home and change into royalty."

Lil. "Makes me feel like I got dirt spots. Look at me. I got dirt? This ain't how we do. What. She answered The Sixty-Four-Thousand-Dollar Question?"

"Apparently." Mrs. Dubrow.

"*Mazel.* Let's play before I get a migraine." Lil.

"It smells awfully like inferiority complex to me." Mrs. Dubrow.

"Yeah and it stinks also." Lil. "You didn't know?"

"What?" Mrs. Dubrow.

"More than you think." Lil dropped her voice. "The man's a drinker. Swung with the boys in Cuba before they married."

"Swung?" Mrs. Slater.

Joan heard it all before, except the Buddy stuff and that didn't sound so bad. She knew how the apartment looked to them, the spewing fountain, the canapés, the fish eggs. Everything Mama had was contained in something else. The milk had a slipover with a plastic handle. Kleenex was packaged in fake fur caskets. The toilet tank upholstered in blue plush.

Mama saw their faces and Joan knew what she was thinking. Two words: *pearl* and *swine*.

The first hand was dealt. Kalooki was fast-moving, nonthinking with enough tricks to hold the attention but not steal it. They'd tried mah-jongg, but maj wasn't their game. New tiles, new rules, click-clack let the Chinese have it back. Maj didn't leave the brain free for sniffing, and the women played to sniff. Joan was never to answer their questions no matter how innocent they sounded.

Was it on purpose how Lil scraped the chair slow across her mother's wood floor? Her feet were squares, her legs two lengths from the scythe incident, whatever that was. She sat heavy and spread, her shoes black hospitals. Auntie Bessie wore orange support hose and left her shoes by the door. Auntie Rose had white KEDS like her feet never grew up with the rest of her. Fran had sandals with socks—the beatnik look. Mrs. Dubrow was loafers and white anklets, no pennies in the slots. Her legs were veined chicken meat. She didn't shave, didn't have much hair. Mrs. Slater slipped her flats off as soon as she sat down, tickled one foot with the other and let her leg kick like Dr. Klein was hammering it. Mama's shoes had sizz. Palace shoes with jewels and the toes came to a genie point.

Lil said what she always said. "We do what we came for gals or the messiah'll be here before we lay fifty-one." The next morning she'd describe the scene to her husband. She'd say Irwina's wig was so black it sucked the light from her heart. Leon would look at her briefly over his wire rims.

Mrs. Slater. "Aces high, jokers fickle?"

Fran. "Only love changes faster than a joker."

"You oughta know kid." Auntie Bessie.

Auntie Rose laid down the Hoyle. "It's double-deck rum aces hi-low fifteen points honor cards ten joker counts twenty-five first meld fifty-one nobody draws nobody lays till they meld. Melded joker pulls for natural. First out collects the table."

Somebody dealt.

Lil insisted on cutting.

"But it's a new deck dear," Mama said, "wrapped and made in the US of A."

"I'll break 'em in. I'll get 'em wet."

Laughter.

Mrs. Slater let her cards lay then grabbed them all at once and fanned. Fran plucked one at a time, reading for meaning. Mama made a double-decker hand, her canary diamond ring throwing it back at them. Mrs. Dubrow picked them up where they fell, her blue-flowered fanny lapping over the side of her chair. Auntie Bessie wore a step-and-repeat print dress like the machine couldn't stop. It was pick up put down money on the table. In the center, a beautiful pile of money Rose neatened between hands. They started at six, would quit at eleven. Woman not talking was the woman on a streak.

"Eat your hearts out girls." Mama's cards come down snap, snap, kalooki.

"So it's early, So the pot's still small." Lil.

"So Fran make a move today." Auntie Rose.

"Put a mirror under her nose." Lil.

"I'm thinking." Fran.

"It's three cents to the pot. Thinking is not involved." Mrs. Dubrow.

"Put, Fran." Aunt Rose. "You're holding things up."

"I already put."

"My ass." Lil said.

"Nothing on this table but dreams." Auntie Rose coughed.

"Dreams. Dreams are sixty percent of the human body," Mrs. Slater.

"You're thinking of water." Mrs. Dubrow.

"Put." Lil.

"I put! You want me to put for the unborn?" Fran.

"I tell Keith we play for the fun." Mrs. Slater laughed uncertainly.

"That a jab?" Fran.

"Someone whose name I don't mention plays for trouble." Auntie Bessie.

"Fran," Mama said gently, "we're talking three cents here. It's not a decision-making moment. Hot coffee anyone? I have real cream."

Lil looked inside Mama's French cow creamer. "It's gone rotten."

"It's not rotten, it's tinted." Mama.

Lil passed the cow elaborately to Mrs. Slater.

Eventually they broke for food. Mama brought champagne, dropped sugar cubes into each crystal glass. The champagne foamed over.

"Like watching a nuclear test." Lil.

"My Jim knows about bombs." Mrs. Dubrow.

Mama's food sat untouched. "Doesn't anybody want anything? Bess? Nonpareil?"

The imperceptible shaking of heads, women's unspoken consent.

"Well what's the matter with all of you? Isn't anybody—"

"I am. Starved. Takes a lot of these eggs to make a meal." Fran shoved a spoon in the caviar. "Looks Halloweeny."

Mrs. Dubrow piled her plate with tiny sandwiches. "Jim's got a new job. Special Services." Her husband had a job a month. Milk man, brush man—he was running out of men to be.

"He is with the bomb department?" Mrs. Slater.

"Administration." Mrs. Dubrow. "Paper, predominately."

"What's he got to do with bombs?" Fran.

"Drop the bone, Franny." Auntie Bess.

"I'm asking." Fran.

"We don't ask." Auntie Rose.

"Ask me anything. I've got nothing to be ashamed." Mrs. Dubrow.

"Looks like Alka Seltzer." Fran stuck her nose in a glass.

"Briosci." Mrs. Dubrow.

"What are you itching?" Bessie to Mrs. Slater. "Can't you take something for that?"

"I used to be a firefly. I was zip zap you know with the scarves on, laughing." Mrs. Slater.

"We heard. And now you scratch." Auntie Bessie.

Joan imagined Mrs. Slater's hands white and smooth like they shouldn't be seen naked.

"What happened to you?" Lil.

"Keith likes me to dress American, but in India each sister had a color." Mrs. Slater.

"What were you?" Fran.

"Saffron." Mrs. Slater scratched at her kilt.

"It itches so you wear undergarments." Auntie Rose.

"Those bother me as well." Mrs. Slater.

The women started slow and ate till the table was demolished. Buddy was late. Mrs. Dubrow told a story about a friend whose husband went down to their basement to fix his wife's freezer and died there.

"In the freezer?" Fran.

"He left her dinner parties to go down there and tinker, but she found out he was peeing over the drain, wanted to inhale the smell of himself, he said. When he killed a mouse and laid it next to her roast chicken she took him to the Printer's Home in Colorado. He worked for the paper, they paid every penny."

"Maybe he didn't like dinner parties." Fran.

"I can't eat with talk like this." Auntie Rose.

"Sorry." Mrs. Dubrow.

"This is real life. Don't apologize." Lil.

Shoes came off, voices blended. Metal. Tobacco. Flour. Wood. Rice. Salt. Joan knew the flavor of every heart at that table and dozed to the sentence-finishing comfort of women in sit-down sport, waking with Buddy's feet stamp stamping near her head.

Seven

BUDDY LIKED GETTING TO temple early so he could get a good shot at the arc. He sat as far as he could get from the cheap seats where pale Jews who knew Hebrew sang unto heaven, which in their case was just above the acoustical tile. Buddy sat up with the cashmeres and had his arms around the velvet seats and was nodding to people.

"Smile at the Hartshorn's, the Hartshorn's are watching you," he said.

"Which ones?" said Joan.

"Over there, elderly couple."

Everybody looked elderly, husbands and wives with sympathetic bald spots. Joan nodded, generally.

"What's that crap around your neck? Is that, Joan. Is that someone's teeth?"

She tucked the necklace in her dress. She was supposed to be perfect for temple. He inspected her breath, her shoes, her.

"Hold it." He put his bifocals on. "I'll be damned."

"They're nothing." Shit shit shit.

"Don't tell me I'm looking at teeth. Where'd you get this?"

Buddy was fast. One yank and the thread gave.

"I know who did this voodoo crap jewelry. Our Miss Fit. Kiss it good-bye."

He slipped the teeth in his pocket as Rabbi Wassermann lifted his arms like a Judy Garland finale. "All rise."

In one slick hydraulic motion the congregation stood, except for Cantor Cohen, who stretched his long legs and yawned.

"Man's his own damn cantor," Buddy whispered. "Look at that nerve."

"I'd like those back, Dad," she said. "Give 'em."

"God's watching."

"All rise," the rabbi repeated.

The cantor finally stood.

"Old trouble those two."

"Dad that's—"

"God's writing it in the book."

"My—"

His dry hand covered her mouth. She tasted glycerin and rose-water. The choir, suspended in a loft above the pulpit, opened with *ma tovu,* a prayer that sustained one word, *a ma* so clean it hit Joan's spine and made her forget.

"Maaaaaaaaaaaaaaaa tow-oh-voo."

From the cantor's mouth came Jew velvet and the rabbi smiled and all was forgiven and the people prayed for what was missing in their lives and told God they understood if He didn't listen right away since He had plenty going on, but if He could take a second for their particular suffering—Joan tried praying, but prayer jumped track and went electric, sizzing and spazzing so her words went to other kingdoms besides heaven. Prayer was only solid when she was riding her bike.

"Quit snortin' and squirmin'," Buddy said.

"Be seated," said the rabbi.

The old men were the last to sit, swathed in the tallises of their forefathers they moaned and rocked until, if they were lucky, a wife touched their arm and said show's over. And then the cantor sat.

Libby Raznik from school was sitting between her parents the next row over. The Shuleman family nostrils flared big as nickels when they sang. Marilyn smiled at Joan. Whine baby. Buddy tapped her prayer book. He could read her mind. She scanned. Lil and Leon over by the giant menorah. Mr. Leonard. The *goniff.* Mr. Horton the footman, Mizer the funeral people, that kid Abe with the one funny ear who was the only boy to flunk bar mitzvah. Even though Cantor made him a record of his own voice.

Kaddish. Things were moving along. Rabbi Wassermann called the names of the dead and people stood. Rosenberg. Rosenfeld. Rose and thaw. Rose in bloom, *V'yaskidoll, vay yiskadosh shamey rabbo.* All the dead roses. Buddy touched his velvet yarmulke, gave it a little adjustment. "Think about the dead," he said.

"I was."

"You wasn't."

Somebody groaned.

"Is it enough for man to pray?" asked the rabbi. He sermoned to the cheap seats like they needed it most. He looked tired and said the tips of things while bigger mounds shimmered just out of sight. He took his glasses off, rubbed his eyes, put the glasses on one ear, letting them dangle mournfully beneath his chin. Kids made money betting on those glasses.

Last Friday his sermon was "Rachmanous and Communism: To Strive or Not to Strive." Week before: "Jew as Salmon Swimming Upstream," poot poots of rabbi spit landing on his glasses when he said an "s" word.

"Is it enough a man should go to his temple demanding an audience with God if the rest of the week he doesn't know God's name?"

No brainer.

"If the rest of the week the man's heart is a boiled egg?"

And the woman's is boiling water?

Sofia Fitt snuck her into Saint Jerome's Church and said close your eyes and see something you want. That's prayer. Works better if it's for somebody else, but don't ask for love or peace. It's vague; it won't get you anywhere. She heard the silent prayers of the rosary people, a massive whoosh of begging, and had to cover her ears.

". . . does he even know what prayer is?"

See it, want it with all you got, kiss it if it comes back ugly. That's prayer. Church had statues whose mouths moved if you stared and blessed water and long-handled money pans. Temple was amber, church was blue with shafts of dust.

". . . when nobody gave the heart the news?" The rabbi was shouting. It was the halfway point.

The cantor shook his head. Clearly he thought the rabbi was a lox.

". . . your Red Sea parts, what will you take and what will you leave behind?"

She'd take her turtle and get her teeth back. They were yelling to her from Buddy's side pocket. He leaned to her. "Main thing is, whole point is—" She used to wait for him to tell her the point, but now she knew there wasn't any point, so she thought about being with Chris Nobel in her pajamas, his taste in her mouth.

"Your mother never learned to pray."

"She prays."

"No she don't."

Mama squeezed lemon on the back of her hands and stuck them out the window and asked god to make her liver spots disappear. According to Sofia Fitt, this was prayer. Now where was she. Chris in her little bed, under the covers with a flashlight looking at her giraffes, kissing her giraffes.

"What's on your mind there?"

"I'm forgiving you for sins."

Rabbi Wassermann's glasses hit the podium and fell to the floor, possibly a new record.

Adon Olam baBOOM baBOOM.

The last prayer and everybody sang loud with relief. ba-BOOM ba-BOOM. Hundreds of Rabbi Wassermanns marching toward the sweet wine and cake in the auditorium. She added her loudest voice to the brigade, and Buddy was pleased. He joined in with his older Hebrew that made t's sound like s's. It was the

Jewish "Seventy-six Trombones," and her body shook with the rhythm of the tribe.

B'tzerim kall baBOOM baBOOM.

Buddy smiled proudly at the fart sitting next to him. "I raised this kid," he said. The man looked alarmed. Buddy spread his arms around the velvet seats, and his chest popped with pride. "My youngest and my oldest."

The congregation was on its feet shouting, backslapping, flinging minks, old people jiggering like they'd been shot with honey through and through, Joan's hand dipping into Buddy's pocket, kids running down the aisles, Cantor Cohen smiling. baBOOM.

Eight

MELVIN FRANKLIN BELIEVED IN straight backs, tight asses and balance. He paced the gym, an excellent pacer, weaving between girls sitting cross-legged in squads under the direction of squad leaders whose job it was to watch for bad posture.

His girls would learn to appreciate the forty-yard dash because they'd earn it. No Phys. Ed. for two weeks. No movement. Pep talks followed by the repetitive singing of Franklin's favorite song, "There Was a Desperado from the Wild and Wooly West."

"We're working on endurance." He paced. "Something you're dangerously lacking like zinc and common sense. Your past performances—" He couldn't find words. "I say run this is what you give me?" He was shouting. "Well is it?"

Squads shouted, "No!"

"This is what you're made of?"

"NO."

"IS IT?"

"NO!"

"Sir."

"Sir."

"No. NO SIR!"

"NO NO SIR!"

He had that rolling Cason rhythm, and some of the girls were rocking.

"WHAT ARE YOU MADE OF?"

Huh?

"TELL ME WHAT YOU'RE MADE OF!"

Girls silently read their names off gym shoes.

"Mind over body, keeping the goal, taking the salt pills." The flies and the clock sounded the same. "I like you. I do. You're good girls, you can take this thing and run."

Maybe because it sounded like a Chinese fairy tale or because he rolled his chair to the center of the gym and played intensely with his metal whistle. Maybe it was the name he gave it, Miracle of the Second Wind. Joan was paying attention. Reserves of power hunkered down inside her waiting to be pounced. Underemployed energy, Franklin said, begging to send them flying over hurdles.

Edie poked Joan. The squad leader shot them a warning.

"And people got it, but do people use it? Do they use this stuff? Look around."

They were polite girls. They glanced within themselves.

"Worst display of physicality in thirteen years as gym teacher of Eugene Field School and forget the dash, this is life we're talking about."

Oh. Life. It was better before he said that. Why such big bites? Why couldn't he stick to crunches or get them some decent equipment like the boy equipment funded by Hortons, Mizers, people with money who moved but remembered the scarcity of Little League before Thillens. Their mitts were so broken in it was their hands that had to be greased and worked. Bats gave them splinters. And how about some bases you could see? Higher than the ground and with some stuffing left?

Melvin Franklin covered the gym, his jaw clicking in frustration.

"How do you expect to get through life with your side stitches and your menstruation excuses some of you three a month?"

Libby Raznik. She had lips like a duck that smacked when she talked and a doctor's note excusing her from movement.

"Picture this, in you this enormous tank and picture you're running you're about to give up you're dying you can't get a breath can't make your legs work and you access this tank. Who can tell me what's inside?"

No sir. They'd seen girls answer wrong.

"Ah come on I already told you."

They had crazy teachers, sure, half of them teaching so long, when they said the Battle of Antietam was like yesterday they believed it. The woman music teacher wore safety pins in her hair, the man music teacher made them sing about dolphins carelessly, fearlessly, leaping away while bomb shelters were being stocked and manned. The boys believed duck and cover might cover it, but the girls didn't, not for one minute did they believe a desk or a jacket could keep the atomic bomb from blowing their faces off.

These teachers were harmless, busy in their own fog. Franklin was another kind of crazy. He hummed "Great Balls of Fire," and when Roxanne Lansky hit a volleyball with her fist he made her stand all period and say why she did it. Why? She didn't know. She saw chance and whacked it. Franklin told the class it was because her parents were divorced. Lansky cried, and after that she got mean.

"Anybody? Nobody? Inside you is a tank packed with energy! Oxygen reserves! A secret wind in your guts and spleens that'll take you straight to the Olympics."

It sounded like gas. They'd been sitting too long. Even Libby Raznik wanted out, and one day he marched them to the schoolyard, tallest first, Joan was second behind Roxanne Lansky. He had his stopwatch, his pilot sunglasses, his whistle. Girls crouched at the starting line he dug in gravel with his heel. Women with a free afternoon moved aimlessly by trying not to look aimless.

"You see everything on his chest through that T-shirt," Joan said.

"I think he irons it," Ruthie said.

"It's too small for him," said Edie. "He wants you to see."

Thirty-two girls kneeling in gravel, salt pills swimming through bloodstreams, goal line sited, tanks flung.

"SPAANGGG!"

They shot out, friends pushing friends, Roxanne Lansky in the lead followed by Daphne Figman, Joan, Edie Slater, somebody called the Thigh Chaffer, somebody named Eileen, nickname, Weeny. Libby Raznik, who ran on her toes, brought up the rear. They tore air, ate pain, stepped over trippers and wished them dead. At the finish line they kept running, pounding into the metal fence. The aimless women crossed the street.

Who won? They wanted, needed, demanded to know. Bets on Roxanne Lansky who had breasts at the start of the race but ran so hard her gym suit burst and toilet paper flew out of her like a welcome banner.

Give them meat, give them victory, give them—bell was ringing. Mary Figman swore she saw a bullet come out of Franklin's gun. He had a gun? A starting gun, Mary Figman said. Lansky, with her chest of unleavened cupcakes puckered at the point, said it wasn't a real gun anyway. Somebody said they saw Joan hit the fence first and Lansky's middle finger rose.

"Perch on this, Fish," she said.

They waited to see who'd be Wilma Rudolph and what stuff was inside them and Franklin wimped. He wimped. Gave them some run like this everybody wins crap, supremely unsatisfying to be let out of cages, given tanks and then have to quietly sit in Miss Sheck's fifth period watching a film of bare-bottomed natives pounding grain on rocks. Or laundry. Grain and laundry being pounded out on rocks. Although pounding looked like a good idea.

Sheck talked over the narrator, whom she felt missed the boat. The boat was maize and misery. Occasionally a native would look directly into their eyes and not seem miserable at all. Unconcerned animals waddled by. Rhinos, hippos. Women and children went down to the river to bathe or pound. Joan scanned the film-lit room for faces.

Turn around, it begins.

Lansky, a bored elbow parked on her desk, finger still raised, Chris Nobel watching her like she couldn't see him, the twins with their heads down.

Turn around, Buddy in the room, her father, like some kind of thirst mirage.

"Libby, get the lights please. It seems we have a visitor," Sheck said.

He was honestly here and was honestly saying, "Buddy Trout's the name, I don't mean to interrupt."

Joan lifted the top of her desk. He'd been threatening this. Bored with the shop, Mama's finery not going anywhere, he craved more, he said, more than Hocus Pocus. A focus. Her.

"Whether you mean to or not is irrelevant because you in fact *are* interrupting, Mr. Trout."

He took off his hat, turning the rim of it like a steering wheel.

"I only come— I want to take my kid to lunch, a father's mid-week treat."

Don't say it.

"That's her, that's my Joanie."

"Fish breath," Lansky said.

Sheck was opening the door, telling him the deal. Permission slips, office aids, principal, passes.

Buddy laughed. "You sendin' me to the office?"

In fact, the office came to him.

A guidance counselor was sent to the apartment. Buddy was furious. Mama served tea sandwiches and tried to make the counselor like them.

"My husband gets involved," Mama said, "which I think can be a good thing, don't you?"

The counselor took notes in a steno pad. She never looked at Joan.

"What're you writin'?" Buddy said.

"I'm noting the interaction," the counselor said.

"Ain't seen no interacting."

"What my husband means, what he's trying to do . . ."

Mama had no idea. She didn't know about his school visit till that morning. She didn't know he appeared places, an accident, a stroke of luck that he should run into Joan at restaurants, make her slide over, wipe his fries good-naturedly through the central ketchup well. At dances he was the father behind the brownies. At dance parties he was the guy in the back with the cigar. At kissing parties he was the voice in the dark. If a phone rang it was hey Fish before anyone picked up. There was nowhere Buddy wasn't. Joan's grades slid. The only kids with worse grades never showed up at school.

"Your daughter's Scholastic Achievement Tests are remarkably high yet her grades—"

"Stinko," Buddy said. "I'm working on it. She's the creative type, gets it from the mother."

"I'm suggesting you take Joan out of the public school system and put her in private. Francis Parker has an excellent curriculum for unique minds."

"Unique. Sounds like it'll cost."

"The school can help somewhat."

"We don't take charity," Buddy said. "Look I get your drift, see, I'm one ahead a you. I got the answer book, flash cards—"

Turn around, he was there.

Nine

KALOOKI AT MRS. DUBROW'S and the air was hammy and underneath that the smell of burnt lemon cake plastered with dromedary dates. Jesus bloomed from the walls. Jesus with his ceramic robe and outspread arms. Rose Quartz Jesus. Shepherd Jesus. Blue Jesus. Jesus the flaky tour guide. Where Jesus wasn't, a depression of Hummel figurines was.

"I heard him talk last time I was here." Fran. "I did."

"Jim is a large talker." Mrs. Slater.

"Jesus." Fran.

"Oh yeah?" Lil. "He give you a good hand? What do you have on?" Lil sniffed.

Fran stared at her slacks.

"The perfume."

"Intimate by Revlon." Fran.

"Stinks." Lil did a finger pass over her chin, found something, worked it.

"Fresh baked?" Irwina.

"I took time with it if that's what you're implying." Mrs. Dubrow's hair was perm fried. The damage compiled could never be undone. "I'm sorry it isn't the deluxe model you serve." She glanced around to see if anyone was backing her on this. "Just plain old honest Midwestern fare."

"Duncan or Betty?" Irwina's mood needed ratcheting.

She was careful to dress down, sloppy Joe sweater, Capri's, and flats but it took it out of her, getting Joan to temple. She hated setting Buddy off. She'd bought her airline tickets, rented a decent

room, had to let Joan wear her own coat with the mink ring collar and promise entertaining things she couldn't imagine herself
doing. From behind, the child would look like her, Joan and
Buddy passing for a couple, which didn't entirely displease her.
What displeased her was the dream she'd had last night where
Buddy and Joan *were* a couple, the kind of alert, socially rehearsed
couple that causes great pain by confirming what others suspect
about their own dim partnerships. A vivid, science dream in which
her family left her and, in the next instant, she was old. Terribly
old with something called brain infarcts, whatever the hell that
was. She took a drug, saw quite clearly the amber Walgreen's bottle and the prescription number: Rx#6681829. It went on, this
dream. She couldn't take a bath without a nurse and a place to
land. Nurse Bebby in a uniform the texture of a Dixie Cup. Then
she had to diagram the trip to the tub, hands to sink, foot to mat.
We live to be put into hands like these. It was New York, she
knew. The New York trip was making her nervous.

"You got complaints about my baking take it up with Sara
Lee." Mrs. Dubrow.

"I'm not complaining." Irwina.

"It is indeed a Duncan, but for your information I added my
own pudding mix. For the moisture and why am I explaining
myself to you? Jim. Honey. Take the women's wraps."

Jim Dubrow was a stiff man who waited for coats like he'd
been rented for the job.

His back was bent. Buddy liked coming up behind him and
poking him hello in the spine. Jim would jerk up then stoop back
where he was. In their wedding photo, Jim was a straight-backed
chair of a man, but the war imposed an endless variety of person-
ality fractures and Jim had returned bent, a ceaseless talker with a
curiosity close to madness.

The women gave up their coats to him one at a time, waiting
in line while he walked each one to the bedroom. They knew
he'd examine the pockets but wouldn't steal. He'd been examin-
ing everything since his last job, a something something with the

Special Services, where he left every day but Mrs. Dubrow never saw the check.

"What'd he do again?" Fran.

"Don't let's start this." Lil.

"Jim was important." Mrs. Dubrow cupped her immobile hair.

"Yeah I keep wondering what he actually *did*." Fran shook out her charm bracelet. Every year she bought herself an 18K gold charm from Schiller's Jewelers and had it engraved to herself. Happy Fortieth! With This Basket of Love!

"Rooskys. Jim did what others wouldn't." Mrs. Dubrow.

Bess to Irwina. "The man slinks around the Buy-Low like the grapefruits are after him."

"So he's got a job now?" Fran.

"He's waiting. To hear." Mrs. Dubrow.

"I think a man needs something more than waiting." Mrs. Slater.

"He's *actively* waiting." Mrs. Dubrow.

Mrs. Slater perked Irwina up. When she talked, there were flashes of India between her words, matriarchy of unneurotic women's hands, bejeweled, chapati flattening hands, and she was beautiful, in a Punjabi way. Keith ruined her with those woolies. She could dress that body.

"So. What did he do at that last job?" Fran.

Mrs. Dubrow was herding them toward the card table. "Missions."

"Missions?" Fran.

"Witness the uncontested thought patterns of the single middle-aged." Mrs. Dubrow.

"Huh?" Fran. "Explain please."

"Jim handled your Nazi Commie element now here, all of you, I'm set up ready to go." Mrs. Dubrow let out an onion sigh, but Fran wouldn't let up. "Officially you mean? All right. Officially. Between me and you he was a seneschal."

"Wow." Fran. "During the war or after?"

"Throughout. Now can we please?" Mrs. Dubrow.

The card table had a paper tablecloth littered with illustrations of playing cards, tilted kings and queens making zany eyes at each other.

"What's his mission now?" Fran.

"Does she come with an off button?" Bessie.

Rose. "Fran shut it."

Lil. "We don't talk behind backs you know."

Rose. "Who made that rule?"

Jim walked another coat to the bedroom. If he got into one of his talking fits it would be a late night. Last year he talked for a month solid, talked till Mrs. Dubrow packed her train case and booked a room at Michael Reese Hospital.

"I needed a little break." Mrs. Dubrow.

"You did right." Lil.

The women understood. Hospitals were a lock a key and a solid routine, hotels only cheaper.

"Nothing closer to salvation than a decent routine." Rose.

"Enough routine the worst life mends." Bess.

"Enough routine the best life ends." Irwina.

Jim had joined them, one of the girls. He bit down on a hunk of lemon cake and talked while chewing. Irwina caught ". . . my mother had long hair till she died—" before she shut him out.

Rose did her Hoyle dance, even though it had been pointed out to her many times this made no sense. "It's double-deck rum ace hi-low fifteen points honor cards ten joker for twenty-five first meld fifty-one nobody draws nobody lays till they meld and a melded joker pulls for natural and first out collects the table."

Lil. "You know Rose you say that garbage but kalooki don't come a hundred ways. Why you gotta say that? We play we play. Every week it's the same."

"Jim. Honey." Mrs. Dubrow. Jim retreated to the bedroom, avoiding the area rugs.

Mrs. Dubrow tried to fill the doubt hole he left behind. "Okay I can say this now. I didn't want to embarrass him. My Jim is selling chocolate for the Chocolate Products Company down there on Division Street." Mrs. Dubrow paused to let the possibility of her husband's redemption sink in.

"They're paying him?" Fran.

They knew each other's thoughts and defended themselves against unspoken judgments. Or maybe they were spoken. Nobody could remember. Six years of kalooki the subtleties melded.

"Kayo chocolate milk in bottles, Stillicious syrup," Mrs. Dubrow was saying. "I saw the place. Huge. They have no less than eight women working the front. Everything is steel and tile so they can hose it down you know. Steel vats of chocolate and enormous Mix Masters, it smells like, well like an ammoniated cow, but he's traveling so it's good. They gave him all the Dairy Queens in Rockford and Peoria."

"How is he doing with this?" Mrs. Slater.

"They're up against Hershey's is how he's doing." Mrs. Dubrow had a minor head tremor, possibly bracing for the next job loss.

"Hershey's built a town you know, in Pennsylvania." Irwina.

"A chocolate town?" Mrs. Slater.

"I could live on chocolate." Fran.

"Patch of yard and nice kitchens." Rose.

"You know about this?" Bessie.

"She's thinking of Levittown." Mrs. Dubrow. "That's an entirely different story."

"Levittown, Chocolatetown, who cares? We're city girls." Fran.

"Rabbi builds Fishmantown that's when I go." Lil.

"But can you imagine a house? I mean actually living in a house?" Fran jammed bridge mix in her mouth. "No one on the stairs but you, nobody walking on your head—"

"You're spewing. Swallow." Lil.

"White Cape Cods a hundred down sixty-eight more gets you stunning architectural equality." Rose.

"Jeezy Rosey, you actually study this stuff." Bessie.

Lil pushed the candy dish away from Fran, who swiped a cat-fast handful first. "We do what we came for gals or the messiah'll be here before—"

Jim was back with a globe of the world. He plunked it in the epicenter of the table and wiped his nose. "Commies testing A-bombs."

Bess. "What's he talking?"

"I'm saying plutonium is what I'm saying and hydrogen's next and we don't build The Super Russia'll push ahead of us and *boom pow* another war and civilization goes under."

"Jim. Please play in your room." Mrs. Dubrow.

Lil closed her eyes and made mental notes for Leon, who liked her to give the kalooki highlights as accurately as possible.

Jim talked to Hartshorn, she'd tell him.

The landlord? he'd say. What did that *pipeck* want with the landlord?

Wants to convert the basement into a bomb shelter.

With the washing machines? No room.

That's what Wenig told him. Lost another job. Got fired for reading *The Post.*

That writer whatshisface?

Yeah.

That Guatemala guy?

Yeah.

That fake-banana-coup-in-Guatemala guy?

Yeah.

Jim spun the globe and put his finger on Roger's Park. The women-in-the-building took turns standing and looking.

"Good. Now at least we know where we are." Rose.

"Do you think that's the South Side right there over Baltic?" Bessie.

"I used to be a firefly," Mrs. Slater was telling Fran. "Firefly they called me."

"Why that sounds so lovely." Mrs. Slater.

"I was zip zap all the time with gay scarves."

"What happened to you?" Fran said. Then, because Lil was staring a hole in her head, "What happened with Leon?"

"He goes in next week for tests."

"They didn't get enough from him last time?"

"Different organs."

"Heart? Lung? Liver? Prostate?"

"Kidney. Bladder. Brain. Blood."

"So he goes. So you'll know what's what." Bessie.

"God knows and he ain't telling." Lil.

Irwina decided. She'd make Lil some sort of casserole to grease the wait. On the other hand, all that mess.

"Speaking of Reese I got to know it good last year when I wasn't so sure I wanted to live." Fran.

"You took the pills, but your cousin found you in time, thank goodness." Mrs. Slater.

"He found me, yeah. I wasn't crazy you know, just tired. You know that kind of tired?"

They knew. They knew.

"How's Married Johnny? He makin' a livin'?" Bessie.

"Why?" Fran.

"She can't ask?" Lil.

"I'm going to New York." Irwina heard herself say, and the room. Only Rose seemed to be moving.

"Why? Chicago don't keep you busy?" Bessie.

"I just thought, you know, if anybody needs anything." Irwina.

"FROM NEW YORK?" Lil and Bessie.

"What can't we get here?" Mrs. Dubrow broke open two new decks, a blue and a red Riderback. Shuffled. Nobody needed a thing.

"Buddy can get it for them." Rose.

Bessie kicked Rose under the table so hard the bridge mix lopped out of the aluminum leaf-shaped bowl.

Fran. "You know, you never know who's the Russian in the crowd. I saw a film. They look like us."

"Such brilliance." Lil.

"Like us?" Mrs. Slater put a hand over her breast.

"Not us exactly, I mean we *know* us." Fran.

"Don't listen to her." Bessie. "We're playing, okay John Chancellor? Feed the pot and rest your gizzard."

Irwina was hoping for a few orders to make the trip pay. It was a strange day. She saw the moon when it was light, but it had disappeared by dusk. Bassackward and that dream was still with her. She fanned her cards. Two jokers and a deuce run. Potential. She talked as she ordered her cards. "Seriously, you might want to think about it. I'm having dinner with Coco Chanel."

Blood halt, except for Rose's hands snapping up cards, scrutinizing their worth, and it was out and they were off and she hadn't meant to; inside her, the dinner with Chanel was snug and glamorous. She'd gone through it so many times: who'd pick up the check, the various desserts, the bond she'd feel with someone at her level. Mrs. Dubrow had a hungry smile, Bessie stroked down the hairs on Irwina's arm.

"A light dinner or chateaubriand tableside?" Mrs. Dubrow.

Bessie. "Buddy didn't say nothin' about—"

Lil was memorizing for later.

Fran. "Somebody filming you?"

Mrs. Slater, breathless from reading faces, trying to catch a nuance, a drift, something shackled with meaning.

"It's nothing really." Irwina.

"We thought that." Lil.

"She—"

"Coco, you mean." Lil.

"Coco, yes, has been gone for quite some time, you know it's probably a P.R. stunt, her meeting with smaller shops. I think she's making some kind of statement—"

"Chanel for the Wee People." Mrs. Dubrow.

"Yeah like Ike's pushing Brillcream." Lil.

"—trade-show-industry kind of deal, anyway, I just thought if anybody needed a specific—" Irwina couldn't stop her mouth.

"—little something to wear around the house." Mrs. Dubrow.

"—or if there was some an occasion I could help . . ." Stop! Stop!

"My sister's the dreamer of us." Rose folded her hand.

"You keep busy these days, don't you Rose. You runnin' the store now?" Fran.

"Those who see, do." Rose sighed.

"Don't Chanel have a Nazi boyfriend?" Lil.

The women nodded in some kind of agreement. Irwina felt a cornrow of sweat forming above her lip.

"There are people who have money and people who are rich. Coco said." Shut up! Shut up!

"There are people who make a mess and people who clean." Rose's face, like she swallowed Irwina's real pearl earring again.

"All right Rosey." Bessie. "Let her look for you gals, she got you nice clothes before, she ain't done bad by you."

"I need a bathroom." Lil.

"Jim's in there, you'll have to wait." Mrs. Dubrow.

"She can look her ass off." Lil. "Look all you want."

Rose picked up her cards again, lifting, inserting, making a project of it, left-right-left-right like reading *Peyton Place*.

"Anybody else you're seein' while you're there?" Lil.

"Dior?" Mrs. Dubrow.

"Well Dior is—" Irwina.

"Dead." Mrs. Dubrow.

"I was going to say." Irwina.

"Bring back some of that art silk if they got it." Fran. "I like that stuff. Maybe a nice boucle knit."

"Can't give it away." Rose.

Bessie. "I need two cards, and I'm down and taking that pot home if somebody don't play serious."

"*Art silk*'s a funny word for Rayon and we got enough Rayon to choke a mule." Rose.

"Horse. I say a lot of things funny too. Pointsettiahs," Fran threw pennies on the pile. "Peemientoes, presperation."

"You got your own way that's for sure." Lil.

The women knew Married Johnny tucked a hundred under her coffee table glass once in a while and bought her orange juice, butter, a carton of eggs here and there but never stayed to eat them.

Fran to Mrs. Slater. "I like your nails. Hey. If Coco moved to Hersheyville—"

"Butterfat." Lil.

Mrs. Slater flashed her hand around. "Do you like them? It is Pink T.N.T."

The air sliced and diced. Irwina had tried to be a woman-of-the-building for a night, to ease into those simple arms and find rest, but there was no rest to be found.

Rose dumped a black queen.

"Dropping the weight early?" Fran.

"Wash your own hand." Bess.

"You ever had a pain right here?" Lil tapped her chest.

"Everybody has pain." Mrs. Dubrow.

"Specially when I bend it's thomp, thomp." Lil.

"Nickel to the pot all." Mrs. Dubrow.

Mrs. Slater looked at her nickel, doubting its sincerity.

"Give it up before they jump you." Fran.

Mrs. Slater grabbed a ten from the face-up pile.

"You can't pick from the faces unless you go down. You goin' down?" Lil.

"I believe I am." Mrs. Slater.

"Did you count dear?" Mrs. Dubrow.

Mrs. Slater laid down her cards, her lips silently counting.

"Kalooki this early? Can't be." Lil.

Mrs. Slater picked her cards up again. "I'm sorry . . . all this talking."

"Lay a natural down or don't pick from the face up." Lil.

"What else you lookin' for in New York City?" Bessie.

"Let's not pursue this." Rose.

"I'm concentrating," Irwina remembered an ad, "on glamorizing the beauty zone. Merry Widow, Pink Champagne, Romance, Lovable, Sweet and Low for uplifting cantilevered support. Did you know I had something to do with cantilevering?" Irwina caught Bessie's warning. "But that's another story. Let's see, foundation garments and the crocodile winkle-picker shoe, if I can find it. Perhaps some spring linen."

"You got plenty of that navy linen look in the back." Rose.

"I know what's in back." Irwina.

"Like you're having dinner with Chanel." Rose.

"Don't you tell me what I've got in back."

"Liar." Rose.

"Rosey. In public yet." Bessie.

"No I will not, Rosey, because she's lied, and it made Ma sick and it's making me sick and you stick up for her and I'm sick of it, that's all, I'm sick of it, and it's preposterous what she gets away with smelling like perfume, me doing all the work."

"Who asked you?" Irwina.

"Your husband." Rose.

"You been there two weeks she runs the place ten years what right you got?" Bessie.

"She hates seeing things as they are." Rose.

Was that true? Was that why the more gilding the safer she felt?

"Spade's a spade." Fran.

"She's got fourteenth-century models and costumes nobody buys. Who can afford her taste? They got no place to wear them, and don't look at me like you don't know what I'm talking about. A funeral? A wedding? How many events does a good woman have in her life? They aren't buying your designer bullshit, and anyways, the knockoffs look more real than your real. Right ladies? Am I Right?"

Eye averting with a consensus of sidestepped mumbling.

Rose spoke to her cards. "Buddy's been borrowing for years. That's right, owes more than Joe made in his lifetime and you encourage her, you think oh she's the good sister and here's her color-book life. You think truth'll break her? Is that it? Well who wants to live like this? Anybody?"

Bessie pushed her chair back. "That's enough. You go too far in front of them."

"I don't give a rat's carcass. Rose, he says, my wife don't know what from what and she's going to New York? To put him deeper in the eight ball? I tell you the truth, I feel for that man."

The women looked at Irwina, who, in the face of head-on hostility from Rose, had a tingling, numb body and a mind that followed. She could yell at Bessie but never Rose. She looked at Rose and saw the cord cut and Louie falling in that elevator, falling a hundred ways. Sometimes he floated, not in an elevator at all but standing on top of it, pausing floor to floor, each one giving him a chance and Louie saying no. Sometimes they snapped his cord, and he fell in the time it took to empty the lungs, still holding the lunch Rose made him. It was a tall building. There was nothing to bury. Rose put flowers in a pine box and her shivah was a charade. Louie would walk in any minute, ragged and with a few things broken, and they'd all laugh, meek Lou who gave Rose the pants early in the marriage and read his girls soft stories. To look at Rose was to see shafts with different endings.

Bessie. "This is bad you talking like this. I'm gonna tell—"

"Who. Joe? Louie? We're what's left, and we should do right by each other." Rose.

"This you call right? Slander in front of strangers?" Bessie.

"I'd hardly say strangers." Mrs. Dubrow.

"Family, almost." Lil.

"Why don't you say something back?" Bessie jiggled Irwina's arm.

"She knows I'm right." Rose.

Sniff, sniff. It was more than the women-in-the-building could chew in a night. Trouble among sisters, meetings with dead moguls, oh joy oh bliss, and Rose's eyes had plenty cooking, but they didn't know the new from the leftovers. They'd have to sort it out later. It could take weeks. It could take a couple winters.

Irwina patted her upper lip with a paper napkin of zany jacks and watched Mrs. Slater peal her blouse off her sweaty skin, beautiful skin. She would bring her saris of orchid ribbed in platinum for keeping her mouth shut.

Fran was the only one concentrating on the game, picking up the card Mrs. Slater forfeited, "As Rome sleeps," dropping a ten face down, her first kalooki in ages, and she took her sweet time laying runs as Mrs. Slater smoothed the skirt that would never be right and Bessie stood there, squeezing the back of her chair, wishing Irwina would fight, and Rose refiddled cards and Lil closed her eyes to commit trouble to memory and Mrs. Dubrow announced, "The bathroom is now free," and Irwina handed her mind over to Blue Jesus, who guarded the store-bought buffet.

Ten

ONCE A YEAR, THE Trouts went to the B'nai Zion picnic at the Forest Preserves and took the extended family with them. They didn't hike. They didn't roast on an open fire. They sprayed each other down with 6-12 before, calamine after and called Nature the out-of-doors and planned for it the way countries planned for war. Buddy mapped and mimeographed directions, Rose turned her straw beach bag into a first-aid kit that could handle everything from snakebite to sudden loss of limb. Joe brought beer, his blue portable radio, and buckets of broasted from the Moo and Cackle.

The meal was a fast play of chicken bones thrown into the empty buckets. Joe's brother Pat—who owned a drugstore on Rush Street and stars like Jan Murray and Sammy Davis Jr. came between shows for Lavoris and Maalox—brought a sack of makeup and medical products he couldn't move. The aunts bobbed for brush rollers, frosted lipsticks, Robitussin. Irwina brought cherries from the Greek, meat from the Kosher, cheese from the Italian. Bessie used to bring fish, she loved eating smoked fish in the out-of-doors, but twice the bones got stuck halfway down her throat. Pike, fishsticks—it didn't matter. All bones found their way to Bessie's throat, and they had to rush her to the hospital to have her neck frozen. So Bessie brought fruit, and Rose brought a checklist and nagged everybody.

The Forest Preserves was a hundred living rooms, every family with their arrangement of lawn chairs, blankets, grills, coolers, baked goods, people staring at trees waiting for them to do something. *Do something!* There was one in every family.

The aunts served lunch, their arms in sleeveless blouses flesh weapons pushing protein. The mouth-breathing cousins picked. Bessie and Joe's youngest, Jeffrey, wore his basketball jersey over his shirt and kept asking Joe to get a softball game going.

"Take a breast why don'tcha," he said to Joan, his mouth smeared with chicken grease. "Take two you could use 'em."

She shoved a drumstick in a Dixie Cup of honey and let it drip on his face. Family, she thought, a band of people thrown together for the sole purpose of disappointing each other. Still, they were outside. In spring Joan tore open the green catalpa pods and stuck them across her nose for a rhino horn. In summer, this picnic. In between was the mystery of empty lots. She could have eaten Nature, so little came her way.

Rose grabbed a wing, thought about it, grabbed another.

"We got a two-fisted wing eater here," Bessie said, "leave some for the *kinder*." She reached under the table for Joe's ring, grown in with swelling. "Still there," Bessie said.

"Couldn't lose it if I wanted, Moose." Joe shook out his arm. "Pins and needles."

"You okay?"

He gave Bessie's knee a thrum, finished his beer, licked his ink-stained fingers, and recruited for a father-son ballgame.

Buddy took off his shirt, his shoes, but left his hat on and stood in the pond, not quite trusting it. He was ashamed of his body but he still had the legs, still had the muscular calves of youth. He stood as kids splashed and made gentle waves that reminded him of before he was married. The water was noisy. Aw kiss me, it sounded like it said. Buddy stepped in to his waist, bobbing slightly, sterning his face and recommitting to God. Women all around him yelling *Rotten egg,* their flesh shifting, refusing to be shut up in gingham or stretch fabric, running with half-eaten sandwiches in the face of polio, flopping in, coming up young.

Come on in Buddy, wife touches his back. He watches her with lust in his bathing trunks and the simultaneous urge to throw a towel over her breasts. Get a little wet why don'tcha Buddy, the wife teases. I'm here. I'm in, he tells her. Wife ducks between his legs—how stiff he was, he goes down in one piece. A slab. His hat floats away, she pulls him under, catches him with her lips and arms, bubbles kisses through his thick skull till he comes up panting. He tries to say what's the meaning of this because he hates swimming, the part where he has nothing under his feet, unknown lips and gills and teeth. Jules Verne crew of multi-limbed pusses with twangers and suckers and snake appendages that— His hat was barely in his scope. He pushes the creatures away and strokes a decent Australian crawl, remembering his Touhy Beach lessons. He knows women watch him. He dives under to assure himself of a bottom and finds a black pit to China and his breathing comes on top of itself inbreath outbreath crashing water in his mouth. Help me, the sand's so far. Lifeguard looks like a pea shoot. He knows he's waving boneless arms and his legs move like a unicycler under water and no hat, dear god, sky laughing, polka-dot white clouds—who cares? One man drowns. Who cares? Then comes the bloat and the shouting and his trunks would've slipped off and he'd be lank and infinitesimal. Children would be averted. They'd lug him in, old, hatless, push on his tired chest, get a few spurts out while he watched the show from a dry place and with his hat on.

He saw Rose. Bess. There was his wife. He slowed his chest down. Okay, the wife was— What were they doing? Dishes. Okay that was good. Dishes were being done and there was ground and he felt his head and the hat was there.

The aunts cleaned dishes in the small pond, their work hands darting in and out, Mama's moving like tropical fish with pond rocks shivering and ducking her shadows. The sisters were a team of scraping, washing, rinsing, their motions smooth with no need for talk. Joan could see how they were sisters. They bent the same and looked like different ages of each other.

"Take a towel make yourself useful I'll tell you a story," Bessie said. "Me and Joe got married the old way. They wouldn't go home till they saw the evidence."

"Evidence?" Joan said.

"Of my original status."

"Your—"

"Virginity." Rose coughed. "They waited in those days."

"We rented a hall," Bessie said.

"A tavern," said Rose.

"Let her have the hall," said Irwina.

"Downstairs was eating and drinking and upstairs the bedroom. Bess, you look so worried, Joe says, don't look so worried, Bess. I was young, see, I was scared shitless and sixteen. You shoulda seen how they had me swaddled in that dress like they didn't want me to move. Here we smoke. Only cigarette I smoked in my entire life and Joe puffs and I see his face. He don't puff, it's black as night. I still see better when he's around. So anyways the people they don't leave till they got proof. They gotta have proof. They want proof, Joe says, we give 'em proof."

"Proof of what?" Joan said.

"Blood," said Irwina. "We'll talk."

Rose looked like she swallowed something.

"So Joe pricks his finger squeezes the red on the sheet and we stand on that bed the two of us jumping so loud the crowd I'm telling you they was hot in the crotch and we're jumping away like kids. Well we were kids. And Joe he's jumping and pulling off his suit. Nice suit. Pat loaned him. And he says take a rest, Bess, and walks out on that balcony a complete naked man. Not a sound. Even the drunks don't remember why they came. They stare at Joe's whatchamacallit, and Joe he don't care. He waves the bloody sheet over the railing like a bullfighter and the cheering—"

"Nobody cheered. It wasn't a cheering crowd," Rose said.

"—on their feet shouting and Joe turns to me, he's got beard like he don't shave for his own wedding, and he says nobody's gonna tell us no more Bess, that's what married is."

"That's it?" Joan said.

"What."

"Joan," Irwina said.

"We finished our business." Mama was looking at Bessie and Bessie was looking through the river and Rose was wringing out the towels so hard they were dry before she finished. They could here Buddy yelling.

"What's he yelling?" Rose said.

"Probably about the photo." Bess said.

"Not time yet." Mama looked so much younger than Bessie, leaning in to her like that. "Talk some more."

The dishes were clean, towels folded in a basket.

"We should go," Bess said. "He'll be mad."

Mama said, "He'll wait. He can't take it without us. Spit." Joan spit in the Kleenex and Mama rubbed her face. She stood dirt still and let her rub her neck clean and pinch her cheeks for glow, the fussing felt so good she wanted to lap it with her tongue.

"We'll sit a minute and you talk," Mama said.

"A minute or a Jewish minute?" Bessie said.

"Jewish," Mama said.

Bessie flumped under the shade of a fat oak and rested her back against it. Mama put her head in Bessie's lap and Bessie rested a hand on her forehead. Rose took off her glasses, looked them in the eyes and put them back on.

"I was a late bleeder, started at sixteen right before the wedding, and now I don't bleed no more. I don't toss the Kotex though or the gear."

"You still got the gear? Rose said.

"I don't want him to know."

"Tell about love," Joan said.

"Tell about love. You want to know about love? Joe spoke the room straightened out. He talked I saw pearly things in the corners. I don't even know what he said. I play the records sometimes, oh sure. The Fisher girls love opera. Like nuts we used to save and sit in the Opera House and hear *Madame Butterfly*, remember Winna? Yeah I tell you something strange."

"She waited for after the music," Rose said. "Paid all that money to hear the voices stop."

"Not exactly, Rosie. When Donnie was growing up we worried he was so pale and always with the books. He don't eat and the phone don't ring so Joe gets him a diving suit."

"A what?" Joan said.

"Outta the blue. Who thinks like this? And Donnie takes lessons and gets equipment and goes on an airoplane and goes to the CaraBEEin and sends us letters with underwater photographs of sea turtle and some girl's legs. A sea turtle and a girl's arm."

"Cynthia," Mama said. Her face looked like she had a good night's sleep. "Donnie married the first woman he was with like the old man."

Joan carried the towel basket, and the sisters walked slowly toward the photo arranging itself. Kids arguing positions on the grass, cousins gathering aluminum chairs, uncles climbing on the picnic table fixing their spines.

"Joe reads the letter and the pleasure in his face, like he's in that water. I'm taller than him. We used to fight it, me without heels, him with the thick soles, and he's gotta stand on something for photos, but now I don't bleed and he's shrinking and who gives a shit. He rests his head here." She patted her shoulder. "I unbutton his shirt talk directly to his chest, no man in the middle." She laughed. "Crazy in my old age, yeah?"

Buddy's trunks made a wet trunk mark in his pants. He was shouting orders. "You? There! You? Here. Sit up. Stand straight. Joan? You're too big for the kids. Get with the aunts."

She took the chair at the end next to Jewel, Joe's brother's wife, whose meat would not stay on her bones. A former dancer, which meant she didn't have to help with the dishes.

"Joan, too tall. Get up with the uncles." Buddy waved his arms.

She took her place on top of the picnic table with the uncles and looked at the auntie's scalps and their bosoms that split at the neck. The uncles left their watches at home and had white bracelets to show for it. Somebody's cousin Ben, a traveling salesman, was tan on his left arm only, like it took vacations alone.

Every year Buddy sent the relatives individual photos, strangers in hats and dark glasses, blurry children with zinc noses. He wrote their names carefully on the back but nobody believed it was them. That don't look like me. It didn't matter because the Polaroid would fade, and there'd be nothing left to argue over but oil spots and sun visors.

Irwina looked up and back, photo to daughter to photo, and said the same thing she said every year. "You look like your father's side, but you got the Fisher hands and forehead, thank god. I don't know, a little lipstick next time and something with the hair."

She wanted to look like the Fisher side.

"And next time smile," Mama said. "I never take a halfway decent picture."

Buddy said what he was supposed to say. "No lens could do you justice doll."

Joan listened to the silence after Buddy talked, waiting for the corners of the forest to glisten.

Eleven

ONE OF MAMA'S LEGS, left over from before the bad news, swung casually over the mustard leather chair. Then sound like great laughter came out of her. Then "No no no no no no no no."

Joe was dead.

Joe was dead and they were getting dressed in a hurried, perfumed way, things dropping, breaking on the hard tile floor and nobody talking about it and nobody cleaning it up. A black car came for them filled with invisible smoke. A man was driving who didn't want to be driving. His suit was poor. His suit made Joan sad. The car had stains and cigarette burns buried in its crushed-velvet seats. The driver was heavy. He farted and excused himself when he got out to open their doors. He didn't exactly excuse himself. He said something that sounded like "Pahmee."

Mama was the one first out, her long black silk stockings and high heels walking into a cluck of people and through the open double doors like it took extra room to get a good look at death.

Rabbi Wasserman greeted people as they entered. He was tan and wore a pressed white silk robe decorated with gold trim so everybody would believe him. People who didn't know Joe well ducked and bowed near the entry. Mizer's Funeral Home could have been a church or a temple, it could have dressed one way or the other. The ark was portable, Joan saw its wheels, the skinny curtain cord, the mobile Torah. The casket was on wheels. The benches had wheels with brakes like a baby buggy. The room could become something else in seconds.

Auntie Bessie, Auntie Rose and her girls, the mother-in-law from the old country, Bessie's sons, Jeffrey and Donnie, and his pregnant wife, Cynthia, Joe's two brothers and their wives and kids and the Trouts sat in the front row. Joan sat between the aunts, who patted her more than usual, touched her for themselves. Mama's eyes looked fierce and gone. She loved Joe. Joe taught her smoking and how to swing her hips to catch a man. Joe never gave up on Buddy, inviting him to the track, letting him sit in on poker night when the *Trib* boys needed an extra. Buddy wore Pa's heavy gold watch and sat with his arms spread like the good seats at the temple. Jeffrey wouldn't look at anything but the casket. He had a juvenile-delinquent face. If the casket opened, Joan knew Joe would be there in Pat's suit, his face—he'd look caught in the middle of something.

The rabbi walked up the aisle, a bride greeting her audience. He stood under a skylight and sun hit him like it was in on the whole thing. The place smelled like a business. Joe was not a temple man. The guys from the nightshift sat together like the unwashed. Their suits were clumpy, their faces looked as bad as Bessie's. Bad for Joe, bad from knowing they'd end dead too. The women-in-the-building sat with their husbands, except Fran, who sat alone because she couldn't bring Married Johnny to public places. Bernice from Beauty Heaven wore a hat with a sequined veil. The Lithuanian seamstress came late and cried through the whole thing. There were lots of hats. The men took theirs off, and Joan could tell who was used to yarmulkes and whose heads they sat on like puffy crooked pancakes. One of the *Trib* guys winked at her. She liked the dark-fingered men, pressmen who like Joe couldn't get their hands clean and had dirt lines in their necks. That made them able to be where she was, where a kid was. They didn't buy the rabbi's gold trim either. The piano lady turned her own pages smoothly ahead of the notes. The flowers were white and blue, the colors of Israel. Bessie's breasts up and down and up and down and wet across her front. Mama had grabbed a suit off the rack for her. It had new folds on the sleeves and the side of the skirt. The *Trib* guys were trying not to cry. There was a shortage of air, the seats were severe. Women pulled Kleenex from purses, her mother's was crumpled and lipstick stained. Buddy gave her his handkerchief.

"*Ahhhhyoy.*" An old man in the back groaned.

"Who invited him?" Auntie Rose said. Her mother-in-law rocked herself.

After the service people gathered in a small room with new carpeting. There was a modest table with modest food, plastic forks and plates that didn't hold much. Nobody wanted to be the first to chew and break the piety. The old man nobody knew drank whiskey from a shot glass. People took to cake. Rose insisted on having the flowers carried into the little room, making a problem of it, making the *Trib* guys help her, telling them they were wrong, making them move the flowers here, no there, back here. Bessie sat on a card chair by a wire wastebasket and kept missing the basket with her Kleenexes so they wadded on the floor like popcorn balls. People told her they were sorry. They said the service was lovely and Joe would have liked the way she handled things.

The *Trib* guys came to her in a group. One of them said, "Joe was a good man. He died a good death." The rest nodded too long. Rose scolded the caterer. Things weren't hot enough, cold enough, cut enough. Her face was dry, her fingertips wrinkled like they soaked in a bathtub alone or did her crying for her. The rabbi appeared in just his suit. His face still held religion.

Joan climbed on stage where the casket was. Brahms played from behind a wall. She stared till she saw Joe through the box resting on a silk pillow looking pleasant and disgusted and about to spit. She touched the wood.

"Bye, Uncle Joe."

After they buried him, the smoke-black car took the Trouts to

Bessie's apartment for the shivah. Hot food, piles of meat, piles of kugel and cake cut in squares. All the food was built up high to show death they knew how to live. People came and went, listening to Bessie's same stories. They'd been on a picnic that very morning. Buddy took a picture of them in the out-of-doors. She and Joe, their last picture. The picture was passed around again. Joe ate three pieces of broasted, a breast and two thighs. He played softball with the boys. She had a kalooki game the night before at Mrs. Slater's. Then the picnic, then she was at Rose's and they watched *The Late Show,* and when she got home there were no lights in the living room, just the peppery test pattern from the TV. Joe left lights on for her, that's how he was, Joe. In the TV light she saw him on the floor with his arms stretched out for something. She thought, of course, asleep. Joe? She shook him. Joe? The test pattern hummed and the hum got louder and Bessie had to cover her ears or maybe somebody covered them for her because there were people in her apartment, people she'd never seen except in the hallway or getting mail. People using her phone, moving her things around. Bessie kept thinking, if only the humming would stop she could figure things out, put them back where they belonged, and she tried, in a nice way, to get the people back to their own apartments. She wanted to turn down the feather quilt and climb in with Joe and stop shaking.

She held up her hand. "Look at me. I'm still shaking," Bessie said. He let her stick the cold feet between his calves. How could he call her Moose with those strangers? "We were on a picnic . . ."

The mirrors were covered with sheets, but a corner of one slipped and mirror peeked out like an illegal shoulder. Bessie sat on the blue, plastic-covered sectional with crumpled fists of wet tissue. Every person who came in the door brought new grief, fresh slices of memory. Donnie brought his pregnant gentile wife a slice of honey cake and a broken rugelach that seemed an insult to her pale, Irish skin. She took the cookies and didn't thank him. Cynthia had red hair and apricot freckles. She'd been a model to help Donnie through law school. She drank lots of water and told

Joan the only soap she must ever use was Savon Clair because it wouldn't leave a film.

Savon Clair. Joan repeated. *Savon Clair.*

Joe's girlie magazines were still under the couch behind Bessie's feet.

Rose stayed in the kitchen cutting things up. People kept bringing food and the food needed to be cut and piled into towers, and Rose didn't want any help from anybody. Mama sat on Joe's chair, pushed to one side like somebody was sitting with her.

Irwina took the unused monogrammed glasses from the china cabinet and filled them with water. She sat on the big chair and darkness sat next to her. She heard Joan speaking to her but couldn't respond. She was thinking of Bess, envying Bess her same story over and over so each time the pain got less, each time Bess could, in the telling, make herself believe it happened. Irwina wanted to cry over Joe, cry like a wife because it had been Joe since she was ten. Her brother, her pa, her push in the behind, a Schlitz, a wink and Joe, holding the quiet center of their family together.

Twelve

AFTER SCHOOL MAMA WAS in the nap position on the couch, her thumb and finger pressing under her cheekbones, *American Bandstand* playing softly. The star couples were on, the Philadelphia regulars. No matter how hard other kids tried you could see the stars.

"Mama? I need to talk."

"Talk's overrated." Her eyes were closed, she moved her thumb between her teeth and bit softly.

"He started this club—"

"What are you talking?"

"Dad and see, I'm not supposed to tell because he wants it secret, but I don't like it. I don't want anymore of his clubs."

"You're lucky you've got a father wants to do things. Think of your cousins, think of me without Pa."

"It's a weirdo club."

Her eyes opened. "Why. What does he do?"

"Sleeps, mostly."

"Oh."

"Tells stories."

"Sounds nice."

"He wants me to tell him things."

"Like."

"I don't know. Everything."

"Is there so much to tell?"

"I think a club should be fun, don't you think?"

"Of course."

"Well this one's not. I don't want him falling asleep in my bed."

"Tell him go."

"I do."

"And."

"He doesn't listen."

"He means no harm."

"Maybe if you let him in your bed—"

Irwina sat up, started fixing herself. "My bed is not your business child."

"I tell him he gets mad."

"You've got a father who's Shakespearean. We are who we are."

Shakespearean? Meaning? He'd recite till all safe places were taken?

"I dreamed he was in this Jeep and this Jeep was sinking in quicksand and Buddy, Dad, didn't call for help. He had this goofy grin like *oh well,* and the Jeep was sinking, Mom, and he was disappearing. The windshield, the sides of the Jeep, his head, his chest—"

"Okay, point please."

"I can't take care of him. He's yours. You should take care of him better."

"Let me share with you my Five Rules."

"Just make him stop."

"Five Rules and that'll be the end. You'll see."

People gave her things. The best they had from lifetimes of living. Things somebody somewhere died for and stuff happened anyway. Nobody gave the Slater twins anything. They'd walk in a room, and the room kept doing what it was doing. People took one look at Joan and gave her their teeth. Nothing worked.

Her mother shut off the TV. "You can take them or not. I really don't care."

HER RULES
1. Don't make waves.
2. Let him make up his commandments. Never question this.
3. Keep a pleasant tone. A pleasant tone goes a long way.
4. Do what he says, what does it cost?
5. He's your father. He's your tribe. He loves you.

Once she made her father king, made him a crown of shirt cardboard that shimmered with Reynolds Wrap points and glitter that fell out of his hair for days. Now she wanted to be left alone. How do you leave a tribe if you're a kid and the tribe gives you a bed?

Irwina didn't cry at Joe's service or the shivah or the cemetery, though Rose said at the gravesite she screamed and couldn't stop screaming.

"You were hysterical," Rose said, "they had to hold you down, you don't remember?"

Irwina didn't hear herself, so she didn't believe it.

Rose said a week after they buried Joe the earth split over his grave.

Irwina didn't believe that either. She believed in cleaning, had never felt so close to dirt. Walked around with a piece of Buddy's old undershirt torn into an oily rag and oiled inside dressers, the scrolly detail of their headboard. Lemon oil was something she believed in. She kept it with her at all times. It was as close as she was willing to get to prayer.

"It's no accident they named it Pledge," she said.

Every drawer screamed to be lined with contact paper in mix and match fruit patterns and at midnight she was still cutting along the dotted lines piecing together apples and bananas.

"You need to eat, Mama."

"I'm not hungry dear. Don't nag."

"You told me never wait for hunger. You need your strength."

Since Joe's death Irwina stopped going to the shop. She didn't care what Rose did anymore. She stopped dancing with the *American Bandstand* kids, but there was plenty to do. The stove burners needed lining and these needed to be replaced daily.

"But you ain't even cookin'. Place don't have a chance to get dirty," Buddy said.

"It's what you can't see that gets you," she said.

"A brother-in-law dies—"

"This is about germs."

"He was family, I understand, but you gotta at some point—"

"He gave me clothes money, got Rose's teeth fixed, filled Ma's icebox, took us dancing."

"I know, I know but—"

"Joe was our pa, our car."

She refined her instruments of detection: toothbrush, toothpicks, tips of knifes. She unscrewed the dresser knobs and soaked them in ammoniated cleaning brine. Her laundry potions—Mrs. Stewart's Bluing, bleach, Sta-Flo Liquid Starch, Calgon water softener, a couple kinds of detergent, and Twenty Mule Team Borax—took up more room than her cosmetics. Their existence had become dingy, she said, they had to act fast.

Joan shook from wanting her mother's haughty self back. Buddy was at the shop all the time, and Mama went around without her wig in the old Hush Puppies that bulged where her bunion was, even when she wasn't in them. After school Joan would find her staring out the window.

"Mama what are you doing?"

"What I've always done."

"Irwina what the hell's with you? I'm tired of life by my lonesome, doll, you're no good to me like this. Women ask for you, Where is she? They're askin' and what do I say?"

"Tell them you're on a roll."

"Aw shit you know it's not the money."

"I thought money was your hit parade."

"Man needs a wife, Rose can't do everything. Joe's gone and he ain't comin' back."

"Thanks. That clears things up for me."

Buddy sat beside her, put his arm around her. "I'm tryin' to understand here, baby, help me, give a guy a clue.

"Someday."

"Sunday? What? Someday? Someday you'll sleep in my bed someday?" Buddy said he'd gone long enough without and demanded to know why she was cleaning so much. What was she trying to get rid of? He gave up after a few minutes. Maybe he was afraid she'd tell him.

"Unseen things," she turned on the ballgame, "eat you up."

Joan set up the ironing board and sprinkled clothes with a shaker made from a Good Seasons salad dressing bottle, winding them into wet sausages that hissed when the iron hit.

Mama ironed, and they listened to the Sox play. She loved shortstop Louie Aparicio, said Louie was fast like a fly and stole more bases than any man alive even when the coach told him to stay put. Louie couldn't help himself. His legs got twitchy, he had to move. This she understood, not waiting for okay.

The game was good sound in the house, Mama doing something besides sleeping and talking about when Joe was alive. Buddy made coffee and never took his eyes off her. She ironed and saw life the way Louie saw life, that honeycomb of window, that sixteenth of a beat opening between pitches when a person could really move.

"Run you little momzer," she said.

Buddy stood in front of the TV. "I rented our same cottage at Edelman's, I want to see you snap out of this, maybe swim, get a load of some trees. Got it all set up."

"You're blocking my game."

"No thanks?"

"You coming with us?"

"Take a rest, you're no good to me like this."

She waved him aside as the second baseman was begging for it, punching his glove goddamn gimme the ball and first base over-threw on an error and Louis took third standing, Mama smiling like Joe was in the room.

Thirteen

THE NEW CHILDREN'S RECREATION Director at Edelman's Resort was changing the way women approached their morning routine. It used to be cleavage packed with Kleenex, cantaloupe-drizzled chins. The worse they looked the deeper the relaxation the longer the vacation buck. Now they were taking measures, tippy toeing the metal stairway down to the pool doing an Esther Williams half-winged butterfly that left their sunglasses and incorporeal hair untouched. Joan counted six sprayed and ratted disembodied heads in daisy formation smiling at the recreation director's butt, shushing each other so they could follow his English accent picked up and carried by the nasal Midwestern air.

The heads spoke.

"Milk black."

"Harry Belafonte mode."

"Don't get it with the sun helmet."

"Didn't know they burned."

Mama should be up. She should be with the heads who said idiot things and screamed at their kids, like the head that was telling her son Stevie to stand up straight or daddy'd put him in a body brace, or the head sailing on an inflatable raft, dog-paddling in sun-stroked waters, or the heads in the kiddy pool exercising with Nan the waitress and her inflatable water wings, their lounge chairs saved by *Marjorie Morningstar* or *The Carpetbaggers* or *Peyton Place*. Heads past caring stained their legs unevenly with iodine and baby oil, stuffed cotton between their twisty toes and waited for their polish to dry, for their husbands to come, that rag flock of tired men looking stunned at the prospect of fun.

"I'm relaxing!" The independently wealthy shoe salesman had been saying this all week, circling the pool, his Al Jolson arms reaching for understanding.

The closer it got to the weekend the bigger the hair the lower the strap the lewder the talk the closer the heads floated to the shallow, where at ten each morning the New Children's Recreation Director held Children's Story Hour. The husbands would put an end to this along with the sautéed bottomfish, spit the pit bing cherries in melting plastic bags, the iodine tans, and after-dinner maj games.

The heads reclaimed their chaises, dried themselves long after they were dry, checked their watches but never saw time. They saw something out an airplane window, something hopelessly beautiful and hopelessly out of their control.

So far, Mama just skipped meals and slept. She said she loved sleeping in the haze of somebody else's washed cotton sheets, and at Edelman's she could relax because they boiled the laundry at 280 degrees.

"Just a little swim?" Joan shook her mother's shoulder to see if it would do something.

"You go hon." Irwina drooled, her mouth tumbled by sleep.

"I've been. It's boring." It wasn't boring. It was flipping pennies in the deep end and making Marilyn Shuleman dive for them like a dog. She'd do anything, Marilyn Shuleman, with her red suit sucked up her crotch shouting *Eureka* when she broke water. It was worth getting up just to think up things Marilyn might do. Strip off her suit and walk naked around the tennis court with a towel turban. Swing naked from the crumbly apple tree letting kids memorize between her legs. Steal bras from the waitress dorm and set them on fire with a cigar. While naked.

"Go. And after that—" her mother turned.

"What after that?"

"Meeting you."

"Okay, but I'm waiting so we can swim before lunch. Like you said." It should be easier to catch a person at rest. She shook her mother again.

"What is it."

"They're banging the activity triangle."

"Good."

"It's activity time."

"You're not going, are you."

"You should come, Mama."

"In my top drawer, get the box. I don't have all day," she said impatiently.

It was her jewelry in a tangle.

"Choose carefully," she said, "one thing. Something that looks attractive on you."

"I don't need this. If you want to give me something give me something madras."

"Madras? Women have enough trouble without a material that bleeds. Pick. I'm not asking again."

Joan chose the gold snake necklace with the fat clasp.

"There. That's nice. Now they'll give you a second glance. Anything else you want from me?"

Irv Edelman was talking through the staticky sound system: "Activity time. Activity time. Children's Story Hour *csk* take place in the fruit *csk* end of *csk*."

You Ma. Just you.

When The New Children's Recreation Director called the kids to come, he spoke in a low voice using his hands like a story was a round thing to make and unmake. And the sound system never cracked. He said gulls. Gulls and boys. A tall man. Taller than the wild plum and ornamental pear trees, taller than Irv Edelman was thunking him on the helmet with his clipboard.

"Edelman's is lucky to have this boychick," Irv said.

Last year they had a desk girl who made them nap on rug remnants while she talked about her period. Irv was trying on the helmet. "Looka me!" He had soft breasts and his belly button was a dark hole in his yellow Banlon shirt.

One of the kids yelled, "Ah th-th-th-that's all folks," and Irv put the helmet back on the director.

The heads were staring at dark skin under a white T-shirt molded to rib and muscle.

A woman said, "Now I haven't seen that oh for at least—"

"Naomi," another woman said, "you haven't seen that *ever*."

"Hey! Relaxing here!" The shoe salesman.

The director leaned back on his arms, the heads leaned forward on their chaises, the kids shielded up their eyes at him, the late kids ran over wet tiles to sit at his feet.

A poker player shouted, "Hey, you kids, what you do now? You don't run it's wet. You run it's wet you crack up your head." He put his arm out to stop them. Every adult at Edelman's was mother/father/lifeguard. The arm was triple tanned and had a weak coat of long silver hairs like an unidentifiable dead animal by the side of the highway.

The director was saying something about a land with bridges built for kings and "in that land lived the Princess Japonica." Anything he said sounded good because of his accent and the loudspeaker, but he usually started with a fakeout to make the real story sound better.

"P.U." Kids held their noses. The teenagers dragged in late and stood motionless in the back.

"Not what you want? I see. We shall cast royalty aside then and walk with me children. Get me a better story. No, Lizzy, we're not *actually* walking. Someone grab Lizzy please."

The teenagers checked the path to the Ping-Pong room. It had a swinging bed on a screen porch that was never locked.

The director swatted at something. They were in a forest, bugs big as camels. "There! My God did you see that body? Look. You think it's a seal?" No kid's mouth closed, no lips were moist, no ice cream while he tapped their half-formed spines.

"Or a rock."

"Yes, it might be a rock, yes, but the shirt, the bugs around it. Half the body is already—"

"Scared!" Lizzy corked her navel with a finger.

Marilyn Shuleman took a loud inhale.

"Stop," a boy said.

"I'm just breathing," Marilyn said.

"Well stop," the boy said.

"He smells like coconuts."

"Stop breathing."

The story was turning into a man who'd become dangerous since they found his son floating in this pond.

Irwina woke to a voice on the loudspeaker and knew before she saw him. She took coffee in the empty dining room where the brunch buffet was spattered despite efforts to gather in the fruit and piece together the sour cream and chive–scrambled eggs.

"Dead," a boy said.

"Quite dead," the director said.

Lizzy took a whiff of her finger and stuck it in her mouth. The teenagers flopped to the grass.

"Can't they turn that guy down?" the shoe salesman said. "I don't see why every goddamned person has to listen to every goddamned story."

"Drownded," a boy said.

"Are you sure? Look. The body was gone over by a forensic man. Forensic? A science of clues to see how somebody died, but here, here children, here it means letting go and the boy," the director raised a fist, let his fingers spread, "foofed."

Joan saw something flick, buck, and spiral to the sky. She watched the director watch Mama spread her beach towel. Her flushed face, hair pulled in a braid, Buddy's shirt tied over her shoulders, silver bracelets up down her arms. Joan knew Mama had seen him.

"The authorities they found a note on the boy," the director was saying.

"On the dead kid?" a boy said.

"Exactly."

"On the dead kid under water they did?"

"Correct."

"And it didn't fall apart or nothing? This is a bullcrap story," a teenager said.

"That's my mama." Joan said this to convince herself this was the same woman, the germ detector who weighed herself on a scale to determine her day. A bad number, Mama shut the door and wouldn't let anybody see her naked. A good number, she ate one poached egg. Bad number, she squeezed lemon juice on her hands and asked god to take her liver spots. Or did The Lion on the loopy bathroom rug with her tongue hanging out and her neck stringy. Good number, Joan sat on the red stool under the sink with her chin in hands, elbows on knees, watching Mama's towel slip down, their four legs two, their toes stroking tile like wet horses loving. Bad, look in the mirror see inside her nose, down her throat, all the holes. Good, she smelled like lemons with pulp and let the towel fall and wiped steam off glass with her hand.

See? This is how I was before I had you.

She did this to Mama, the soft ropes playing her belly.

Mama pushed her flesh around to show where everything once belonged.

In those days they went to Edelman's as a family. South Haven Michigan, the smell of Jew in the air. Lox, chlorine, all of them in one shower tinted blue like Mama's dot-the-dot pencil. In the little shower with her father's legs.

Beautiful, Mama says, real good pair of man's legs you got there, Buddy.

Soap was in the hair of all of them, soap tipping off arms that held, swarmy family in the car puddling down grained roads, *tinka-tink-tink* summer, the lake tipped white, sand hiding shapes,

Daddy back from the store with nuggets to split or save for later, bits of chocolate falling apart on her tongue, in the same cottage they were sleeping in now.

The director watched Mama. Children surrounded his pink-soled feet. His safari hat looked solid as cement. Joan saw the dark man see under the blue-and-white umbrella with the poker men proud of their tans and their summer shirts open at the top. And she saw him see under Mama as she dropped her shirt and walked in one piece to the diving board, bouncing twice, entering splashless, shooting across bottom between the heads and petaled caps, bobbing like Ju Ju bees.

Irwina was counting seconds as the chlorinated water bleached her brain. Ten. Fifteen. Time was loaded at the bottom of a swimming pool. Twenty. Twenty five, the underwater pleasure of his voice. She came up spitting water, found her daughter amid the slump-backed sundresses and ruffled behinds.

"Hey baby." She ducked in a headstand and waved with her feet.

When Irwina first heard him, she took it in the chest. The New Children's Recreation Director was the man she imagined, the friend she carried since she was old enough to know there was more than Mama's house. He was Unseen Partner. Not a dead ringer or a facsimile or what a weird coincidence but him. These things don't happen. She marched straight to the check-in desk of Sheila Edelman, where prices rose and rooms shrunk and a woman had to have her wits. The Frankensteinian world of Edelman's drifted and lobbed.

The Mai Tai Lounge was wide-mouthed women drinking side-cars and Singapore slings. Thursday night, Hawaiian/Amateur

Night. Waitresses in hula skirts, busboys with coconut bras riding crooked over their shirts. What was this crêpe-paper connection with Jews and the tropics? Teenagers were trying to talk the bartender into spiking their Cokes. Tiny lanterns swung lazily from the knotty pine bar.

When the husbands came, Edelmans paid for real entertainment. Comedians were bussed down from Detroit, the fabulous Honey Bear Sisters from Chicago, and the Chinese chef sliced prime rib under an infrared light as Irving and Sheila chatted up the tables.

Tonight Irv and She kicked it off with a little number.

"Here's a little number for you," Irv said, a song they wrote, a song whose only words were their names accented on different syllables.

Ir-ving *Eh*-del-man.

She-lah *Eh*-del-man.

They looked into each other's eyes and shared one mike so Irv had to double over.

She-la Eh-del-*man*.

Ir-ving Eh-del-*man*.

The shoe salesman himself relaxed into a dress and lipstick for his performance of "Fever." The walls of the Mai Tai slid open and six electric ceiling fans blew that crazy rhythm, but still the loudest sounds were women's thighs peeling off the wooden card chairs.

The New Children's Recreation Director sat at the bar, his shirt the whitest thing in the place. He leaned over, said something to the bartender, who laughed and poured something gold into the teenager's Cokes.

Joan and her mother shared a table with the Shulemans, the same table they shared for the past ten years. Marilyn Shuleman was singing *Oh we ain't gotta barrel of money* under a yellow gel light. The tired drummer from the Sleepless Knights Band slapped a cymbal behind her. *Through all kinds of weather.* Crash.

"Doesn't your Joan want to get up there?" Mr. Shuleman said. "Joanie. What do you like to do Joanie. Tricks? You like tricks?

Do a trick. You like jokes? What does she like?" he asked his wife.

"Sid, she's happy just sitting," Mrs. Shuleman said.

"How 'bout 'Que Sera Sera.' Every girl knows 'Que Sera.' "

Mr. Shuleman could shove it. He was a dentist from Wisconsin and every year he'd tell her to sing "Que" fartball "Sera." Last year when Buddy was here . . . Buddy should be here. He should be here now the way Mama looked with her hair going crazy over her naked shoulders and behind the straps of her sundress that white skin. He should be here right now, and he'd be so Shuley, still nursing the tooth racket? You like teeth, Shuley? Get up and do some teeth for the crowd. You like plaque? Shuley. Scrape off some plaque for the crowd. On the way home they'd stop at the A & W and he'd let her drink a root beer float half down then call the car hop over and say, oh miss? Say miss? My kid got gypped. Bottomless floats.

Mama whispered, "Pie, it's time."

"Why? Things are getting good." Things were bad. Mama didn't talk about Joe anymore. She wasn't herself. She slept late, ate three meals, and was happy. Things were rotten.

"Remember we had that talk?" Mama said. For some reason, they both looked at Marilyn Shuleman singing her ass off.

"Where's she going?" Mr. Shuleman asked his wife, whose breasts rested on the table like vegetables whose names you can never remember. Her tiny hands peeked out from underneath, her frosted nail polish stopping in the middle of her nails like she'd done all she could and could do no more.

Her mother, Joan realized with a shock, was stunning. No wigs, no suits, no germs, and her skin was hot. It was on fire. She could feel it scalding from the next chair. Her body was shaking. Mr. Shuleman grabbed looks, but he wouldn't talk directly to Mama. Please let this mother stay. Please let this mother stay when we go home. Joan took a swig of her mother's Manhattan.

"Oh. Well. We have this prior engagement," Mama said. "Right Pie?"

She was supposed to say something, but how good it felt not to, to see Mrs. Shuleman's hands shoot out from her wahpumpahs and dig into Mama's arm. For Mama to need her. She felt her own skin warming. She slurped. She felt Mama's beautiful rub off on her.

"Surely you're not leaving us." Mrs. Shuleman made a sad face.

"Where's she going this time a night?" Mr. Shuleman said.

"My supposed to know everything? Ask her."

"Pie? Ready?" Mama pulled her drink back.

"You need to go, go. Joan's welcome to stay with us." Mrs. Shuleman dug deeper. They had the cottage next door. "Seriously. We hear everything. You come in from wherever it is you think you're going at this time of night, we'll send her right on home."

"This is a rural zone. Nothing's open." Mr. Shuleman said.

"Who's taking care of her?" Mrs. Shuleman said.

"Nan." Mama reclaimed her arm. Mrs. Shuleman patted it. Give a hurt, take a hurt.

"Waterwings Nan? She baby-sits?"

"She is actually a very good babysitter."

Marilyn finished her song and was waiting for further instructions. Take your clothes off, Marilyn. Toss that sundress to the crowd.

"We got a cot, she can sleep on the cot by Marilyn."

Mrs. Shuleman's head moved up and back like she needed to shake water out of her ears.

"Our cottage gets a lovely breeze. She can enjoy the breeze. On the cot. With Marilyn. While you're out."

The Shulemans were hypnotizing them. Mama made small jokes and laughed to wake up. The director was gone, Joan's legs were heavy, eyes getting heavier. Soon she'd be up there singing "Que Sera Sera" till somebody whacked her over the head, but Mama was pulling her out in the country air with stars splattered all over the place and they were running past the shuffleboard court.

"Why're we running?" Joan said.

"Just do it."

They ran past the lobby, the basic cottages, mid-rangers, ultra cabanas, running to the waitress dorm, that green room of metal lockers and cot beds with potato chips underneath. Joan looked back, the Mai Tai was a swatch of laughter. Mama stopped like she'd come to the edge of something.

"I need to talk, Pie. Sit with me."

There were things she didn't need to know. She hoped . . . Mama was pushing the hair off her forehead, picking up her chin to the moonlight, kissing her on the mouth. Warm lips. Lemon pulp.

"I'm sorry, baby," she said.

"It wasn't that great in there."

"I'm a lousy mother, and no don't argue with me I am. I try, I know you see me trying, but I can't get it straight in my mind this whole mother thing. How do they do it, I ask myself. How do women get up, make a nice bowl of oatmeal, clean the pot and keep a positive attitude? Maybe smoke a couple of ducks."

"What?"

"Mrs. Shuleman you can just tell she washes the bottom of her pots."

What was she talking about? Her pots were immaculate. She never even used them. Was she crying? They were sitting on a flat rock, and Mama was crying with her hands folded, her head bent. "And look. I'm not saying there's anything WRONG with a secret life of satisfaction these women seem to THRIVE on, I mean, if they thrive, it's good. Right? I see that. I am not a stupid woman. They're not PERTURBED and I say bravo," she sobbed.

"I don't even like oatmeal."

"Oh, Pie, I know, I do, I'm running out of tricks is all. Isn't that silly?"

Ducks, tricks. Actually it was horrifying.

Mama hugged her. Joan never could fall asleep till Mama was in safe, her key in the door was when she could breathe again. Joan filled her lungs and held it. She'd keep Mama on the rock.

"I need this vacation honey. I need this night, and that's all I'm telling you. You said sure you'd be all right because Nan was a really fun person. Remember? Are you holding your breath? Listen to me. Tomorrow is another day . . ."

Why did people say that? Her chest hurt, and she didn't know why. Her chest knew but wouldn't tell her.

"—and we'll get up early and pick fruit."

"They give you fruit. Fruit's free. You get diarrhea from all the free fruit." Her voice through sucked breath sounded like a monster voice.

"This will be our fruit. Fresh-off-the-tree fruit. Pie, just can you please accept and don't make a scene."

"I don't want fruit. Where're you gonna be? What if I need you?" she rasped.

"You go to the Shuleman's."

"I'll croak first."

Mama sniffed the air. Waited. "Oh for godsakes breathe, Joan!"

She coughed air in. Mama pushed her head against her shoulder till the shoulder went soft. She pulled the bangs out of her eyes. "Pie, you strange creature you. All right look, never mind. I don't remember what was so damn important. Me and you we'll climb in bed and cuddle and Buddy will come and everything will be over."

Her staring-out-the-window face was back. A pebble of grief did a back flip inside Joan and rose to meet her mother. The moment, something discovered against the odds. Okay she'd go. Okay she wouldn't fall asleep staring at Mama's photo of the three sisters on the beach, skirts up, knees pointy to shore, their beautiful synchronized cancan legs, Auntie Bessie before she got fat, but she'd do it. She could do this, give this one thing. Tomorrow would be another day.

A sign reminding him to wash his hands before leaving was the only decoration. There was an unopened bottle of Old Overholt, some books, a transistor radio, paper. What did he write? Who waited for his words? So many socks, clean and white piled heel to heel on top of the dresser. A travel alarm clock, a helmet, a shredded mat breaking up the white painted floor. His bed made a sound. Reeega. She watched his face. He didn't let her touch him. He told Irwina stories in his bed, and she was afraid to sleep, afraid to miss a minute.

He said, "Walk with me woman and see the moon on water calling fish up from the bottom of the sea."

He talked to her like she was a roomful of children.

He said he found her body beautiful and she wanted to serve him her breasts, radish rosette her nipples. Eat this honest flesh.

In his bed staring at the ceiling she saw high moon tide rush to meet sky and his hand moved up her leg and his other hand, he had another hand! covered her belly. She felt this in her back. He didn't rush. Let the sea rush. He was slow. He made her wait. A drop of sea trickled down her leg and his hand detoured. He wanted his flesh cold. She stared at his profile in the skimpy curtain light.

"So then, Trout," the director said.

"I sound like part of your story."

"These fish have a meeting about the tide and what it will do to their ways. Older fish of course remember about high-moon tide, a treacherous thing, horrible phenomena, but they remember it happens every month, lifts them from their homes and leaves them blood splattered on the shore."

"I like my stories bloodless."

"Oh I don't believe that." He fingered the length of her arm. Up close he didn't look exactly, his nose wasn't, but it didn't matter. "You have a good arm. You swim like nothing will make you stop. That's what made me love you, watching you get from one side of the pool to the other."

"Oh heavens, we're not talking about love here."

"*Shhhhh.* Don't tonight."

Like there would be other nights?

She was trying not to think about why she was here or that she was here or if she was here or how it felt like she'd already been here. Joe would not stop by unannounced and sit at the kitchen table with her smoking his Luckies, and she stamped seconds into a memory of this man's mouth. Remember this mouth, she told herself, when the thoughts come back you remember this mouth. Love. Was that what she'd been swimming in? She must remember to save some for later.

"The wisest fish is not a fish at all, you see, but a whale."

He said *whale,* and his hand fell between her legs and held her there. The heat from his hand, its stillness. She would write a postcard:

Dear Mr. Kinsey Report, There is only a hand and where it comes to rest.

"They've seen this phenomenon many times, and the whale tries to say how it will be, how each fish must swim out further than they've been before or die. Easy. They must do opposite what their baby fish brains tell them."

"Sperm?"

"Pardon?"

"The whale." She reached under the blanket to graze the tip of him. He moved aside.

"Big blue he comes way up from murky moon water just like that."

Heat between her legs and sea, and if he moved, her body would float to him in pieces. Shore wreckage. "Do the fish listen?"

"You cannot believe, even the dumb ones born yesterday dead tomorrow they every one of them listen so that night all the poor moon takes to shore is grit and rock and a few empty crab shells. Not one fish gets caught in the moon's net."

"The moon takes what it wants." She said this after a long silence, pretending to analyze his story and still remain in this bed.

"You don't believe me," he said.

"That isn't how things work."

He was offensive, addictive, coconut under her skin. She wanted to take him inside every part of her that hurt.

"You learned nothing." He rolled her over, put his lips to her spine. "You think I memorize? My god, woman, my words *are* you. You are the fish who couldn't get stuck in any net no matter how you try."

"That's not how it ends."

"Give me another."

She turned to him, above her his sad human face.

Fourteen

THE WOMAN IN THE rat-fur jacket, the same woman that was watching from St. Jerome's when Buddy gave birth on the sidewalk was stalking the meat section of the Buy-Low, a carton of Salems shoved under her arm. It was the weekend. Germans were buying sausages, Japanese lined up behind the bok choy, Jews argued over Sabbath chicken. Feathers? Feathers? I wanted feathers I'd go kill a chicken my own self. The store was full of people trying to eat their homelands.

"So what do kids call you?" She started right in like they'd been talking.

"Joan."

"Nickname?"

"Pie, when Mama's in the mood. You?"

"Sofia Fitt. Sounds like they eat slices of you. What kind of pie? Not a meringue or pecan or mincemeat or pumpkin. Let's see. Nothing particularly sticky. A good and tart cherry I think, no top crust. You're young to have a shopping list with this tiny writing. May I?"

Not a question. She grabbed the list Joan had balanced on the child seat of a shopping cart and was walking up the baked goods aisle *"ach, ach, ach,"* moving fast. Joan had to push to keep up.

"Your mother wrote this? This is your mother's wish list? Sure doesn't want anybody reading it."

"Yeah that would be her."

"Kraft mac and cheese, frozen limas, frozen corn," the woman read. Jeeze she never realized what a rotten list it was.

"Am I getting warm? Fels Naptha. Aqua Velva. Now what please is a velva?"

Joan sang, *"Because there's something about, an Aqua, Velva, ma-an."*

"So it's—"

"Aftershave."

"This is no shopping list, kid, it's role call for the dead."

Shoppers were staring at Sofia Fitt, then snapping their heads back so they didn't get caught. They kept doing it. Looking, snapping like suddenly the soup cans and flanken could do without them. Joan grabbed the paper, which seemed so small and terrible and such a sketch of her family. Where was the mother who waved her feet from the pool? The laugher? The eater? The Mai Tai conspirator?

"I didn't mean to offend," Sofia Fitt said.

"Look it's how we eat, okay?"

"I live alone. The mouth outruns the brain when nobody's around to say different. A list, well sure, a list. It's your list. Hang on to it."

Sofia Fitt was leaving, waving her Salems, letting the dismal world of Buy-Low shoppers rush to fill where she'd been standing. There she went, out the door, on the street, something important moving out of reach. The woman who wasn't cobbled by a husband or beauty. A talker. Who talked. Who might say something that would explain a few things around here. Who was fifty or seventy or forty. Who walked the streets at night, alone, with no *destination*. Who said this? Fran said this. The fishermen on Farwell let her sit with them, and nobody ever sat with the fishermen. She was getting away, leaving with things Joan needed to know. Suddenly the approval of fishermen was everything, and Joan was running and yelling for the woman to stop and wait up. And then she did. Stopped dead and looked her full in the face the way other kids did. There was something wrong about this, like didn't she have anything else to think about. What should she say? What could she say? The woman was waiting.

"What did you need?" she said.

Answers. Not to be alone, not to carry all the secrets alone and eat this crappy stuff. "Nothing. Wait! I don't know."

"Look I don't take to most people and it's likewise. I give it out straight or shut the hell up. Two gears, Pony, and most can't take it. Don't blame you a bit. Well then, righto."

Slow women passed making a day out of street conversation. Pony?

"What were you doing, with the list thing."

It didn't matter what the woman said. She said something and it didn't make much sense, but there they were, the two of them standing in the sun and it was good again and somehow they were back in the Buy-Low and the butcher said, "Hey Sofia," and smiled at her. He knew her name. She wasn't alone. She had butchers, she had fishermen.

"Say I give your Mama a real shopping. Say I rewrite this little list so she dances in the street."

"She already dances enough."

"Anyway let's throw this scrabble out."

"She'll kill me."

"You're the firstborn?"

"The only."

"She won't kill an only. You don't worry."

Sofia plucked delicacies from the aisles, making loud sounds of satisfaction. Clucks and clicks. Joan stood far enough away so people wouldn't think they were together. Maybe Sofia Fitt could help. Mama had been edgy since Edelman's, worse than before.

Irwina, what the hell's the matter with you, Buddy said. I'm in the shop by my lonesome and they're askin' me, they're sayin' when she's comin' back? Whatem I suppose to say? When you comin'? Are you? Comin'?

She didn't know.

Come to bed let a man make you feel something. You don't like bed no more either? You want a Posturpedic? What the hell's up? But he gave up asking after a few minutes. Maybe he was afraid she'd explain.

And she don't even cook, Buddy said.

But she did. Spaghetti with bloody ribs stabbing for air. Pike with her angry red sauce, frozen pot pies gashed in the middle, some kind of green pea and chicken mush erupting and burning onto a cookie sheet.

Germs, Mama said. What you can't see will eat you.

Issat so, Buddy said.

The unseen and unheard. One must watch.

He didn't ask why her laundry potions grew to three shelves or why she started ironing his underwear, the sheets, newspaper clippings and why, with all her cleaning, the house still stunk of smoke. She ripped the filters off cigarettes and lined up the stubs like tiny armless bodies. Buddy would find them and toss them out the window, but he stopped asking. She'd be staring at absolutely nothing in the hallway, a piece of Buddy's old T-shirt soaked in lemon oil hanging from her hand.

Mama, everything's clean already. You can stop. STOP!

One room at a time, each room—? was how she talked. Sayings that fell off at the end like by that time, she didn't believe them herself.

Sofia was tossing things in the cart. Who'd eat them? The three of them hadn't sat down at the table in forever. The Slaters ate from six bowls and two countries and Lil had her schmaltz-jar coin bank and Mrs. Dubrow had stinky pig and pudding cakes and Buddy ate at Rocky's Diner and Joan made Kraft macaroni and cheese and peppy-sounding things from *The Betty Crocker Cookbook for Boys and Girls* that turned out brown and gloppy.

"Tenderloin Mr. Z.," Sofia Fitt was telling the old butcher, "don't weigh me no fat."

People were standing in line, clenching plastic numbers, tapping them on the glass case, but Mr. Zabaraz ignored the hell out of them.

"I want to see you cut it fresh young man." Sofia Fitt picked up a bloody ball of cellophane something. "What are you calling this?"

"That there's lamb."

"Looks like your grandmother's mutton."

Mr. Zabaraz said not only was it lamb, it was grass-eating government-stamped grade A baby lamb.

"Hey," a woman said, "I got a number!"

"Since when is lamb anything but. Gimme that slab of short ribs.

Mama had everything spread over the Formica table. Raspberries, ribs, lamb chops, filet mignon, anchovies that looked so interesting and funny in the Buy-Low, Belgian chocolate, a coconut, figs, Neapolitan ice cream, an ice cream cake roll, white asparagus, a hunk of apple-smoked bacon—evidence.

"I gave you a list. You think a list is an exercise? I WROTE THINGS OUT FOR YOU IN MY OWN HAND. What— God I need a cigarette."

"You need these raspberries."

Mama lit up, fishing for a piece of tobacco on her tongue. "I wish it was that easy.

"Here's your money, okay? You're entirely uncooperative." Joan threw the bills on the table in an adult way, and Mama looked at them like something was wrong but she couldn't figure out what.

"How did you get this stuff?"

"It's not important."

"What? I can't hear you."

"I said it's not important."

"I'm asking you a question."

"I can't. I promised." *I can't I promised.* She should get out the knife and cut Mama a big hunk of ice cream cake roll smothered in raspberries and force her to chew and be regular.

"Look at me. Did you steal this?"

"Oh Mom, just take the stuff as a gift, okay? It's a gift from someb—"

"Who?"

"It doesn't matter."

Her mother's cigarette arm whacked out, stopping just short of Joan's face. She was a yeller, a hair puller, but no direct hitter. "I'm pooped. I've got no stomach for these games." She picked up the coconut, and her face relaxed. "What's this?"

"A coconut."

"I can see it's a coconut. I am not asking you if it is a coconut, Joan, I'm asking who gave— She did this, didn't she. It's her."

"No."

"Who?"

"Nobody."

"Tell me."

"It's not her."

"Who?"

"Nobody."

"Tell me."

"Sofia Fitt."

"Oh, Pie, you're a lousy liar on top of everything else, thank god."

"She meant it good."

"You took from the Loomer? You know what it means getting involved—"

"Nobody's *involved.*"

"—how dangerous? No. Because you don't think about things like *after* or safety or what people think or what she'll want from us." She was saying all this like the coconut would answer back.

"She doesn't want anything from us, Mom."

"And you know this."

"Yes."

"With your twelve years of world wisdom you know this."

"She's got good in her heart."

"Oh Joan. And you probably think what an interesting person. How interesting and fascinating to look up and she's there. But why, Joan? Did you ask yourself why she's always around?"

It was a fearful idea, always being around. "Doesn't matter."

"Stop saying that."

"Well it doesn't."

"Where is her life Joan? Don't you wonder? Where does she live? What does she do? She has nothing, no job no family no life."

"She's got me."

"You."

Squirm.

"Take this out of my house this instant." Mama put the money in her fist and squinched it tight. She pawed the bottom of the shopping bag. "Where's the receipt? There's no receipts in here. Did she take the receipt? How'll I pay her back?"

"I wasn't watching."

"Find her."

"I don't know how." *Wah wah wah.* It was right, this food was right. It would make a delicious dinner, and they could laugh and feel full and watch Uncle Milty and forget. Well she didn't know what they would forget, but it would be a nice night, a night like she saw in the other apartments, people chewing, listening to each other. Pass the peas? And somebody passed the peas.

"You wanna hand that over?" Joan said.

Mama was cradling the coconut, smoothing its hair.

"Just take the rest of the crap."

"No, you said everything."

"Don't Joan."

"You said." *You said.*

Mama looked hard/sad/tired/not here. "I have a daughter who can't be trusted. One night I leave you and you said, 'Sure mama, fine Mama.' "

"It was. I didn't care."

"Then why?"

"Why what?"

"You had to get . . . get back at me with, with fruit."

What? "If you're talking about Edelman's I didn't tell anything."

"There's nothing to tell. Do you understand me?"

"Yes."

"Then we understand each other?"

"Yes."

And off Mama went with her fruit, an invisible agreement made. The groceries stayed. She didn't even take her money back, and Buddy was so excited to have interesting food in the house he cooked up the lamb himself with Mazola and fried onions and hash browns like it was liver.

Fifteen

IRWINA WAS LOSING THINGS. One of her Hush Puppies but then it showed up again. A gunmetal pump, her good tweezers, a particular eye shadow she found on sale at Carson's, peach and with a glow that made the underbrow important. Things too small to name were slipping from her, and it was Rose, she was sure. Those damn earrings she remembered like yesterday. What did Rose say? You want it back? Wait. It's only a process of elimination.

Irwina made a cup of black tea with honey and wrote a list of the missing items and taped it to her closet door. Then she spilled some lavender oil in the tub and pulled the shower curtain tight to compound the steam. She could breathe in the bathroom. Chunks of porcelain, metal radiator, frosted windows. It was the only place she could think, and where lavender steam rose, she was safe.

"Bathroom fixtures cannot be gunned down," she said. To herself. Wondering if it was true.

She filled a metal bowl with water, dumped in African violets from the kitchen window, set it on the radiator, put the coconut on the toilet lid, then more steam so the flowers chased each other. So much steam the bath was fire, her arm a smear. A *shvitz* like the old bathhouse where Buddy and the boychicks sweat it out. Pauvich, Manny, that sad Mr. Witz—concentric men soaking worries and getting rubbed down with eucalyptus oil.

The coconut—what a witch The Loomer was—made Irwina want to be beautiful, for Buddy to see her as beautiful again and what could he do but love her? They'd be in the same room in the same game, and she could put her Edelman's Experience to bed. Well. Anyway. Shoot it dead and rest in her marriage the way she rested in Cuba on their honeymoon. A mindless rest with Buddy climbing trees, short trees yes but the coconuts fell and the natives closed their eyes to another American wearing their weather on his shirt.

She stepped in the tub. Hot. She had to take it in stages.

Buddy didn't care what they thought, never did never would. He carried a knife in Cuba, and the knife kept getting bigger so by the time they got to the good hotel it had become a bayonet. She worried he'd chop his leg off. He didn't. He shimmied up trees—a city boy—and tanned beautifully and took her in his arms and said whatever you got on doll you'll always be naked to me. And he looked at her. And he burned her dress off.

The family would never understand.

What Irwina had, what she'd find again, was true romance, better than the magazine. Did Rose ever do it on a palm-scented sheet? Did Ma run with Pa in the moonlight? Did Ma run? Did Bessie even consider washing with papaya soap instead of LAVA?

Rose had taken her place in the shop, and the place looked like cheap dresses in plastic bags tied at the bottom, like there was something to protect. And the window. No theme, no shoes on the models. It was Kresge's.

Snoring. Hers.

The bath was cold, the radiator cursed, the March issue of *McCalls* was facedown in the water, its pages fat and wavy. She dabbed Arpege on her hot spots.

"Promise her anything." What a slogan, and they used it for years.

Without her wig and makeup she looked old, Chinese, mildly confused.

She opened the doors to her medicine chest and stood before

her court of curlers, wands, bottles, clips, powders, pots, rouge pats, pan sticks, liquid shadows, mascara boxes, nets, waxes, stencils, rinses, sprays, salts, oils and got down on her knees before them and begged for the return of dangerous beauty.

"I'm begging you."

Silence.

She turned to the coconut head on the toilet throne. "You. I want beauty a man could bruise himself on." Then she added, "Buddy," for clarification.

She stenciled in a face she could live with, placed her breasts in the secret cups of the black negligee with the champagne lining that encouraged cleavage out its dark lace rim, brushed her pubic hair fluffy, sent Joan to the Slaters.

"Let's put the joy back in the old Almond Joy." She chopped up the coconut and hid the chunks behind her pillow and waited. Waited till ten o'clock and was just about to call the shop when the phone—

"Wanna know what I'm doing?" he said.

"I've got something for you. When are you coming?" She tried sounding beautiful.

"Why? Something wrong?"

She laughed in a negligee way.

"What's wrong? You sound funny."

"Does something have to be wrong?" She kept the smile in her voice. "You're my husband, I want you home."

"Oh. I got a truckload of stuff you're not gonna believe this, seconds they call it, but you can hardly tell. A button, a thread, nothing, and they're buying like . . . we had another six-hundred-buck day. Rose is beat, bless her heart."

"Rose is there?"

"She worked her ass off."

She had been rubbing her eye, her finger was black.

He was saying, ". . . couldn't get the stuff on the rack they were dragging it out of boxes."

The underwire itched.

"Irregulars, seconds—it's all semantics I'm telling you. I gotta clean the place up or it'll be hell tomorrow."

"Is Rose there?"

"What?"

"You're deaf suddenly?"

"No I heard you. She's here. She's in the back I think. Rose? Oh Rose?" An untired voice coming from the land of seconds. "She says to say hello."

At midnight she cold-creamed her face back into a tissue, put the wig back on the wig head, and wrapped toilet paper around her hairdo even though there was no hairdo and toilet paper never saved a single woman's hair. It just kept her head from splitting open.

She woke early, and Buddy was sleeping so hard she touched him to see if he was living. There was time. She took a shower and thought, he hears me. He knows what I'm doing. He'll be up and dressed when I'm done. It wasn't even five thirty and she was hearing voices.

Lil: Not even dark she wears see-through.

Mrs. Dubrow: On a weekday? A child on the premises?

Lil: Kid lives at the Slaters with the mice, in the Corningware.

Buddy: Winna you gonna stay in that toilet all day?

Irwina: Ta-tah!

Buddy (singing): Crooked hems and they don't care.

Irwina: Ta-tah!

Buddy (singing): Broken buttons and they don't care.

Irwina oiled her body, put on the white peignoir set, and felt like a play that couldn't stop. She was Scranton. People paid good money and would see her even if she flopped.

"Winna you stayin' on the throne all day? Guy's got work."

Sixteen

IRWINA COUNTED OUT PATS of warm water and spread
the eggplant soap so many motions per cheek because age was a
sneak-bellied crawler who didn't come if you watched.

Bessie called, her voice ragged. "I'm getting better. I don't wake
up so much at night."

"That's good." She pictured the cookie jar Joe bought her a
week before he died. Aunt Jemima with a split under her sternum
where the cookies came out, how it shook when the El passed.

"It's not so good." Loss through phone. "Rose thinks I oughta
take his clothes to the Hadassah, you know they got that rummage sale."

"You want me to help?"

"This is silly, but I'm thinking if Joe comes back he's gonna
need his shoes, he paid so much money and hardly wore 'em.
And his good pants. There's a pair with the label still on. I keep
waiting for him to walk in that door."

"Honey don't cry, it's all right, you're not ready that's all.
There's no law that says get rid of a man's things. In time, when
there's time . . ."

"Rose says—"

"Fuck Rose."

"—men could get good use of 'em. She says she gave Louie's

stuff away the day after the shivah. Remember? So lots a men could walk around in his pants." She was crying.

"Rose is very organized."

"And my friend Roz, you remember Roz," she blew her nose, "the one who moved after the husband went? Sent everybody cards with her new address. He had a heart attack and she cremated him and put up new wallpaper. I don't know how they do it. I can't do like them."

"Honey."

"Brass urn Roz kept him in, in the den. On each side she put a china dog."

Last week Bessie made her come over and look at Joe's clothes to see if there was anything Buddy needed. Slouched shoulders, stained vests, Irwina took a tie and shoved it in her bra drawer.

"Yah so I'm not crying so much so that's good, but it don't mean I don't hurt. I feel like we haven't talked in years."

"We talk every day."

"No, talk. What's with you?"

"Good. I'm good."

"Buddy?"

"Good."

"The kid?"

"She's good."

"Winna?"

"Yeah."

"This ain't talk. Somethin' stinks over your way. Is it too much, Joe gone?"

"No no no, honey, you don't think about me. I don't know where time goes, that's all. It slips and falls and I don't know what happens to the days." This wasn't what she meant to say. She wanted to dole comfort, put a blanket on her sister and rock her pain. Why was it so hard to get to these things? "On the other hand there are entire weeks that are simply perfect."

"And you ain't even lost a husband, Rose is helping full time she says, sounds good Rose."

"Yeah I'm taking a rest from the store."

"You had a vacation now you're restin' from the vacation?"

"Something like that."

"Go to work, Winna, you need work."

"They're pulling six hundred a day."

"Shop don't look like you no more. You gonna let that slip away? I'm saying hold what you got 'cause it ain't gonna stay put otherwise. Know what I'm sayin'?"

She knew. "We'll have dinner soon, we'll have you over."

"Hang on. I gotta go check my social calendar." A beat. "Guess what? I'm free every night."

"I'll call."

"Make an appointment. Get in line."

"I'm going to Bernice's. I'll call. I love you."

"Love you."

Irwina threw on the old ice chiffon, once a star now a stunt girl stained and cut so the dye wouldn't bother her, and the blue Hush Puppies. No. Missing. Who takes shoes? No girdle, hooks, chains, pulleys, hoists, harnesses. On Friday the body breathed because she was a thirteen-year-old standing at Bernice's Beauty Heaven, where nothing was expected of her except to dump her head back in a shampoo bowl.

She packed her wigs, one in the pale blue snap-on case, the other in the off-white. Shampoo, cut, curl, and dry for succor, backbone, and the pluck to go home and try again.

She took the alley way that smelled like ethnic potpie and wound through back porches with eyes, and Irwina knew those eyes, those grandstand seats of Rogers Park housewives, kalooki players, temple goers, Rice-A-Roni phonies, balcony after balcony of cement and soot, La Scala de Chicago, the Met of Mop 'n' Glow. Men owned the streets, women commandeered porches. Look at them sitting wide-legged between chores, watching their kids play in the concrete courtyards, watching her as only *they* could watch from apartments and tenements where holding tanks of people soothed their limbo with whiskey from utility sheds. Shake a rug sneak a shot.

With her wig cases and her pointy sunglasses and the Kim Novak red scarf double tied in back, they wouldn't recognize her but they wouldn't mistake her for a porch lady.

Only woman alive disguises herself so nobody'll miss her, Buddy said.

She sucked in the Mother Russia undertow past women with homesickness stuck in their throats pulled as sleeping children from beds in Lithuania, Romania, Minsk, Pinsk. And their longing. It flew down and it pierced her. She had to rest against a building, put the cases down.

Didn't they have anything else to do, watching her like this from their sad porches, their little renters' whiff of real estate? Friday things were as they were. Garden balconies? Basement porches. Porte cocheres? Piss-stained entries and the only thing kids learned on those dim concrete slabs was how each other's genitalia looked by flashlight. Women on folding camp stools, women on turned-over buckets. This was their patio furniture. A woman leaned over the railing like Romeo oh Romeo. The endless soot of their existence—

A child of about six with clear green eyes was smiling at her.

"Hi."

"Hi."

"What're you doing?"

"Resting."

"I'm playing hopscotch."

Each box was a different color, and BLUE SKY at the top was beautifully colored with bluebirds and clouds.

"You did a nice job there."

"Where you going?"

"Sherry, what'd I tell you about strangers?" a porch woman screamed.

"Beauty Shop. I'm a standing."

"You're standing? I'm standing. What do they do there?"

"Wait for you and take care of you and make you look pretty."

"Can I go with?"

"No sweetie, you play your games."

"Here." The girl pressed a damp, broken-off piece of gold chalk into Irwina's hand.

"And how are you *doing* Mrs. Trout?"

Eva at the front desk who remembered everyone's name and said it like they were in recovery. Pay the bill, Eva handed you a dyed carnation. She had a gold plaque on the counter said EVA. But everybody called her Eve. Evie. Edie. Edith or Evelyn or Angela or Enid.

Eva was making a thing of her appointment book, following dates with the sharp tip of her pencil, bifocals sliding down her nose. She had the same appointment for thirteen years.

"Ah, here you are." Eva drew a line through her name. "We're out of coat pegs, dear, just hang it over somebody."

The room was hot pink with motion. Moist, sweety smelling, shimmering with female well-being. Irwina blinked and took her place in a leather chair compromised by years of women's bottoms. Soon Bernice would spin her in the chair till her feet dangled and the worries left her head.

"I swear you get different weather than the rest of the city," Irwina said.

"Bernice's got pull."

"She taking new heads?"

"They raised her again and two shampoos quit."

Bernice's voice from the back over water running into something metal. "With you in a Shake 'n' Bake, and there's coffee and *kolach*. My ex in-laws made it to take me out of the game."

Her voice filled the shop, which was already full of Pauls. Bernice had a thing for Pauls. Photos of every pope and glossies of Newman and Anka. There was order here, among the Pauls. Irwina picked up a *Photoplay* but found herself staring at the unchanging wall of calendars.

Louis and Helen Witz. Reap what we sew.

Hortons. The shoe fits since '50.

Al Corush Life Insurance. When you need it most.

Mizer's Kosher Funeral Home. Dedication.

Ashkenaz Restaurant & Delicatessen. Better than this there isn't.

Cynthia the manicurist rolled by in white. The other girls wore pink smocks with HEAVEN embroidered on the pocket, but Cynthia dressed like a nurse. A redhead with a wax strip on her upper lip was sitting at her station, her diamond ring on a towel. Cynthia never smiled, never missed a cuticle. On her table was The American Red Cross First Aid Handbook. Bernice kept telling her they don't come here to learn about snake bite, but Cynthia had a kid with problems and clung to all things medicinal.

"Color?" Cynthia said.

"Fire and Ice."

She plucked from a tower of reds without looking, gave the bottle a flick like an IV. Shampoo girls stayed about a month, then either vanished in the night or had good-bye parties with beer and sheet cake. More sinks than girls and every sink full. There were three snorers, wet cats straining for harmony. Bernice taught them well. The shampoo girl from last week scratched Irwina's head like she was mining for gold, but today's was soaping her tenderly, her black arms startling against the magenta basin.

"You should let me dress you in black crepe and magenta silk, that's how I'd dress you," Irwina said.

"Mmm hmm."

"You'd look stunning."

"Mmm hmm."

She fell asleep at the bowl dreaming of a church that smelled like sex, the holy water a mixture of sperm and Ajax. She was eating something salty, Buddy said it was wolf. He whispered graffiti about her thighs, nudged them apart, in and out of her in one retracting motion. A telescoping umbrella. A collapsible pill cup. Bernice was lifting her head, turbaning her tight in a towel neat, no edges.

"Hon how's she doing with the hair?" Bernice said. "I'da let you sleep babe but you were making sounds."

She let the hand lead her to the chair and then the hand was gone and she was spinning, stopping, that woman in the mirror.

"I got an idea," said Bernice.

How small a head looked when wet. Not big enough to manage the job at all. Bernice dropped a copy of *Modern Hair* in her lap.

"Take a look at those Lennon sisters. Huh?"

"I don't want to be a Lennon sisters."

"They've got pageboys; I'm talking pagette. I'm talking knife-sharp crease along the sides and not so much bang." Bernice pulled a clump of dripping hair across her forehead. "Bangs to the side, see? New look. We'll do it with the wigs too."

She liked the knife part and she wanted to take Bernice's hand back; talk to it a while, kick life around a while, but Bernice was all business, making her bend her head over her lap, lay her forehead on her knees so she could cut from the bottom.

"And remember you've got cheekbones like iron and a strong chin is good so we'll emphasize that today. I'll start and Larry'll finish."

"What?" She could hear Bernice swig from her Thermos. Swish, swallow. "Who's finishing me?"

"Larry. He's new. I got him from beauty school and I'm telling you he is the leader of the pack."

"You're giving me to a Larry?" A short man in all black drinking from a mug with his name on it. "I'm a standing," she said weakly.

"Everybody loves Larry."

"I don't want, Bernice, I think a thirteen-year standing should stand for something."

"I got some advice for you."

Irwina braced herself. She'd be given to this Larry, like a slave.

"I want you to go darker on the lips, lighter on the powder, not the other way around. Here. I've been saving a lipstick for you."

"Cherries in the Snow?"

"It will be your perfect red, I promise you you'll want dozens."

Irwina put the lipstick on to please Bernice, to keep Bernice at her side. It was. The perfect red. Hot with a flash of blue underneath. Her face seemed to fall into position around her mouth.

"And Cyn has the polish to match. Then you don't look so ready for the pine box. I tell you I've been having dreams lately?"

"Tell me," she said. Stay, talk.

"The old comedians have been coming to me. Burns, Benny, Beryl—we all sit on a park bench."

"This is fascinating, this is funny. Were they funny?"

"No."

"They didn't say anything funny?"

"I'm getting Larry. You'll love Larry."

She was desperate. She stuck out an arm. "Feel this!"

Bernice touched the arm.

"It's dry don't you think?"

"Not so bad for a winter arm."

"All that radiator heat's sucking me dry. Can't you feel it?"

"Look, they're all dry this time of year." Bernice ran a test hand up and down. "Doesn't seem bad."

"Try the elbows. The elbows are parched." In the back room, rows of oils and lotions she wanted them.

"I'll give you five minutes."

"Great. Wonderful."

"I'll give you my apricot kernel oil to get that vitamin D going. I got some in back."

"Apricot, just what I was thinking."

"Then Larry."

"Of course."

Bernice rubbed, pinched, pulled, and measured how long skin took to find its way home while Larry worked on a blue hair at the next station.

She knew the woman, what was her name? From the store. Fourteen top, twelve bottom, they had to split suits for her. Auerbach. This Larry had his hand on old lady Auerbach's shoulder.

"What are we doing today sweets?"

The woman had six hairs. Was choice involved?

Old Auerbach closed her eyes and waved her speckled hand in a vague way.

"No, now I need you with me." Larry lowered himself to her height, and they looked at her together. She lifted her chin. Lunt and Fontaine. Rogers and Astair. He didn't say, she didn't ask. Her hand instinctively shot up with a blue curl rod, a yellow, a pink.

"You see? How the skin drinks?" Bernice was massaging in the last of the oil. Irwina let her shoes pigeon to the floor and looked past Eva to a fat woman in a uniform with a white patrol belt directing children across the street, the way she put her body between those cars and those kids. The old church seemed to be gathering women in the basement. Lutheran. They had a lot of meetings. Bernice was talking about vacations, Acapulco.

"Thirteen a day all the air conditioning you can stand."

The New Children's Recreation Director called only once since her vacation. She never gave him her number. His voice in her apartment. It was late. He'd been prepared to hang up. He was in L.A., he'd been having thoughts. He talked about her hands. She looked at her hands. He sounded drunk. Trout. Do you know what I am looking at right now? he said. I have three very white rooms at The Beverly. Then Buddy got up to go to pee, and she slammed the phone down. She wanted him in South Haven, god knows she wanted him now. But in her apartment? On her phone? Just hello was a gun at her head.

Mrs. Dubrow was standing at Eva's desk waiting to be crossed off the list.

"What's *she* doing here? She's a Wednesday every other." Then she realized she was speaking to this Larry.

"We perming you today?" Eva took Mrs. Dubrow's coat. Evidently pegs were now available. Irwina felt her arms. The oil had sunk below the surface without a trace.

Mrs. Dubrow was being seated to Irwina's left and given tea and an aqua oilskin cape. The only gratifying thought, she was having her overpermed hair permed.

"Oh, Irwina, hello, I didn't know you were here," Mrs. Dubrow said.

"Here I sit for thirteen years."

"That's long in one place. Well. So. Good to see you. What are you having done?"

Irwina held out her arms. "Bernice oiled me, that damn radiator heat."

"Ah. The calefaction factor." Mrs. Dubrow used a continental accent in public places.

"Let's get cutting, Lottie, I know you've got a schedule," Bernice said.

A schedule? The woman made soup.

Irwina wanted to pull Bernice in the wax room and slap her straight. A standing! She had a stomach knot. She could feel her ovaries filling, sloughing, filling. Did Bernice bow? Was that a little bow? Definitely the head bent, and she walked backward like that waiter at the Drake who wouldn't let anyone see his ass. For Mrs. Dubrow. Who boiled pig.

"We haven't seen you. What have you been doing to justify your life?" Mrs. Dubrow shook out her cape flicking remains of powdered sugar from the *kolach* she gobbled.

Pick something. "Oh relaxing for a change."

"I see a lot of Rose. Lots of bargains at your store I must say. I purchased three dresses, and it cost half of what you charged me for that French number in the old days. You know the one."

"Chanel endures." Mrs. Dubrow's continental accent was creeping into Irwina's voice. "A Chanel never loses value."

"I'll have to remember that when I sell my wardrobe. We missed you at kalooki. You're not leaving us?"

A suggestion? She was losing things, things and places. Places in line, her standing, her seat at the table, a decent night's sex. On both sides the urine smell of perm and Bernice bending low to a Breck Girl in the waiting room, handing her Kleenex, getting to the bottom of her thin, blond life.

Cynthia had finished the redhead and old lady Auerbach was asleep under the dryer, her head slumped against the hood, a red crease cutting a half circle into her forehead. Larry picked up the wigs with a wink, and Mrs. Dubrow was reading *Saturday Evening Post,* the *grrrr* of dryers, the impermanence of waves. Last time she was here Bernice brought her kibbe and leftover leg of lamb studded with pomegranate seeds, that divine meat wrapped in crumpled foil, its au jus running in silver canals.

She'd get old in this chair. She'd have to hunt for a place on her cheek to dab rouge, find it like Braille. Repeat. Isometrics push anger away. Tense, release. Tense, release. She'd have an old bottle of Oil of Olay, the oil permanently separated from the olé.

Bernice was unraveling her tissue collar letting it sail to the floor, sending apologies zooming through Irwina's bloodstream.

"Wait while I go mix you some of that oil to take home. I want you to rub it on wet skin after you bathe so it soaks in." And she said her pagette looked trés trés and filled her a to-go bottle and Eva was ringing her up when, falling, falling, a great distance away, the memory of her daughter.

"Oh god," she said.

"What is it Mrs. Trout?" Eva said.

Larry set her wig cases at the desk and waited, pointedly.

"You haven't seen my daughter, have you?"

"I haven't seen her," Larry said.

"Joan? No," Eva said.

"You're sure?"

"I haven't moved Mrs. Trout. I would have seen her had she been here."

"Oh shit, sorry, may I use your phone?"

"A local call?"

"No wait. I can't. I don't want to scare him."

"Buddy?"

"This never happens. She never does this."

Larry gave up on her.

"Oh all children—"

"Not Joan. We were meeting here, she loves doing things with me. She's . . . an hour late." Sick dropped belly lost child.

"There's a good explanation somewhere I'm sure."

"You are—"

"Joan is a good girl, you'll find her, then you'll kick yourself for worrying. Here." She handed her a kelly green thing. "Take a flower."

"Hey lady where's the fire?"

Keep walking.

High-waisted men collecting like sand flies at Morse and Glenwood, small stepping people slowed by longing, refusing to move aside. The mystically stupefied Orthodox. The open-mouthed women whose naked bodies Irwina knew by heart. How doped up the world looked when there was a child to be found. What was the world on anyway?

She took streets this time, past places Joan might be. Caswell's? Loyola? The shop? Slaters? The day had been laid out neat as dinnerware. Wanna go with Mama to the seamstress? Of course she wanted to go. The kid jumped. It was almost painful. The Lithuanian would be a good lesson, she said, any woman who could pull off invisible stitching was pure Beluga. That sounds great Mama: Great, she said it like that, like she'd be here. They were supposed to have dinner after. And the bra thing. She promised to find something without "Angel" in front of it, something that had expectations of a chest.

Walking, walking. People trying to slow her with chatter, but she couldn't be bothered. A woman was given so much time to do things right and she'd gone past it and her child was gone. Oh, Pie, don't give up on me, you just got too far from my thoughts.

Wig cases bruising her hips, sensible bruises, decent pain, crime follows punishment, inhale panic, exhale fear. Running past women—such bad deportment—reading two-for-one signs at the Buy-Low.

"Slow down lady, we don't run here. Run, you call the evil eye."

Hey! Eye! Trouble here! The last time any of them ran they had silver candlesticks and nightshirts inside their pants. Anyone could be Nazi for a day; their disguises were brilliant, fluid. To run was to wake the Third Reich. She ran. So late and the child could be— Don't think it. Think about the seamstress. Small thoughts. The seamstress sullen, and she would offer no sweets. A bitter woman really, with her metrically composed stitches. Oh, Pie, don't be nowhere.

Irwina looked in the window of Caswell's, Mrs. Caswell waiting for the end of life to slap her in the head. That children should come to this cave and bargain with a mute for sugar pleasure. Irwina threw her cases down and leaned over the grimy shelf.

"Was she here? Joan. You know my daughter." She held up her arm to show height, up, up. Her daughter had grown taller than she was. A tiny head motion. Could be yes, no, a fly.

"This is urgent!" She acted out urgent! with her hands.

"What kind of candy she buy?" Mrs. Caswell said.

"Does she buy? Well I have no idea. Pez I think."

"Can't help you."

Froiken's Knishery, all that potato nonchalance. Anybody? Somebody? My child? Was she imagining or did women take one giant step back from her like some underworld Simon Says. The man behind the counter, his skin thickened from complaints. Too much oil, not enough meat, she knew! She was on his side! My daughter, have you seen her?

"Any of these yours?" *Kishke*-tranced children, oil running down their chins, plopping onto wax bags.

Leonard's Juvenile Shop. "You got an instinct, Mrs. Trout." Mr. Leonard revealed his lower teeth in some sort of smile. A cataract clouded his left eye, making the right an unreal blue. A gifted fitter, he could drag down a child's size from hundreds of garments dangling from the ceiling, snag it with a hook, never take his eyes off the mother.

"I haven't got time. My daughter."

"I marked twenty off as of ten minutes ago. Good value on the tights also." He was sizing her up. The questions, the sweat, she was a lousy bet. He worked his ivory toothpick, rubbed his hands together. "Not a ting."

In Morry's Store for Men, where Joan was always saving to buy something for Buddy then losing her down payment. Once she had an oxford cloth on layaway so long they had to sell it before it went out of style. She should have helped. She would help. A woman had only so much time before they called the game on her. Aparicio caught between third and home.

Ashkenaz was hopelessly packed with *shav* slurpers, and she'd have to go to the shop. It had been weeks.

The place looked like somebody bleached it and sucked up its remains with a vacuum. Her window, later. Take a picture, click, look later. Joan was not here. The reality of this punched her hard. Plastic-bagged dresses. Muffled sweaters, gagged arms. Click. Click.

"Irwina." Was all Rose said.

"Rose I haven't got time."

"For what?"

"Has Joan been here? At all?"

"Why, she missing?"

"Missing? Missing? Are you kidding? Ha! I just assumed—"

"I'm getting Buddy, he's in back."

She grabbed her sister's arm. "No. Don't. You've been here all day?"

"What do you mean? I'm here. Every day I get up I work till it's done."

"Till it's done? Till what's done Rose? Tell me. What is it you'll finish?"

Rose slid a dress into a plastic bag and knotted the bottom. "You haven't been very effective lately. Those are not my words."

"Whose words?"

"You been making mistakes, Winna, it's costing."

"What do you mean?"

"I got work to do, and you got a kid missing."

"What mistakes, Rose, tell me."

"The receipts, the ordering, figure it out. What you buy don't sell and he don't want to tell you, Buddy, so he lets you order your fancy stuff, lets you hang it up but it don't move. It don't move a muscle so after you go," she leaned on the cash register. "I don't think you want to hear this."

"I'm delighted to hear this. This warms my heart to see how in weeks you seem to understand what it took a life to build."

"I come I work. I don't look for no problems. Buddy—"

"You that lonely, Rose?"

The shop bell. A customer. The sisters lowered their voices. "So you haven't seen her."

"Was there an accident? Look at you. You're sweating."

Half the room was tied and sealed, and Rose was looking: She dying the hair? Rouging? One customer half out the door. A morgue. Perhaps Rose had sealed the customers in plastic too. Later. Racks jammed at military angles. Costume jewelry in a heap. Meat-locker cold.

"Don't tell Buddy I was here."

But Rose would. She'd flap the minute Irwina shut the door. She'd ask her sister later if she thought women no longer needed to feel the clothing. Feel the goods, own the goods. A sale waited in the lining. But the money, Rose would say, the husband. No. Rose would say Ma gave her a curse. Presses is dresses. Or she'd say nothing, that's what Rose would say. In her holiest of voices.

Running with these damn wig cases, she wanted to fight for her child, but all she had was hair. Running, a dark scrap of dream running with her, helping her against the traffic on Sheridan Road. Who was she kidding? Lift the neighborhood, carry it on crêpe de chine. Pull women from West Rogers Park, Highland Park, Kenilworth, Skokie. Restaurants would sprout, restaurants that didn't stink of onion. Viennese pastry shops, bone china, thousand-layer strudels. She thought it was life she'd been living, but she was the perpetrator of a dream that started with a decent suit, some gardenias, an idea on a napkin and now it was over. If this was waking up, there was no grace in it.

Ring the bell, let the seamstress buzz you in. Wait. The intercom, foreign fuzz. Static. Don't say anything. Don't ask. No reading this voice. Let the child be here, I will cook. I will make meatloaf with butter mushrooms and three meats and tomato sauce from scratch. I will sit and eat the meatloaf with them. I will teach the child what took me years to know. Wig cases are so heavy, I'll tell her. Why lug them up these stairs? I will let her stick her hands in my flour and bake messy things, terrible things. Papier-mâché breads. Four flights of putrid door decorations. A cross, a mezuzah, a dead straw wreath from old Christmas, a dime-store brass name plaque, a mat, shoes. See their different lives?

The seamstress, recrimination.

Don't listen. Let her be here. Scan the apartment that is all livelihood, no furniture. No child. Three sewing machines, two bent Luxo lamps, bent like the seamstress' fingers, clothes with names pinned to them, a wall of threads, radio on—"Hudson three two seven hun-dred"—old black Lab on the sunporch, old, stinky, hardly moves dog. Mad seamstress, something about something and her breath is chalk, not the pure gold chalk from the beautiful child. Ghost flint.

Her breath is sour and cold. "You are so late Mrs. Trout I could cut a thousand hems in the hour you make me wait." She shook her nun mother teacher head. "Why are you do this to me?"

"I'm sorry."

"I cannot for you today cut."

Seamstress licking bumpy finger, flipping pages of the blue receipt book. There would be a charge, Irwina would pay.

"And why not a call then?" The book close to her glasses, scribbling, licking, frowning, something torn from a book and handed to her. A number. Pay up, pay anything. A faded hassock. Gray? Pink? Sit. Open the purse. Pay.

Joan was standing in the kitchen doorway with a plate of windmill cookies, powdered sugar on her lips, her red knee socks.

"Hi."

Something breaks, blood moves, numbers fall, cookies fall. She has a child! Is holding a child who, after all this, is bigger and stronger than she will ever be. Her cheap cookie smell, her hair that needed washing. The child was not hugging her, the arms limp. No. Holding a plate. She never grabbed the child like this, has frightened the child who looks like Buddy's side, his older sister, Edith, who became an interior decorator and had a stroke in the window of Gump's. The child was not apologetic or wet in the face or glad to see her. Who is mad? Who is mad? Who is mad?

"Cut it out," Joan pushed her away "You're hurting me."

"Leave her alone." The seamstress was picking up cookies, dusting them on her black dress leaving a comet of powder, handing cookies to the child, standing between she and the child. Why? Do they think?

"I said leave the girl be. She was here on *time*."

"Yeah," Joan said.

"Waiting for you so I gave her something to eat."

Picking up the numbers, shoving number at her, cookies at her child.

"I . . . I've been on the streets Joan. Don't you realize how difficult this has been?"

"Why?"

"Why? Why? I've been looking for you. We had an arrangement, and you weren't there."

"I was here. You said meet here."

"She's been with me the whole entire time here," the seamstress said.

"Well thank you. I realize that now."

"So why on the streets you were?"

Joan chewed daintily around the perimeter of a windmill cookie, staring at her, burning at her. Perhaps this day, this minute she started menstruating. Irwina felt as if her entire life was standing in doorways, asking for things that would never be found. She swatted the cookie plate to the floor, cookies on green shag, powder everywhere.

"Listen, you, I said meet me at Bernice's. I was running up and down Morse, I was at Caswell's, the shop, I went to Morry's and that Leonard's filthy cell of a basement. I was worried sick you didn't call. I didn't know what happened. Stop looking at me like that."

"Why'd you come at all?" Joan said.

Her daughter's face was a burning she couldn't turn from. A woman's face. They were locked in a deadly game of who blinks first, the seamstress standing near Joan, protecting her.

"I'm leaving and you're leaving with me. Young lady."

"I am not."

"You'll come or else."

"No."

Irwina reached for the girl, but Joan raised her hand, no longer a child's hand, and slowly, as if she possessed some magic implement, drew a line in the air between them.

"What do you call that?"

"You can't cross this. Ever."

"This is silly, do you hear me? There's nothing there." But she felt it. The daughter lowered her eyes, yet this was no victory. Quick before it dries. Things dry in place and can't be moved. Lives are mortared in a moment.

"I'm sorry, Pie. I was wrong, okay? Maybe I got it wrong but look I can get things wrong, can't I? I'm a human being."

"Hmph." The seamstress.

"I was sick with worry because . . . because I love you, Pie, and you never do things like this and I know how much you like— liked—doing things with me and what would I do without you? I mean I made a mess and want us, I want us to go on from here."

The seamstress shoved a pile of unhemmed dresses at her. "I don't care for your business, Mrs. Trout. I don't cut for you like this."

"We can still get the bra, I mean if you still want the bra, and Ashkenaz, it's early, there won't be a line and we'll get a good booth—"

"Mom stop." Joan breathed out. "You keep these," she told the seamstress, "we'll do them next time."

"I don't want her work," the seamstress sulked.

"Sure you do. It's good work and there's more from the shop." Joan said.

"I got all kinds of work."

"You'll miss our bread and butter."

"I don't miss."

"Our nice dough-re-mi."

The girl sounded like the father. The seamstress took the clothes with a priss face and tossed them over one of the sewing machines. Joan picked up broken windmill pieces and put them on the plate.

"Seriously we could still make a day out of this if we push. We can save this."

"Mom."

"What time is it? Five? Six? It's six already? My god, well isn't time a funny thing." She was sick with relief. It was getting dark, the heat was going from her daughter's eyes.

"Let's go home," Joan took one of her wig cases.

It didn't seem right, all this and straight home. They needed a way station, something in between.

Ashkenaz had a line out the door and people crammed against the wall behind the velvet rope barricade. The windows were dripping, fresh-labeled ryes were piled like bricks on the deli counter, bagels and onion bialys filled the deep wire bins.

"Let's take a minute here and decide things," Irwina said.

"There's food in the house, it'd be better if we went there."

"Aren't you starving honey?"

Joan took the other wig case from her. "There's too many people."

"I think, you know, after all this business we might have a little celebration. That too much to ask? Something to cleanse the day?"

People waving tickets at the deli counter. Sam pulling the Now Serving sign string and the number flipping to 88. You couldn't get a sesame seed at Ashkenaz without a ticket. Irwina swiped the window to see in better. There was the photo of Cubs' pitcher Kenny Holtzman hanging above the halvah, there was laughter. When it came down to it, Irwina couldn't make herself go inside.

"Mom. What are we doing?"

"Shh. Watching."

"What's so great about seeing people eat?"

"It's not the eating, per se."

"It's like we can't get tickets to go in."

"I could make us a meatloaf, maybe make a double batch freeze one for later. Would you like that?"

"Sure. Yeah."

Ma's grinder, the breadcrumbs, three meats if you wanted to get it right. Beef, veal, pork but don't tell him about the pork just let them enjoy the fatback salt of satisfaction. It wasn't easy, feeding the bodies, clothing the bodies. She had so little room for gristle and beans. Irwina felt her lungs pushing out her ribs, everything inside wanting out. Food would be a mess, she'd have to clean. But the child. "I could make fries. You love my fries."

"Okay. Fine. Can we go? Can we just go?"

Irwina wiped the window down with a Kleenex. There were things her daughter didn't know, things she could still teach her. Look carefully. Families gathered over brisket, a family of five in the good booth, booth two, each with a chocolate phos and cheeks hollowed from sucking. The sky had turned a bruise color, a waitress passed by the window with hot plates lining both her arms, arms of steam.

"Beef. Pastrami. Tongue. Soft Salami."

"Mom what are you doing?"

To say the names, witness the names.

"Are you reading the deli sign? Mom stop."

"Medium Salami. Hard Salami. Sturgeon. Bar-B-Q Salmon. Sable."

"Stop. Let's . . . Mom, let's go in or home or can we not just stand here like this?"

Not yet. Not yet. The thing between them, the thing her daughter had drawn in thin air was lighter now, of a different material. Water? Glass? But still, it was there, she could feel the line her daughter had drawn blocking bone and flesh like the thing between she and Buddy, she and the shop, and Rose, and all that was warm and called back answers. When Joan was a baby, the soft muzzle of her lips pressed to that neck. The thing must not go home with them. Who knew what words carried wings?

"Peppered Sable. Cream Cheese. Chive Cheese. Munstett. Münster. Wisconsin Brick."

Seventeen

IRWINA FILLED THE KITCHEN sink with hot water, hot as she could stand, and soaked her arms to the elbows while Joan ate her oatmeal, red kneesocks swinging.

"I need to change the window as soon as possible."

"Can I help?" Joan said.

Winter's back was breaking, and Irwina knew what women needed. They needed what she needed, but she'd give them a good second. Pastel shorty coats, sailor suits with white gloves. Irregulars? Seconds? She'd rip fool heads off with joy.

"Can I help you?" Joan repeated.

"What? Oh."

"With the window."

"I'm sure I'll find something."

"What's the theme?"

"You know I have to stare till it comes."

"You should use your old dresses, the fancy ones."

"My—"

"From the garment bag."

That was good, that was interesting, don't even use his store crap, use her own things, things so splendid they forgot how to make them let alone wear them. Things women would beg for. Her backless lace, the tuxedo the Lithuanian remade in her image, the aurora-borealis sequined number that outweighed a dinghy. There they were, waiting to help her, and she could share, even if they had no place to wear them. Even if they slipped on the knots and angles of a Dior and wanted to be her. Gay Paree. Let him try selling farm stock.

"You know, Pie, I never was a woman you could count on to make things come out okay."

A Greyhound bus passed, silver and red like the dog, and Irwina saw herself climbing on that bus wearing the periwinkle sateen, sitting behind the fat-necked driver, a busload of sateen women behind her, city blocks whipping by. The occasional Dairy Queen.

Irwina made a meatloaf and was reading a box of rice when Buddy came up behind her.

"Still like lookin' at you doll, you know that."

She held the Rice-A-Roni between them.

"Winna I'm trying here."

"Well don't."

"Why's it so dark? You savin' electricity?" The light above the stove was on and candlelight from the dining room table.

"I wanted to make it nice, we don't eat like a family anymore.

"I'll make it nice." He unbuttoned her blouse.

"The kid's here, I've got a meatloaf."

"Stranger things I seen in kitchens."

"Four cups water, two rice, pinch salt—"

"You got potatoes, what do you need rice? Who eats potatoes *and* rice? You cookin' for the army?"

"Bring to boil."

"I'm talking here." He kissed her neck. "Cook me."

"I tried. You weren't interested."

"Aw last night? Last night I was beat doll, don't make a federal case. See I try talkin' to her, but she loves that gray; long as things are gray she's the pissed-off right one." He lifted her hair, said this to the base of her skull.

"Stop it. Leave me alone."

"Make me your good little meatloaf man."

She halved the potatoes the long way and cut the halves into spears. Her cheek had sleep wrinkles on one side from her nap. She'd been sleeping more, sleeping too much. Mazola sizzled in the skillet. She tried to think.

"Still like touchin' you doll."

"It's not the time."

"It's the time it's the place I'm the guy." He reached out to her, a gesture. How many times she'd tried for that hand.

"Please."

He pounded his fist on the table, potato water sloshed out. Her blouse was open, he untied her apron, it fell on the linoleum. She didn't pick it up. He was biting the inside of his cheek, his lips pushed to one side. "I'm looking for the good in today."

"Look tomorrow."

He put his hand over her mouth, she ripped it off. "You don't EVER touch me like that."

"Tell me, show me where you wanna be touched."

She picked up the apron.

"I can't have this."

"I know," he said quietly. "I know. You want me to spell it?"

"Spell what."

"Edelman's."

"I can spell Edelman's."

"You gettin' tired a runnin' me through your mind?"

Her blouse, she realized, was off.

"Joke. Kidding. Ha ha. You laugh till you got wet panties with the sisters but with me . . ."

She closed her eyes and saw the New Children's Recreation Director, his bare room and fishnet tales and hairless chest and he didn't sweat till it was over and when it was over it became a new story, then another, then another.

"Look at me when I touch you."

"You want burned food?"

He lifted her breasts out of her brassiere, one in each hand and talked to them, said how he loved his titties even if she wasn't a faithful wife. They were different breasts for the director, firm, attentive. These breasts got dropped and hung over the rice water, nipples gathering steam. Oh, he was saying, he had no proof, sure, because if he did, if he knew, she'd be sayonara. "Guy suspects when the wife digs a nighty outta mothballs."

Saltwater, wait for boil.

"I went to a bar one time, I tell you this story? The woman, Jesus she was small, looked like she needed protecting, like she was lost. Little lost blonde thing, emergency room nurse. And they talked, and he took her to his car."

"You were in the car with her?"

Because everything was closed you see, so they had to talk in something.

"Front or back."

"What?"

Why did she insist on details? These things were minor. "She had some hard life this woman, I'm telling you, natural redhead."

"I thought she was blonde. Why are you telling me this?"

"Red-blonde, you think a door'll close on her and she'd crush like a pepper. Kinda woman somebody steps on you don't hear a noise. See? You wanna protect her, that's how guys think, it's only natural. Teller in a bank, lost her job."

"You said she was a nurse."

"Long night. Anyways she lost her job had a kid to feed . . ."

He unzipped his pants like he needed to pee, lifted the back of her skirt. The rice water was *ping ping ping,* Joan two rooms away. Twice she'd gotten him so mad he went yelling his story to the courtyard. Mention was made at kalooki, lightly touched on between hands. Buddy the performer. He should try out for the local theater group. This time he'd have something to say and the women-in-the-building were hungry. They'd shut off radios,

they'd open windows. She didn't have the strength. Think of him
as something antiseptic to wash her mistakes. Buddy the piper.

"People got real problems. She was married to this big guy
with a huge *petsalah,* he carried a snapshot in his wallet. When
the guy's father was dying he picked him up, bathed him. That's
when he realized. You listening to me?"

She'd stopped at bank teller.

"Guy inherited his father's *petsalah,* what a time to find out.
How'd you like to be married to a guy who carries his dick in his
wallet?"

She had the terrycloth mitt, the Mazola was hot, spitting op-
tions.

"Some guys they got sprouts, poor shmucks, this guy had himself a hole in one. Stick of a blind man. Burden of the overen-
dowed."

"All right. I get it."

"Trust Fund Fucker. Majority a One. Yes Vote. His Ace, Your
Hole."

He snapped down her underpants. If she stopped him, he'd
yell her dirty laundry like the neighbors paid to hear. And the
kid. Better to turn on the radio, turn up the flame. He was trying
to push inside her, she was dry, dry, he spit on his fingers and
dabbed at her and fucked her and she bit her lip and the candle
flame slanted and the table was beautiful and the meatloaf glis-
tened with bacon fat and she wiped something off her mouth
that wouldn't come off and when he was finished, when he was
zipping up, she put her mouth to the faucet, rinse, spit, rinse, spit,
rinse, spit she saw the oil flame jump the pot, cross the counter,
lick up the white cabinet leaving a soot line in its path.

"JESUS WINNA, FIRE. YOU WAITIN' FOR THE PLACE
TO BURN DOWN?"

He was grabbing for the extinguisher, baking soda, anything.

Flaming skillet in hand, she saw her child.

Eighteen

THE NEIGHBOR'S APARTMENT MOVED at the speed of onions laying low in an electric skillet.

Joan didn't know these people, nobody did. They were temporary people, friends of the landlord staying while their home was being built somewhere. Their walls were lined with cartons, not the boxes Mama kept in the shed—old Del Monte pineapple and Chiquita banana crates—but thick cartons with American Van Lines printed in fat letters on all sides. And tender instructions: This End Up. Handle With Care. Their furniture was a card table, cloth director chairs, a piece of wood balanced on silver buckets. They wore shoes in the house. They had sports equipment, tennis racquets in zippered covers, a golf bag, skis. These temporary people, it seemed, could do anything. They'd been to India, kept dogs in the apartment, dogs with Indian names. Mrs. Slater baked them something, which they accepted at the door.

"Meet Shakti, Govinda, and Chai. Airedales." The woman nuzzled one. "We're terrier people."

The father nodded to Edward R. Murrow like they just finished a satisfying conversation. "Hello Joan. You should have seen her last bunch. Holly, Ivy, and Yule. Meg's a theme parker but she won most respected breeder in the Midwest. Didn't you." He gave her a squeeze.

Govinda, or maybe Chai curled his well-bred lips and snarled at the man, who picked up a cheese-and-cracker tray and was holding it above his head, bumping dogs aside with his knee. "Oh cripes the cheese'll get spilly."

"You need me to do something?" The older son, Timmy, on Lassie without the country boy.

"Relax, pups, I'll put the babes down, oh yes, oh yes, oh yes, you are my darling babes." The woman wrestled three beasts to their cages, which was most of the dining room.

"Mom believes in crates, but I'm saying what's the point? Big dog small crate barking in misery? I believe in freedom and justice for all." He wasn't Timmy, he was Spin of Spin and Marty. She had to stop from putting her hand over her heart.

"What are you doing *here*?" Joan said.

"No offense but we're not really here. Dad's a cheap bastard and Hartshorn's not charging him. We're building in Kenilworth." He whispered moist words in her ear. "Mom picked it because it sounded doggy. They're late of course."

"Late?"

"The builders. Builders are always late. We should've planned for this."

Right. Now they were stuck. There was another boy, a wanna-playboy with a pile of board games and a large head and glasses. Without the glasses he had a girl's face. Spin was tossing and catching a tennis ball.

"You go to high school?" she said.

"Prep. Sorry about your fire. Anybody hurt?"

"No, oh no, it's just . . . it was messy." Her apartment, it was in Mesopotamia.

"Shoots and Ladders?" the boy said.

"Scamper, she was in a fire."

"On fire?"

"Don't answer, he stops eventually."

This apartment had a Scamper and a mother who recited the evening menu like poetry. Roast loin of pork with mustard crust.

"By the shores of Gitchigoomie." And potatoes Anna, string beans with caramelized onions, lemon pound cake, your choice of whipped cream or vanilla ice cream or even plain with the lemon glaze would be fine. In her apartment, turtles dried under couches and weren't found for years. They would eat on paper plates, no big deal.

She put her ear against the door.

"I'm telling," the boy said.

She gave him the why-I-oughta fist.

"Go to the Head of the Class? I'll let you see answers."

The man gave a bow, or no, he was setting the crackers down and had a stiff back. There was a brown leather photo album beside the cheese. The man opened to a shot of a fountain pen lying next to a blob of something.

"Kenya," he said.

"Elephant excrement," Spin whispered, sending warm curly air throughout her existence.

"Wow."

"Dad shows it to everyone, it's a size-relationship thing."

She took a cracker with blue-colored cheese that smelled like baby vomit, but Spin was whispering again. "The dogs will bark through dinner. Would you like earplugs? I prefer taking Anacin with a large beer."

"Au jus or should I flour?" the woman said.

"Go gravy, Meg," the man said.

"Righto."

After dinner things took a dive. Spin had to go, and the dogs were still howling, the boy was pulling on her, and she couldn't stop thinking about Mama holding that pot lit up gold as god.

"I better go too. They need me over there. So thanks so much and all," she said.

"I'm afraid we got the go-ahead," the man said.

The go-ahead?

"Dear, your mother has her hands full and wants you with us overnight, you know, clean things up a bit. Patrick is sleeping at a friend's and you can bunk on the bottom." Was this woman kind? Joan tried to picture her as kind but able to tolerate dogs crying.

"I'll just check and be right back," Joan said.

"Stay dear, you know how things left undone have a way of finding you."

What? What did that mean? The woman handed her four Saint Joseph baby aspirins with water from a shot glass of pigs being chased by a wolf and waited while she swallowed. These temporary people, there was no way to argue with them. In a few days or a week or the next time she thought about it, she'd knock on their door—yellow tennis ball, Spin in her ear, rack of lamb on Chinette—and they'd be gone, replaced by a young family with struggle in their faces. She'd ask but nobody would remember them.

The bottom bunk had a red flannel quilt and a bunch of toys. The man swept the toys to the floor, pulled the covers back and tucked her in and he said *Lights out!* as he turned the lights out. The room was orange from a Mickey Mouse nightlight, Mickey's orange eye winking at her. The blanket pushed her lungs, she stared at circles of metal holding the mattress above her.

The boy's upside-down head appeared over the side. "I got Marlin Perkin's Zoo Parade. I gotta flashlight. We could play—"

"Can it."

A corner of his sheet struck through one of the circles. The outside world was cold, exploding beauty. She let herself remember.

Something meat in the oven and Mama making fries, her apron double-tied in front, peeling Idahos over the trash, fast straight strokes and the white skin came out clean. She dumped the potatoes in a bowl of vinegar water so they wouldn't brown, fast stacked plates on the dining room table, set out candles, salad forks, fast fast bowl in the fridge, grabbing bacon, shutting the fridge with a hip like she was on *Beat the Clock, Truth or Consequences* with that chimpanzee in the dress, Beulah with the buzzer going off any minute and Mama'd have to stop where she was, unfinished, deal with judges. She stripped the carrots in four strokes each.

Joan was afraid for her fingers. She looked small, her feet tinted blue from the wet shoes drying on newspaper by the door. Buddy touched her mother's arm, lightly, the way Bessie did to bring her out of a dream. Then he touched her another way, and Joan went to her room and played the music.

Her bunk dream. Lake Michigan was a river, skinny enough to cross but full of wolves that were dotted or wearing flannel. The river was on fire. She drank from it. Somebody opened a dam, and wolves rushed her. She cut them into fish and peed the fire out.

Nineteen

IN THE MORNING, JOAN stuffed dog treats through the cage bars and snuck out before anyone got cheerful.

The kitchen showed no trace of last night's fire. The burning skillet held two smaller skillets nestled logically inside, the oven was immaculate. Buddy in her bed—he must have slept there. Mama's door was closed. Rest, Daddy. You look tired. Rest.

With his eyes closed, without moving, with his back to her, "Home early? Didn't have to call no fire department, she wants to argue, little baking soda and common sense I took care of it." He rolled over, his balding head on her pink pillowcase. He had something, he'd been waiting.

"Tell me about the fire," she said.

"C'mere." He smelled like Juicy Fruit and booze under that. Tooty Frooty Buddy.

"Why aren't you at the shop?" She hung on the edge of the bed.

"Sit like a real person. Relax. It's early. Don't go in yet let her sleep."

He looked like he'd been up for days. Forgotten limbs flooded with memory. She'd been in this moment before. Nothing in the apartment was missing, only air moving faster looking for places to land. Mama must have cleaned like mad. Buddy gave her a halvah covered with a thin layer of chocolate.

"Before breakfast?"

"Sesame seeds don't hurt you. I had it last night, but you wasn't here. What's the good word? Gimme the good word. How's whatzitz the turtle?"

"Mike. He's got a name."

He got her a turtle, its shell streaked with red lacquer, a Jell-O mold house with an island of colored rocks and a plastic palm tree jutting from the center. The other turtle, the nice plain turtle that dried up under the couch, she wanted him. Things were missing, gifts disappearing. Mama didn't like his gifts, she'd find the hiding places and throw them out. Nothing had locks, everybody helped themselves.

"How's Mikey?"

"I fed him spaghetti yesterday, you should see how big he opened his mouth. Tell me about last night."

His face changed. "Nothing, she got crazy with the Mazola that's all. She's not used to cookin' got a heavy hand. All taken care of. Point is, what'd they feed you next door?"

"Pork roast."

"Figures. Guy's a high-up at Quaker. VP of Oats. What'd you do?"

"Eat, sleep."

"Whattya do at the twins'?"

"What? Why are you asking?"

"You eat there?"

"Dad."

"You play Scrabble?"

"Let's talk about last night."

"That takes, what, half an hour?"

No evidence of the fire. There should be something, some reason.

"Leave all night for something that takes a half hour don't

make sense. I want you to lead a good life, Monkey, I want you to have snacks. Snacks take what, fifteen minutes? Dinner, half an hour tops. You got a decent bed, use it. Sleepin' at other people's ain't normal. I want you with us."

"I didn't want to go."

"That's last night, last night's different. I'm talkin' . . ."

It was harder to do things, harder to get away. Last week Mama let her sleep at the Slaters. She and the twins snuggled barefoot reading Archie three to a comic and Mrs. Slater was practicing English to *I've Got a Secret*. She adored Kitty Carlisle, adored the diamond heart Arlene Dahl wore, put duct tape on the TV to cover occupation of mystery guest. He was the man who held the canary in the coal mine and Buddy was standing next to the hamsters saying she didn't have permission and Mrs. Slater was packing her things and Keith was quiet in a bursting way.

Sofia Fitt said leave the family, find your head. Only she called it a tribe and said they wouldn't like it. Said there'd be mourning in the village.

"Who's opening the shop?"

"She's worried about the shop all of a sudden. Rose. Rose takes care of business."

"How come I had to go?"

"That was your Ma. Ask her. When she wakes up."

"Don't overfeed him."

He was dumping too many fish flakes in the turtle water, a clump of beige floating sludge.

"Guess he ain't interested. And don't tell me don't."

"I wanna know about the fire."

"You see black? You see flames?"

The halvah was delicious. She put Spin and his tennis ball in front of her father's face. A funny smell was coming from Sofia Fitt's teeth, or maybe it was her pants. She'd let a little pee go last night. He'd smell it on her. She wanted to change before he smelled her.

"I found this, whattya make of it?" He had her Pink Ponytail diary. On the back cover she'd penned different married names. Mrs. Chris Nobel. Mrs. Gock.

"Where'd you get that?"

"It's locked." He was laughing, playing keep-away. "We got no secrets in this house."

"It's a diary, you're supposed to—"

"I'd like the key. Please."

"That's why they—"

"Fine. I'll help myself."

He went through her drawers, her nightstand like it was his.

"What's so special you gotta hide?"

"They only give you an inch a day to write."

She could see across the courtyard, Mr. Slater in his undershirt, Lil at the kitchen table with Leon, a woman she didn't know brushing her hair in a bedroom mirror.

"Decent families don't keep things from each other."

He nudged the lock, something fell out.

Shit.

The naked people drawing. The Melnick babysitter who studied at the Art Institute, she'd drawn a woman with grapefruit breasts, a man with a charcoal penis so Joan could *see*. It was beautiful how Melnick could draw. Legs with muscles underneath. In his hand they looked like people in the JCC shower she didn't need to see.

"My own kid."

"It's artwork."

"Filth."

She grabbed the diary, shoved it under her shirt. He laughed, tapped his nose. "Detective takes what he takes. Melnick's fired. Kaputsky."

The leatherette was sticking to her chest, her keys gave off a metal odor. He'd smell her soon. She picked up the edges of the plaid bedspread Mama sewed when she was trying to quit smoking and wrapped herself.

"You used to tell me everything, 'member? Hocus Pocus nothin' to hide. Clean slate. Take that mutton-colored sorry thing off, it's ugly and you're ugly in it."

"It's cold."

"Stale air. When's the last time anybody cracked a window?"

"It's freezing."

"No heat in Amana."

The Lunt Avenue bus passed. Sometimes it was that easy, everyday things shaking him out of it.

"A father wants to know how his kid's doing, can't visit school—"

"There's Parent Night."

"Parent Night."

"For teachers and parents."

"I know all about their book reports on the wall."

"The other—"

"That ain't learnin', that's show biz. The key."

Joan swung her legs against the bed. There was no mapping his moods. She made a box of onyx and pearl, he climbed in. A box of chrome and red, he was there. She was a cell hiding from its nucleus.

"Well I'm disappointed, didn't I show you how babies come? You need books I'll go to the library get books."

"I want—"

"Take it up with your mother. You finish your homework?"

"Yup."

"Extra credit?"

"Nope."

"You double-checked?"

Extra credit she made up to keep him happy, keep him away. Color Asia Minor. Paste seeds in a book according to how they reproduce. By air, by land, by glue. She was very busy.

"I want you to succeed."

"I'm succeeding. I succeeded."

"The key."

"Could we—"

"What was your homework?"

"Story problems."

"You got a G minus in math. You wanna be a candy striper empty piss pots a buck a day?"

"It's story problems not a career."

"Smart mouth. The world's a story problem, don't you know yet? Guy with the best story wins. Your work please."

Cars passed like tape recordings of cars. The temporary people were eating cereal with wheat germ and fresh berries, the everyday of it slapping her. Look how far you've come from me, their lives said.

Her father's finger passed lightly over her ear, and she found herself above the room looking down on a bed, a girl in KEDS, a man in boxer shorts with threads of elastic growing out of the waistband.

"What's funny? I like a good joke. Crazy people smile at nothing, nuts in nuthouses."

She had two record albums, *Greensleeves* and *The Kingston Trio*. The Slater twins had Pat Boon, Peter and the Wolf, Neil Sedaka, but Joan knew every note of her albums, every instrument. She could be the oboe in *Greensleeves*. *Kingston Trio,* third groove, longest song: "Down by the mission San Miguel lives a great house wherein dwells Don Carlos Y la Doña Maria Elaina Cantrell."

A worker saddles mares, falls in love with the lady of the ranch, but they can never be together, he can only oil her chairs. It was confusing here in Mesopotamia. The temporary people with their dogs and boxes had the same size apartment as hers but so much room. They could use their arms and legs. They were wild with their arms and legs. She wanted pork roast and wet whispers.

"*Shhh,* you'll wake her."

Scratch, off. Buddy opened a window, iced air rushed the room.

"Lemme see your homework."

"I gotta go to school."

"Family emergency. I'll write a note."

She had half an hour to get to class and he had her math book, the red cover was an illustration of a boy's and girl's smiling faces peeking out from behind a brick wall. Fractions. Halleluiah come on get happy.

"Why must you?"

"So you can be better than me."

She gave him her math paper, let him act like he was thinking it through. He had the teacher's answer book like she read *Argosy* behind *Life* waiting for him at the barber's.

"Farmer's got apples, ten bushels and two pecks a apples, and his cow eats six . . . You got it wrong. How many apples does this guy take to market?"

"I don't know."

"Pick me a number."

"Six."

"Wrong."

"Seven."

"Jesus."

"You've got answers, you say."

"Nevermindme."

"Got the damn teacher's book."

"What's that? Something about a book?"

Without answers he was nothing. Anyway what kind of farmer lets a cow eat his apples? The guy should be a vet. He should sell pies.

"Work it out, show Daddy you gotta brain."

She scraped together farmers, cows, bizarre unrelated events as Buddy's thick fingers undid her tangles one by one.

" 'Member when you played like everything in Marshall Field's was yours? Lunch at the Walnut Room, shmancey, you wanted Waldorf salad. Try the snails, I said, hot roast beef. Waldorf, Daddy, you said." He touched her shoulder then retracted as if her skin electrocuted him, lemon on tongue.

"You ever seen a dead person?"

"What happened to the farmer?"

"Here's a story problem for you."

"Dad—"

"You and Ma make me a funeral."

"I don't like this problem."

He'd never died like this, stretched out on her bed had a grand funeral, the grandest king on the grandest island in the ocean, and she and Mama gave him this. Horses, a rosewood casket, Rabbi Wasserman, Cantor Cohen—

"Still fighting," he laughed.

Mayor Daily, Meyer Lansky, Arthur Goldberg, Studs Terkel, Melvin Beleye, Mike Royko who suddenly became their first cousin, the rich uncle who invented chocolate milk, the relatives from England. Zumka, Rumka, Mollya, and Sollya. This was supposed to be funny but, in truth, they had relatives whose names sounded like this. Everyone came. Big names, big Jews, Midwesterners, and, for some reason, the good folk of Ireland.

"Four pall bearers, muckety mucks from *shul,* oh, and Mizer's does the food, chap did a decent job don't you think?"

She could puke.

"*Bang!* My casket lands in the hole and you're crying and Ma's crying—

"Can we stop?"

"Everybody's a sob sister because NOW THEY KNOW WHO I REALLY AM."

Who are you, really?

"My old girlfriend cries—I won't mention names—drops to her knees rabbi's afraid she's gonna jump in with me"

"That's horrible!"

"That's love, kiddo, unto death."

He was scratching her back, his dry fingers up and down one line. He wanted her to look in the casket. So peaceful. So worry free. Look how nice they folded his hands. Feel the hands, come on touch the hands. They felt like the rubbery things people leave under seats at movies. The bathing of the body, the prayers, the shroud. He wanted her to succeed, and she had to know things. Death, for example.

"Apples ain't worth shit if the farmer kicks," he said.

He grabbed for her, missed, she ran to Mama's bed. Still sleeping?

"Mama? You gotta get up."

Something felt wrong. Joan pulled back the covers. Towels and a bathrobe wadded up. She wasn't even here? All this time? Who stuffed the bed? He did. Why?

"Aw what're you doin'?"

She didn't know. Find her. Open her jewelry box, the fat-legged ballerina twirling to tink music, three ballerinas in the mirror behind her, pearls strangling brooches. Not this. Her closet, shut the door on him, soft on her eyes and forehead, the bottoms of dresses stroking death away.

He pulled the door open. "I wasn't done."

"You lied."

"You callin' me a liar?"

"I can't believe you did this."

"It's Friday. She's at Bernice's Beauty—"

"You lied!"

"Step outside. Don't make me come in there."

"Liar! Liar! Liar!"

"Wha?" His voice thick as powder.

She felt for the teeth, the second-wind tank, life making life squeaks, anything. "Liar! Liar! Liar! Liar! Liar! Liar!" Watched his color drain, his tendrils and tongues recoil.

"I just died, show some respect. I go, you're alone kid, remember that. Show's over."

All alone.

"I could do somethin' but . . . Hey listen, Ma says meet her after school at the Lithuanians."

She slammed the door, held it. He spoke through it.

"Are you getting this? Three, Mama, the Lithuanians."

"Why Dad, why?" she said.

"I needed a little time."

Twenty

AT FIRST SHE PRETENDED it wasn't Rose, pretended dresses in plastic bags with knots on the bottom were the work of enemy hands. The Balenciaga in the back. Sweaters with arms tied. The hidden Yves St. Laurent trapeze. Her Jordans of Paris. Ferragamos marked down before they could walk. The window had become a fluorescence of class struggle with Tricel dusters on two models and Celia in the original beaded Mainbocher. It was over. The housedresses won. A shutout. The battle garb of the powerless. Some of them no particular color or pattern, others with detailed lives played out. A kitchen, a boy on a tipped stool, a black dog, a pot on the stove, apple trees, a mother, father, neighbors grilling, neighbors cutting grass, howdy! a cumulus sky, two small planes on an uncertain trajectory, all playing out on 50/50 cotton/poly.

Once upon a time, Irwina would sell no housedresses. Now the women-in-the-building had twenty a piece. It gave them suspicions of richness, this abundance of cloth. They wore them over sleek ribbed nightgowns, zipping in breast, hiding mounds.

"I seen the sun rise retail," Buddy said.

"We lost our philosophy," Irwina said.

"Yeah but we're makin' dough."

What happened to you can't sell what they can't see? Build on the good names, you got something to build on? Doesn't matter what you have on doll, you're naked to me?

Irwina set the alarm for four, slipped out to change the window while he slept. She kissed her child, who had unmistakable breasts, large breasts and a smell coming from under her arms. She walked the predawn streets feeling like Sofia Fitt, inhaling night plants that went inert by day. Nicotiana? Honeysuckle? Dawn people looked at her frankly, said hello like they shared something. She didn't answer them, but still.

She ran through some of her best windows: The Morse Avenue Easter Parade. Women After Dark. Linen Lunchtime. Bing Crosby Chanukah. Boardwalk Babes. All those memories transformed into rag gowns and muumuus with rickrack and wide pockets for chattel. Her designer names were being smuggled behind the velvet-curtain border.

Cheap dresses came off the models like paper. Irwina could see how a body was hinged, what it was asking for. She started over. Silk panties, full slips—fine things nobody would see.

In the three-way mirror, straight pins in her mouth, she looked like some spiny animal, arms hugging a steamer full of dim water. She used to freshen the garments every day, taking pleasure in flushing wrinkles from the just-shipped, but the cheap stuff held no joy. Plus it didn't wrinkle. Wash 'n' disintegrate.

Bessie played dumb. "Well things don't move by themselves. Maybe you put them away wrong." Her voice was tight.

"What's the matter with you?" Irwina said. "You sound funny."

"Me? I don't say nothing."

"I'm saying I do the windows at four in the morning and the next day . . . When does she come? At midnight?"

"Who?"

"Don't give me this who."

"You ask him?"

She hadn't.

"Maybe he's got answers. It didn't happen in a day."

It did though, Bess, never mind the laws.

One day and things slip, the gardenias, the cold love. On their first date they designed their way out of the old neighborhood.

Paris he said.

Schiaperelli he said.

Rose had love; it went down an elevator. A good man gone in a day.

Her marriage was fourteen years and one idea. Well two, the kid. It happens, Bess. They wiped her hand from the store.

"Things change," Bessie said. Bessie was tired from working at Pat's drugstore on Rush, selling Mylanta to second-tier stars. And she was lonely and interviewing for a new roommate because the last one stole from her.

"But only bracelets, go figure. You makin' money?" Bessie was impatient.

"Yes."

"Stop whining take a Miltone."

"So I can fly through the housework."

"Something like that."

Irwina put on her good suit and stood behind Rose pushing rags that wouldn't survive a washing. She tried watching women spread their purses and throw away money. The same women who once bathed and spritzed like it was an occasion, a destination place, now came to the shop expecting cut rate. Stuffing garments in shopping carts with their Davidson ryes.

Okay so she didn't turn as many sales as she once did.

They still memorized the way she dressed, copied her on Singers. Just yesterday a woman—imitation was food. It was her bank. They still bought her expensive hat pins, she wasn't dead yet. And, she knew, they hid them in Kotex boxes so they had something.

She still understood the rhythm, the wait, the lighting, the mirrors. But Buddy and Rose knew it better. And she couldn't natter about the drinking because the more he drank the more he sold. Years dripped off him, women shy in the door knowing Buddy was there to receive them.

"What are you doin' in back Winna all the action's out here. And Rose needs help."

"I've got something in mind for the window."

"Stop would you? We got it figured, or haven't you seen? They want this stuff, who are we to argue? Whitey Ford has a slump he takes a break. They pull from the pen."

"Is that what you're doing?"

Buddy examined his pen, played it head to toe on the wooden surface. *Ttt.*

Sttt."That ain't the point I'm tryin' to make here."

She sniffed. "I can smell it on you."

"You got nothing to complain, I got an opening in my gut—"

"I know."

"Pa the same."

"I know, I know."

"Man could drink never get drunk, Pa taught me good, dog eat dog and you wanna keep up, knock a few back like the big boys."

"Breakfast of champions."

"A mild suggestion I'm sayin'."

"The pen."

"Take a break. How's that for direct?"

"A break? I haven't been here for weeks."

"Consider it. Seriously."

"You don't need me." She started explaining herself he turned on the CB, the talk adolescent and menacing.

"Well I'm not going anywhere." She said it loud so Rose could hear.

Stripped off her slacks while he watched her, his expression unchanging. Pulled on one of her three Chanels. Pencil skirt, navy single-breasted cardigan jacket, beige trim, blouse with the pussycat bow.

He scooped a pile of something.

"What's that?" she said.

"Our next five-hundred-dollar day."

"No what it is?"

"Poppets. You don't know Poppets?" He ripped a necklace apart, popped it into four bracelets. Plastic beads splitting and dividing like feckless cells. "It's versatile, it's cheap, it's what they wear. Read *McCall's*."

"I'm not leaving." A confirmation she'd never go anywhere.

He and Rose did the rotary sweep, making sure the customers were hooked on something.

Six women in the shop not even nine-thirty. One had thyroid eyes, an Irish baby face, a back she carried like it had been broken, fixed, broken again.

"What's the occasion?" Buddy smiled at the woman. Drunk, sober, he had it. Buddy smiled, the world's static cling let go.

"I've got a funeral and I don't want to dry-clean," the woman said.

"Mary is it then?"

The woman hesitated, pulled herself in. "Mary Catherine."

Buddy brought forth garments like a medic, and the widow smiled. Was she a widow? Irwina didn't need to know. They were opening their clutches for him, digging out cold cash, and Rose was ringing them up.

That sound, how she used to love the fat snap of zipper, the laying of coin.

Look at him, he loved all women, wouldn't let anything happen to all women, but he took her while the Rice-A-Roni boiled over.

"I'm not going anywhere," she yelled.

Buddy was sweating and talking in head motions. Rose was gliding on her birthright. They were calling her, they needed another set of hands.

"Oh Win-NAH," he yelled.

She stayed in back. If she went out there, she'd make them put on their good shoes and walk up the mountain of cloth-covered buttons and try to make them believe what she no longer believed.

The widow was faltering. Buddy, the soft-mouthed host.

"Now quick before you say no." He smoothed his bargain frock. "Mary. May I call you Mary?"

"You already did."

She watched for a day and week as they bought by the pound and strutted out the nouveau poor. They held magazines at him: make me this. He nodded and gave them what he wanted. Three dressing rooms going at once, garments flopping under doors, pooled around naked ankles and how he looked at them. The women were his. He stood behind them at her three-way and sold lies. A handsome man still, she couldn't help seeing this, couldn't stop watching him like the only suit on the dance floor.

She painted the shop, picked its shelves clean of varnish, created windows Michigan Avenue lost sleep over.

Didn't the *Daily News* write her up twice?

She advertised to women in bathrobes stalled over coffee determined to make something of their lives, a thing they'd forgotten about. She named the shop and had Sid the Eighteen-Caret Gold Leaf Man paint that name in three places with a lifetime guarantee to do it over when it flaked.

Here at the shop she was not a borrower. Here life bulked up and added years to itself. She wiped the mannequin's faces every morning like they'd eaten the night before and taught Buddy: keep heat up to encourage disrobing, the lights down to rub out the ache of disappointment. All her love poured into the hosiery.

She had to get out of here, had to think. She took the back door out the alley. No destination. No destination. Like The Loomer. A train. She needed a train to think.

She took a backward seat on the Morse Avenue El going toward the Loop, the electric motion calming her, the tired people in the car who carefully avoided each other. Looking in people's windows calmed her, half-dressed people pouring cereal. A city was an intimate thing. People a foot away and not bothering with curtains. All her life she dressed women. Knew where a thigh was headed, how to play a shoulder, where a skirt should end, and why.

Wait on a woman once and she could forever create that body from memory. Take a break? How? Hundreds of women were engraved on her, their uneven legs and different-sized breasts and blown out bellies.

Her hands ached. She had been clenching the jacket of her suit. Strange to be in the Chanel outside of the shop.

Chanel closed her salon in '39, but she was back with a new line. Sleek, entitled, understated tweeds, boaters, her infamous white-fabric camellias. Coco who disappeared from the fashion eye completely. Now she was back, staking her life on practical, timeless, garments.

What did Coco say?

Fashion fades, only style remains the same.

Right Coco? Oh Coco.

Then she saw it. New York, dinner for two at the Waldorf. No. Russian Tearoom. Something red and vibrating, deals all around them. Phones hand carried to leather booths, tablecloths stiff with bleach.

She and Coco, white wine and Dover sole. They'd talk, Coco would sympathize. Don't tell me darling, she'd say, they call it fashion but it's faith. Faith, darling. Have some more wine.

But would it sell in Rogers Park?

Dearie. Lovey. Experiment. Play. Money I simply won't discuss.

Then there would be raspberries with clotted cream.

"We don't have no dough for no New York eleganza," Buddy said.

Rose, thankfully, had gone home.

"You said take a break."

"Not a spending break, I wasn't talking intercontinental. What are you doing?"

"I want the window special before I go. There's a show and it's big. A once-a-year fashion event. I'll just look."

"Shop's already crammed full. Will you leave that thing alone? Get down outta the window."

"I see the whole thing in my mind so clear."

"Why don't you leave it there."

"Resortwear—all whites and creams, sand, shells—I'll hang glass for stars and you could put the gels—"

"I'm not putting no gels when there's real work, hell. You never hear me anyway."

"Celia will be drinking champagne. I'm calling it my Cocoa Butter Bon Voyage. Don't look so upset, I'll go to New York and look. It won't cost you."

"You got your plane, your hotel, you got cabbies. What if I don't want you goin'?"

"I'll use my own money." Mad money. What else but to keep a woman from going mad?

He pulled the arm of the cash register down and slammed the drawer for effect. "Kalooki pay high these days?"

"You won't even know I'm gone."

The window was shaping up. She found an old piece of mirror and piled sand around it. It could look like water with the right lighting and she'd brush their hair so it looked windblown.

"What about the kid?"

"Bessie."

"I'd rather Rose's."

"Fine." Sandals. They needed sandals. "Then it's settled."

He made a thinking face but was using up time. He could hardly cover his relief. "Just don't go bringing back the Taj Mahal."

"Then we agree then."

He shrugged.

"Are we agreed?"

She wanted him to fight, was braced but he demanded nothing of her.

"Just don't go bringing back any Taj Mahal."

Twenty-One

IRWINA TRIED CONCENTRATING ON kalooki, but Mrs. Slater's Van Gogh posters were screaming and somebody let the pigeons loose under the table and she smelled mice from the kitchen. A little wall space please, some quiet please. What was this woman thinking? Colors hit her head and neck, bullying, ear splicing, airborne colors, and not an inch of white. It was like drinking five coffees and having no toilet. Foreigners, they tried so hard.

Keith wanted her to be an American so he had her cook Sloppy Joes and dress in Goldblatts kilts. This one drifted unflatteringly below her calf, made her look like she wandered off from the bagpipe brigade.

Bessie was stroking her arm.

"I'm here," Irwina shook her off.

"Yeah? Everything okay? Where's Joan?"

"Joan's here. She's with the twins."

"I don't hear a peep. Like mice—"

"Don't say mice. You got everything for the picnic?"

"Joe's picking up the broasted tomorrow."

"I got a list in case anybody forgets." Rose.

The buffet so unmistakably gentile. How kosher meats could be made to look Christian, the stacked corned beef, dill pickles sliced like coins. Where were the pointy spears that could slide in the mouth, that sour satisfaction? She knew Mrs. Slater kept notes on how to do things better, kept a notebook with that ridiculous picture of the family magnolia bush taped to the cover. She was forever talking about that *bush,* that mystical *bush* that supposedly pushed out skin-colored blossoms the size of heads the year Chandra Devi Slater was born. What was appealing about this? She should go home to her magnolias. They should all go home to their Warsaws and their magnolias and their blown up stories. She'd seen Mrs. Slater's notes by the telephone table.

1. Leave knife in mustard, pop bottle cap off so no gas from the fizz.
2. Rolls—do not slice through.
3. Serving dishes. Reynolds Wrap. Says thrifty.
4. Alka-Seltzer, Jews, Briosci-Italians, baking soda Fran.

All this *trying* made Irwina tired. There should be an American Manual and she should write it. The harder Mrs. Slater tried, the more her place looked like Punjabi alley. She scratched at that kilt and was probably dying for saffron cream saris, saris the color of cayenne and orange peel that barely touched her skin. Keith spread her clothes out on the bed with his cowboy hands and she wore them. She was trying. For Keith. For the twins. For Ike.

Mrs. Slater shuffled.

Irwina saw her night after night in the window shuffling after Keith went to bed, practicing her air shuffle, her two-pile-off-the-table face-up shuffle, her one-handed slap-back draw shuffle, the famous gravity-defying accordion shuffle.

Americans need thick wool to hide their cranks and deliberations, Mrs. Slater once told her, but in India people pray for these mechanisms to be gone. So go. Be gone. Leave me white space. Apartments told everything, only the rich could soundproof truth.

At Bessie's she smelled Joe and years of earnest dinners. Bessie's china cabinet was a prison for monogrammed glasses.

Use them Bess, she said, use them while you can.

But Bess was saving them for a good occasion, which so far hadn't happened.

At Fran's there was nothing on the walls and the place was dirty, dirt she couldn't see like a grimy little mustache sneering from under the Murphy bed. A studio apartment, one room boxed by a round table piled with coupons and articles like an old woman who lives on paper. When the game was at Fran's, the women-in-the-building peed at home and nobody drank coffee.

When they played at Lil's she was up and down, deedle-dumpling around trying to make the apartment brighter, more complex than it was. And what was it but a stove too often cleaned? A fridge loud in its business? A Mr. Bubble–scented bathroom?

It made her tired moving from apartment to apartment taking in so much of a woman. If they could have played in a hall, a smoker's lounge, it would have just been cards.

"Lillian has made a special request tonight." Mrs. Slater.

"Now what." Fran.

"That trip," Bess whispered to Irwina. "Look out below."

"Does anybody mind?" Lil. "It's not long.

Mrs. Slater turned off the lights.

Lil said in the dark. "We took a car, a bus, a boat, and a number of planes to get to *eretz havak chalav.*"

"Where?" Fran.

"Land of milk and honey." Lil.

"This ain't kalooki anymore," Bess whispered.

"Stinks," Irwina whispered.

"See you had to start something." Rose.

"Me? How is this me?" Irwina.

"With your caviar and . . ."

Leon bigger than life squinting at the Gaza Strip. Smiling like a Dagwood as two hostile-looking sabras walked in front of him. The film was black and white, the projector sounded like fighting glass. Leon suddenly waved at the camera. There was desert behind him.

"The ancient sands." Lil.

A soldier walked by. Leon herky-jerky put his hands in his pockets.

A camel led by a small boy. The camel stopped in front of Leon, looked into the camera.

"I was yelling at that thing wouldn't move." Lil.

"I want a Clark bar." Fran spoke for the camel whose lips moved.

"What is he saying?" Mrs. Slater.

"I told him to act natural. We didn't pay for the one with sound." Lil.

Leon at a market place, presenting the marketplace with a sweep of arm.

Leon in Bermuda shorts with bowling-pin legs and sad sandals, spices and grains low and swirling on the ground.

Leon standing above a pile of rice, presenting The rice. Picking up a leg of something, a hunk of a leg of meat of something and shaking it in mock anger.

A man grabbing the meat and holding his hand out for money.

A swarm of people around Leon and the man holding the leg.

Lil and Leon with water behind them.

"Where are you now?" Fran.

"Tel Aviv."

Lil wearing a flowered dress that shook in the wind.

Leon feeling for something by his mouth.

Lil talking but they can't hear her.

Lil leaning against stone.

"The ancient stones," Lil said.

Camera plunging to the village below, back to Lil walking bigger, bigger, a smear of flowers and the camera goes off.

Lights.

"How you must have loved this trip." Mrs. Slater.

"Wonder what they paid for that?" Bessie whispered.

Lil stood, took a small bow. The women clapped uncertainly.

"Aright, aces high, jokers fickle, same as last time." Rose.

Fran. "Only love changes faster than a joker."

"You oughta know kid." Bessie.

"Then it's gonna be double-deck rum aces hi-low fifteen points honor cards ten joker counts twenty-five first meld fifty-one nobody draws nobody lays till they meld. Melded joker pulls for natural. First out collects the table." Rose.

Mrs. Slater dealt. Nobody cut.

Lil laid down a ten run waiting for a nine of clubs.

"Sixes missing the heart, I get forty-eight." Fran.

"She can count." Lil laid four deuces.

"Throw me something good. Jack spades? Trash." Fran.

The doorbell.

"It's Buddy." Irwina.

"How do you know?" Mrs. Dubrow.

"I'm psychic." Irwina.

"What's he want now?" Bessie.

"Wants to take the kid to temple."

"Again? She went last Friday." Bessie.

"Wants her to go every week."

"She wants to?" Bessie.

Irwina shrugged.

"Why don't you do something?" Bessie.

"Do what?"

"Reason."

"Reason. With a man like that?"

Bessie clamped her mouth. She promised Joe.

"It's your husband, Irwina." Mrs. Slater.

The women fanned their cards facedown on the table, there was a run on corned beef and the bathroom. Only Fran stayed put, staring at Buddy out of habit, the way she watched all men to see if they needed her for anything. Keith came out to shake Buddy's hand and settle things down. He was a large man with a large Nebraska boy grin and held his hand out a long time before he accepted the fact that Buddy, in his dark hat and coat, would have nothing of it.

"I come for the kid," he said.

"Yep she's with the girls in there, in the coat bedroom cozy as rats. They've got themselves a new pile of comics, you remember how that goes?"

"I'd like you to get her for me, please."

Keith spoke in a careful tone. Mrs. Slater woke up to a rabid squirrel in the bedroom, and Keith used this tone to talk it into the Tupperware with a dab of peanut butter on the bottom. "Now I can't see the harm in just leaving them have their fun for the night. The child said your wife gave the go-ahead."

"Is this the case Irwina?"

"She doesn't want to go, Buddy. I said she could, yes."

Buddy took his gloves off, flexed his hand, Keith talking in a sleepy pleasant way about Archie and Veronica and kids needing time to, hell, just look at the sky move.

"You gonna get her or do I go in?"

"Let her stay why don't you." Bessie.

A pigeon walked over Buddy's shoe. "I didn't come here for no gang bang and no discussion. I'm just a father takin' a kid to God. Step aside."

Keith did.

Rose went into the bedroom ahead of Buddy. The three girls were laying between the women's coats reading three to a comic, swinging their legs.

"Troubles," Edie said.

"Joan dear how bad can it be, temple? Go. Say prayers and make things easier on us."

"I'm waitin'." Buddy.

The women-in-the-building stared at Irwina, who said nothing, whose arms felt light, whose chest squeezed, who felt a cold settling in the freezing network of her body, who saw her daughter's face hanging there, begging, who tried to remember the Five Rules and instead remembered Unseen Partner, his hands on her shoulders, stroking her hair—

"They had plenty of dinner." Mrs. Slater.

"They always got a situation, these Trouts." Lil.

"Winna, do something." Bessie.

Buddy was putting Irwina's coat on the girl, her arms stiff, shoulders high to her ears.

She wished Joan would grow up remembering a different life, an apartment with photographs and the smell of cracked leather and old magazines, *National Geographics* boxed and labeled, fresh cookie dough with chocolate chunks—hammer cracked, never Toll House. A mother kindly and overqualified for mothering, with intelligence—she could have been a chemist, a research assistant—this was aching and evident in the intricacy of her fruit-plate mandalas. She wished Joan came from money and the refusal to talk about it and a large home with a workshop where no screw went unlabeled and tools were outlined on a pegboard and they had five o'clock drinks, civil, and then no more. She wanted Joan to remember love as something direct, not implied, not the bait, the bribe, the endless promise. The sensitive talk of a sensitive father staring into the fireplace, presenting—

"I'm not going. Don't let him make me, Mama."

"Win." Bessie touched her arm. "Kid don't wanna go."

—the world order of things, and she'd remember being born on the fourth floor of Marshall Field's, where things never faded. A daughter from no-load money funds and T-bills that grew fat on themselves. A family that wintered in Chamonoix and summered on a boat. She'd address that nautical mildew with a weak bleach solution.

"I thought," Keith was saying, "you know bring her back first thing in the A.M., with your permission of course."

"God don't take attendance. You go because it's right."

"Do something." Bessie.

"I am." Irwina.

"It don't look like much."

"Go with your father." Irwina.

"God in heaven." Bessie.

Two dark coats left the animal palace. The child left with the man. The women, no longer hostages of uncertainty, restarted the game, slapping cards, discussing some other man's rapid slide to hell.

"Fella talked about his own private parts—" Lil.

"You gotta be kiddin'." Fran.

"Some things are not for jokes." Mrs. Slater smoothed her skirt. Day and night and her skirts were wrong.

"—and nothing was said about the incident except—"

"Open a window somebody," Fran. "It's thick."

"You see how he treats her Winna? Do you see?" Bessie covered her mouth with her cards. "Under your nose, girl like a wife, sits with him, wears your coat. She needs kids more than *shul*. Win. How come you just sit there? Forgive me, Joe."

"It's not what you think." Irwina.

"Thinkin' is stinkin' but to feel is for real." Bessie.

Rose laid down an ace high spade run to the jack, three tens, a flush of hearts, and sevens looking for a club, satisfaction riding on her cheeks. She looked at Irwina and added the club.

"Kalooki," Rose said, adding the pot to her small towers of silver.

Twenty-Two

IRWINA LET BESSIE WALK her across Broken Angel Courtyard and wait while she pulled out her key, but she never went home that night.

It was late. Clouds gathered, threatened, dispersed without explanation. Remnants of light clung to the sky. The gloaming, powers of lightness and dark conferring, waiting for one to give in to the other. Not a soul and the heat of the day hadn't budged, but she didn't feel it till she saw the shop window. Her Cocoa Butter Bon Voyage was three models in crap dresses with stiff necks. Rose Rose Rose couldn't you wait till I left?

It was cooler in the store. She slipped into her work clothes, dungarees that held the shape of her body, and she felt in the pockets for her familiars: lipstick, compact, keys, tissue, why these should comfort her. The steamer was heavier than usual. She dragged it and heard Ma: You push their presses you run. Presses is dresses. The steamer gave an old-man sigh, and Irwina lifted the hose and steamed herself. Warmth melted anger and plumped her against the crepuscular world.

She poked a few dresses, they hardly moved. Everything was packed tight, nothing in the back but her designer clothes. She tried thinning things out, moving them around, but it didn't change anything. It was the window. She had to make it something that couldn't be undone.

Radio on. Everley Brothers were singing *"Wake up Little Susie."* She pulled the dresses off the models, pulled her work clothes off and slipped on a Chanel. Then the Dior. Then the phone. Screw the phone.

Edelman's was the last time—Edelman's when he—don't think about that—bent her back but never let her fall, not even if she wanted to. Her better dresses were city dogs begging to be walked. It would take hours to satisfy them, make each one her own, smooth it down from her hip, the long journey across her belly. She would turn every collar, kiss every metal zipper before morning, try on every decent dress love them as best she could.

----

2 A.M.

And she hadn't touched skirts and jackets.

Irwina switched the radio to WJJD and shook out a knockoff Jean Dresses and the Everley Brothers were back doing a medley, a Ray Charles number.

> *This little girl of mine*
> *knows how to dress so sweet*
> *This little girl of mine*
> *stops the traffic on the street*

Serendipitous rush of hope. With the music came the storyteller, but she turned him away. Tonight she had work.

She would integrate the store by feel. The orange double-layered Loretta Young hobnobbing with the Garbo drab. Silks enhancing rough linens, blacks made blacker by having explosive prints as neighbors. She let the Everley Brothers design. When Phil felt a brand-new heartache coming on, Irwina brought forth winter whites. When Don asked, why can't I trust you, darlin'? she answered in petite mandarin blouses.

Celia with the auburn waves and lie-detector eyes stood bare in the center of the room, waiting for something.

"Say bye-bye, Rose. Bye-bye, death window. Celia, who do you want to be? Darling, which of my dresses is you?"

The mannequin who once called to her in Paris (well fed, touristed, drunk on Left Bank beauty) spoke in boxed lunches, Carter's Little Liver Pills.

"Oh baby, what did she do to you? For real tell Mommy who you want to be in this world."

Celia was tense perfection. She was trim wives, trim husbands, trim my meat.

"Baby, I know you can do better than that. Woman's got a right to more than lean meat."

Irwina removed Celia's left arm at the elbow joint, refastened it to cover her heart. She clicked her head up twice so the mannequin gazed expectantly at heaven and gave her legs the wide stance of strength.

"No shoes today baby. Today it's barefoot, nude, African amber and fifty bracelets charging up and down your arms. Let's see them figure that out."

She dressed the other two in sober elegance, the colors of cloaked winter: tree-branch brown, sidewalk gray, frozen-star white. Set them in gunmetal shoes, rolled cotton in the heel to stuff the gap. Hat and a handbag, hanky in the hand. Faintly haughty, nicely disapproving. She lifted the models one by one, set them to rest on either side of the naked bejeweled Celia.

"Now my babies, is this it? Is this what you wanted so bad?"

Those models didn't so much as smile.

"What's wrong?"

Models weren't talking. Phone was ringing.

Irwina stood outside for perspective. The first rain of summer was falling thick and heavy. She was soaked. She saw her mistake.

She hadn't designed a great window, she'd put her own life on display. Pent up woman surrounds herself with women-in-the-building. She had to laugh.

3:15 A.M.

She began addressing wrinkles.

Irwina didn't quite have the window, but the steamer was inspiring her. She turned up the dial to high and water bubbled in the glass container. Lovely hiss. She lifted the long hose from its resting place and let warm mist smooth things till she finally heard what Celia wanted.

"Okay, baby, Mama hears."

There was a box in the utility closet, lush with glitter, antique glass, sequins, tinsel, gold-leaf spray. She laid Celia carefully on newspaper.

Rose: Paint? Color? Haven't you learned anything from death?

Lil: A big production. Feh.

Rose: We will talk sidelong about you and never run out of things to say. Rooms will go dead when you enter, strange creature.

Irwina opened the can to the Righteous Brothers singing *I hunger for your touch* and spray-painted Celia gold. There wasn't a germ of French porcelain left. She did the other models, fast now, because her hand was sure.

----

6 A.M.

Irwina set the models in the window, placing a tiny spotlight at each of their feet and stepped outside for a look.

Luminous fire, the models gold naked with breasts thrust, legs firm. Something more. What? A touch. At their feet she dropped her familiars. Lipstick, compact, Kleenex, that they may find comfort.

6:48 A.M.

So many garments crying to be saved.

Irwina was exhausted. Her back ached as she filled the hungry steamer one last time pulling the jug to the sink, dragging it across the room.

"Well I did it, Ma. Such beauty even you might smile."

Ma: Run Winnala.

"Run where? Pie's young, she hasn't even gotten the curse. Chanel's waiting, Ma. Always run TO something."

When her arms could lift no more Irwina climbed on top of the counter, laid her body on all the unpressed dresses and slept.

7:19 A.M.

A bum wisecracked a brick building sashaying between the blank and barred windows of Schiller's Jewelry, Blum's Store for Men, and Mizer's Funeral Home with its dusty window plants that leafed on one side only.

"The fuck?" He lowered his bottle, thought he heard something.

The sound of women pushing kind words. Saw a light that turned rain to gold. Got afraid. Looked at his hands. A three-legged dog hobbled into the alley. He could feel his fingers for the first time in months. He stepped closer to the window. Something forced itself under his damp hair, his tired mind. Three golden women were holding their arms open to him. Him! Him! He pressed his body against the glass.

Twenty-Three

O N THE THIRD DAY of the fashion trade show Irwina Trout had three decent conversations—the Sarah Coventry woman, the Jantzen man, the Butte Knit man—and one of them even took notes on her ideas. She didn't care anymore that her feet ached to the knee, that the hotel room was a black box with no air conditioning, no breeze, her shower a joint venture involving half of Manhattan. The bored sportswear man gave a half-wave of recognition, the Sarah Coventry woman nodded as she passed that skinny aisle for the umpteenth time looking for something, anything to buy besides undergarments. And it didn't matter that Coco Chanel was nowhere near the place and Irwina had to take a horribly expensive cab to House of Chanel, where she was told madam was resting. In back? Abroad. And oh, such reluctance. She was shown a piece or two of madam's line and knew instantly. The boaters, the camellias, Chanel's entire comeback collection was sewn for French bodies, not chicken-fed bosoms lopping out the sides of brassieres.

And it didn't matter that for three days New York smelled her lack of budget or that she spent her mad money betting on understated tweeds and was ready to leave on the first day because nobody so much as offered her a free pen. Maybe all it took was time and coffee, but things were changing. She found people to lunch with, people who listened to her. She was part of the greater garment family. A man in a blue turban, tennis shoes, and a good business suit was holding out his hand to her.

"Sufi Sid. I've been watching you since day one. You're a woman with a lot on her mind."

"I'm a buyer, of course—"

"I can peg 'em. You're Midwest."

"Upper East Side."

"Don't kid a kidder. You got a home to go home to?"

Why would he ask this? She had a blue fountain, a family. She checked her skirt for lint, tried to catch somebody's eye.

"It's okay; it happened to me. Ten years at R & K Originals and one day I'm sitting in a park and nothing makes sense. Not the wife, not pushing rags so some other guy gets the dough. I quit on the dime, went to India, met a man. I see I'm boring you."

"No no, I'm actually—" thinking about what she was going home to.

"Here. Gimme your shoes. They're killing you. No? You like suffering? I used to be that way. I tell you selling's easy but giving things away? It's a bitch. I sent you a package, figured you'd need it."

He was handsome, in a Belleview glint kind of way. His suit was double-worsted wool. She flushed.

"Won't it be nice, something to come back to?"

"Yes well it's been—"

"I know 'it's been.' S'okay lady, no strings. I'm probably the only one in the biz whose god is nonattachment. This is my booth. In a year dominated by cashmere and monochromatics, I'm pushing saris, djelabbas, kirta shirts."

Exhaustion seeped through her bloodstream taking her will hostage. He could kill her by the Butte Knits it wouldn't matter.

"Sid picks he never picks wrong."

"But you don't have my address." She sounded like a child.

"Sign their lists sweetheart you are public domain."

Twenty-Four

HE PUTS IN HIS time at temple, a few words with the lord, drags the kid who could care less about forgiveness and a man comes home expects some response in the bed department, some kinda greeting and he's yelling and he's calling the shop. Nobody, nothing.

"Hello ello ello! Anybody home? Oh Win-NAH?"

And nothing on the stove so he yelled a few more times just in case. Didn't they know by now? How little it took to set him going? Called the store, called the sisters, woke the world up, got it fussing. Bessie swore she saw Winna go in, walked her to the door well the Hellwithem. Provide protect defend fuck.

He emptied his bladder.

He could be at the Greek's now. He could be playing pinochle with the boychicks. Wife don't make order home goes down the toilet, bathroom looks like a science project all his prediabetic pissing gear. Gotta take a goddamned litmus test every time he goes. And those tiny strips, who made those tiny strips? Has to get the pee smell off his hands with her lavender soap so now he smells like piss flowers. He was a tight rig, didn't they know by now? See how he was rigged? How little it took to knock him off?

In his nightstand, some airline bottles of vodka, such a little opening to put his mouth around. Oooh good taste warm. He cleaned out his pockets, rubber-banded Uncle Sam's receipts, clipped his bills, shoved everything in the drawer, sipped another baby, thought about nightstands, look in their nightstand you know it all. Did detectives do this? They should do this. He'd tell 'em. Start with things people sleep to, wake up to.

His nightstand: compass, coins, fountain pen—Italian filigree— bought on his only trip to Italy, bunch of adults following a tiny teacher through Umbria, Florence. What else? He pulled out the drawer, threw it on the bed. Hair pomade, those were the days. Cuban cigar with the ring on, airplane vodka, good, expired passport, Pa's Old Testament with the cracked spine, wedding ring too heavy to wear, gave him eczema. Photos, signed, big names. Handkerchief and his latest portrait. Five Buddies at a table. Don't she even hang it? SHE DON'T LISTEN SHE DON'T LISTEN SHE DON'T LISTEN.

What's she got in hers? He saw nothing. Sentimentalia, snippets, fear. Shoved his portrait in, let her think about it.

He showered, stared at the drain where his hair caught in clumps, his hair that once held a brush no-handed, hair he used to comb it and give himself a little salute and test-drive the old wink hoo boy.

He'd stop taking yearly portraits if she didn't give a shit, molting anyways and didn't need no record. He slid the hair off the drain with his foot and flipped it in the toilet. Place for everything only nothing was where it belonged. Wife goes, kid slips away. That's right, kid was a born sneak slipping out of his hands wearing that mink-collar coat of her mother's having a nice piece sheet cake Oneg Shabbat one minute, next minute gone. He's lookin' around, he's askin' people, but last thing he wants is a scene in Oliff Auditorium so two are missing. He has to call the Slaters and wake 'em up and get them hysterical because no no no she wasn't there and where was she? Why wasn't she with him? Askin' like they don't remember he's the guy who called them.

His word, it was nothing.

That's okay, that's fine.

He'd think up something the kid wouldn't forget, give her time to get her mind straight. Go to your room with no supper business was useless. The downstairs shed, who'd hear with all those dryers and yakkers? Anyways they hear a voice probably soak their panties. Give her time to see things, make sure she didn't follow the mother steps.

Buddy combed his hair back with his fingers and finished another vodka baby. He used to slide those fingers over pomade, now he's moving his part half an inch a month. Fucking part'll be in his ear by summer.

Wait. He heard something. Nah. Apartment rubbing on itself.

Kid was growing up too fast. When they had Hocus Pocus he could tuck her in give her back a massage so she don't turn out frigid. It was a venue. He lost touch. Stay in touch with touch, he always said, lose touch you get Rose. Christ she never took a break. The Ice Queen Sisters. Coupla queens. Did the wife ever like sex? He wasn't sure of nothin'. Man couldn't be sure of . . . One more bottle and he felt like praying, felt God waiting for him to touch base.

Oh lord they don't listen. I give you an example. WHERE THE HELL IS EVERYBODY? Me and you Lord, me and you we work out our differences and I'm faithful and I don't hit like other men. Plant trees in Israel. You know that, right? Musta populated a few forests by now. You see me getting up, making a living so I'm saying, no note? No nothing? See where I'm going with this? Help me here Lord. I wish she wasn't so cold. I wish she broiled a turkey once in a while. Okay, that's enough.

Buddy dropped his bath sheet and looked at himself full in the mirror. His belly was vegetables in a sack, but the legs, the legs were still strong and they could carry him and he had one more vodka sweetie pie to lengthen the mood, then he flopped on the bed so the old body—Christ! Banged his elbow. Serve her right if it broke. Hellwithem.

Close the eyes. Relax the throbbing. Man comes from no

heat with coal scarce as garbage, man can live through anything. Letemgo. Where he came from only the rich had garbage. Letemgo. Guy got lucky guy could sly coal from the coal lady. He was twelve. Pa had already lost the dress business. Dress business. A cart and a rack. Pa never had a kind word for him, and Ma didn't talk. Only his kid brother, Natey. Natey was their light, their oyster. Natey they couldn't shut up.

She was lifting two buckets and those things, man, they were heavy.

Need a man to help you? his twelve-year-old voice said.

And where would I find one of those? She laughed at him.

He couldn't remember how he answered her, probably tried to make himself sound older than twelve.

Her wool sweater was a gray button-down and he carried her buckets and she said she'd give him half a bucket to take back, make Pa proud. Clean deal, even a kid knows a clean deal. He knew the coal lady would give him coal like he knew she'd open up that sweater of hers. City kid with no money eats instinct for breakfast. Sure enough she's unbuttoning those suckers one at a time never takes her eyes off him. Never. Those eyes are his and she stops talking about the neighbors, the heat, female troubles, and he can see that chest like—

In bed, his aging hands fiddle with two little dials in the air.

—yesterday. Guy don't forget his first chest. Freckles all down there and small breasts, nice breasts finished off in pink, same pink like her mouth. Those three pinks made him have to pee. She took his head, pressed it to her chest. Her skin was damp, that soft nipple rubbing across his face, in his mouth, hard nub sweet juice coming out. She had milk! She fed babies at home! His twelve-year-old crotch thickened.

He comforted himself, felt a little thickening even now.

He sucked off her chest and she let him. Encouraged him. Held on tight to his head had her fingers sunk in his hair he couldn't move if he wanted.

Put the buckets down Benjamin, she said.

She touched his hands to remind him where they were because by then—

Ben, she said, put down the buckets.

So he does. And he comes up to her lifted skirt and that made him want to laugh, but what if he laughed and couldn't stop laughing?

He's laughing now, who the hell hears?

This coal lady she was no mother.

Bulky stockings crawling up her thighs, nothing thighs, not like Ma's thighs that made him sad, made him think he couldn't do things right. The lady was dark in between, he'd tell Natey but Natey wouldn't believe him. Natey probably thought women had clouds down there or nothing, like dolls. The coal lady wore no underpants. She pushed his head between her dark and he fought with all his might because she was smothering him to death. Dead and he didn't even have face hair. And to come home without coal was to piss in their faces. She kept pushing him around, tiny movements that made her talk from the soft place under her throat, moving his head and talking till the taste of her went wet through his mouth, then BOOM BAM THANKS SAM it was over and she was pulling down her skirts, pulling his hair so it hurt. Ouch he says, hold your horses he says because he wasn't ready to have her covered over like everything else in the neighborhood. What could he do? His voice was thin. It didn't reach. She got dressed and didn't smile and he didn't get no coal.

You say anything Benjamin Trotsky and I will tell them you're a filthy little liar. Or worse. I'll tell them you broke in, made me . . . She went on. Had it all worked out.

I ain't gonna tell nobody. Who'd she think she was dealing with here? But her eyes were like any other women's eyes that's had kids and chores and not enough dough.

He wouldn't tell nobody. They couldn't beat it out of him, hell, so he's walking home with no coal and no garbage because it's dark and he's late and got no time to rummage and Natey, that *putz,* shooting marbles in the snow, in the dark with that dumbfuck gang of marble shooters, and Natey holds up the burlap pouch Ma sewed for him. Only Natey got the pouches, but he had to wear that thin plaid jacket stuffed with sweaters and with the snot running down his face and so cold the snot freezes, but Natey, he don't care. See Benny, he says, I been winning Benny. Shooters, cat's eyes, boulders but don't tell nobody Benny 'cause I'm savin' up. See? What I got?

Natey's burlap sack tasted wheaty when he slashed it open.

He can still taste the wet straw.

Slashed it with his teeth and that stream of marbles disappeared in snow leaving empty holes and then he feels better, then he can walk home to their faces without the goddamn coal.

"Thing is," he told the bartender at a place called Aaron's on the Gold Coast as he poured from two feet up without looking, "I dreamed I had a car business see, old cars that never worked from the get go. Name of the business? Get this. Lemon Aid. A-i-d. You good with dreams?"

The bartender knew—did he know?—but the guy let it alone. Nobody took no chances anymore.

"Buddy," bartender swapped peanuts for roasted cashews, "you're a good man."

"A tired man. Hey they're closing the old synagogue down."

"Yeah, I heard that somewhere." Guy had arms. Stood in one spot and sent out those arms like Mercury.

"A question of money they say, but personally? You got a cantor and rabbi in a cock fight where's it gonna go."

"That right."

"A man's tryin' to concentrate and holy men trippin' each other on the pulpit—they still got a brass plaque for my pa, they do it up for the dead. Amber light, whole bit. Say, you Jewish?"

The bartender was slow to answer, but if Buddy needed him Jewish, he'd accommodate.

"That's a shame buddy."

Knows names. They better hang on to him.

The stools stayed full till the 3 A.M. closing. He could've done without the negro and the guitar but the woman next to him was a Marion. Clean face. Greek, Italian, something in there mediterranean like. She smiled it took half her face.

"What's the good word?" Buddy said.

"Ha ha ha ha."

"You like this place? They work hard."

"Ha ha ha ha."

Not much furniture in the upstairs but nice teeth. On the other side of him, a guy who worked in the Wrigley Building, studied horticulture before that, drank with his coat buttoned, whiskey man, short glass, short words, Frank. Had a lined face, but not from sun or worry. Lines in odd places like he spent a lot of time practicing in his room.

The bartender refilled Buddy's glass and slipped a fresh Aaron's coaster underneath, wiped the bar, spiked three olives on a toothpick and kept the garnish bins neat and tidy. The abrupt shortness of the Marion's dress as she lifted herself off the stool made him dizzy. City of gifts.

"Ah it's a grand life anyways," Buddy said.

Across the street an empty window box was filling with snow. Irwina used to tell him what his dreams meant so he could shake 'em off. Used cars, people lining up to be fixed, people showing him veins he couldn't tap to save their souls. He kept thumping their arms, but they all croaked on him. Anyways.

"Frank, my man? Dreams. What's it all mean?" Buddy said.

"I'm short on meaning tonight. What business you in?" Frank said.

"Gizmo man." He wanted to say detective.

"Gizmos huh."

"They got museums for the stuff I got."

"No kidding."

Ask me something. Ask about the wife.

"What kind of gizmos?" Frank finished his drink, put his hand over the glass.

"Museum of Science and Industry has my stuff in their basement."

"The coal mine?"

"Who said coal? Cobblestone. That old town downstairs with the shops and the jalopies they take your picture in. Heirlooms of mine in those windows." Natey got the silver candlesticks, Edith got the furniture and Ma's meat grinder. He got there, one drawer was left for him to pick through. Pens, Pa's glasses, temple giftshop stuff, a broken up bible.

"Oh yeah?"

"The wife's got appliances they ain't even invented yet."

Frank looked away.

"Frank, my good man—"

Frank threw a couple bucks on the bar and was gone.

"I'm talking here," Buddy said to his drink.

Sour smell coming up his tailbone. He was seeing clear into vodka now. He's laying on a sidewalk nothing to connect events and his mouth tasted like a fuckin' subway. Missing: a shoe, a sock, cashmere blend, leather like cream. His elbow, he must have bashed it. Coat on the ground next to him covered in snow. Freezing. It was freezing and he saw the shoe sticking out of a juniper bush, sock was gone, cop was drinking coffee, steam from a Styrofoam.

Buddy got himself upright. Act natural. Shove the shoe under the arm, morning *Trib*.

"How are you? Man going to work picking up the news." There was a stripe of vomit on his tie.

"Pull your pants together Jaysus Merry and don't we have enough of our own kind puttin' on the show."

"On my way home, sir."

"Take a little nap along the way did ya?"

"Why—"

"Yer in mick land. I ever see yer kike ass on my street I'm booking it."

"Just a man goin' home, sir."

"A stinking drunk outta his element."

"I got a shop. I got a wife and kid, sir."

"S'wonderful. S'marvelous. Don't show me yer face again."

Apartment so empty it wasn't breathing. In the bathroom mirror, guy with a stone beard looking back at him, thousand tiny pebbles embedded in his face and the barn door looks like a stroke victim's mouth. Jesus and the vomit. He swiped pebbles down the drain, he'd give the wife hell but the kid? The kid? All night gone? The kid stood between him and trouble, he'd give her what for. Shower and a shave, take the cardboard backbone out of a clean shirt, blue oxford cloth feel like a man again. In the nightstand, the signed photo. He set it against his reading light. Mayor Richard J. Dailey in the nightstand, you're not some asshole on a street.

Twenty-Five

JOAN LEFT BUDDY STANDING in Oliff Auditorium working his way to the Mogan Davids. Sheet cakes were melting in the
intense synagogue heat. Somebody propped open the double
doors and the first snow of winter blew inside. She followed it,
slow at first and with no intention, then it tasted good and cooled
her face in wet splotches and she was outside.

She'd see Mama before New York, he'd yell or pull a Pocus and
Mama would be seeing what wasn't there but what the hey?
Home.

The apartment looked mentholated, Vicks Vapo Rubbed,
something aliens would rent. Blue night lights, no Mama. Her
suitcase was by the bed, at least she hadn't taken her suitcase.

Joan called the shop. No answer. Come on.

She kept calling, checking rooms she'd already checked, turned
on the gooseneck reading lamps above their bed. One fell over.
She ratcheted the blinds over Buddy's desk. What was going on
in beautiful Broken Angel Courtyard? Leon was sleeping on a
couch with his opera mouth slung open. The Dubrows were using the toilet, the wall was filled with knocking, a single flush
could take ten minutes to stop. Fran and Married Johnny, the
backs of their heads lit by TV, bag of chips between them. Okay.
Fifteen minutes and Buddy would be back. She didn't want to be

here if Mama wasn't around. Knock on any door they'd feed her, take her in. Act fast. Turn on the *Phil Silver's Show*. Phil, yelling at his men. Mean Phil. Turn him off. She'd ring twins' bell. Mrs. Slater though, she'd want to know things.

They left you all alone? she'd say.

No. I left them.

But your Mama went home after kalooki.

No. She didn't.

But I saw her go inside.

She's not here.

You looked everywhere?

It's a small apartment.

In the drain pipes? Shoe boxes? The oven?

I gotta run.

Your father?

I gotta run.

Your mother?

I gotta run.

A family leaves with no word?

A family stays with no word?

You must wait for them. You're a child. You on your giraffe jimmies and with open arms, tirelessly ceaselessly wait for them.

Mourning in the village.

Pardon?

Never mind.

Joan ran the streets, the streets would tell her. Plenty of girls wouldn't cross Sheridan Road, they stayed so completely on their own blocks they'd crystallize if they touched new pavement. Snow whitened her mother's coat. She was a pirate, a Magellan.

She crossed the tavern street, haw haw stink beer smells leaking from jukey open doors. In this neighborhood, eyes caught her and squeezed and the wind whipped up a good one and she couldn't tell if snow was falling up, down or crossways. She sent breath through her mittens signaling her numb fingers to hang on. Pressed each knee to her chest to bribe it into working.

Howard Street, Morse Avenue only serious. Buddy used to come here for live music. Club Silhouette. Club Detour. Mama wouldn't go, she was a fancy dance hall person.

Neon lights fought with each other promising the end of thirst and pain in blue and pink vows. All You Can Eat. Why Go Hungry? Bill The Friendly Loan Man. Bargain Matinees. Happy Hour. Ladies Night Free Drinks at the Black Cat. Pan Dees. Howard Bowl. Checks Cashed, No Questions.

Joan walked till men were thin and copper-haired women stood open coated using their breasts as ornaments. Maybe some Howard Street woman with big upper arms in a second-floor apartment was watching her.

Why Al, that girl's alone, let's take her in Al, we can adopt her, give her that canopy bed and that chest of mohair sweaters. Honey, come in where it's warm.

Honey, come in where it's warm.

Honey, come in where it's warm.

Honey, come in where it's warm.

"I'm so tired."

I'll run you a bath, scoop you in my fat arms. There. How's that? You like my arms? Aren't they nice.

"My arms hurt."

Why?

"From holding the family in one piece."

Why are you holding them?

"So they won't fall or go away."

Al. Are you getting this?

She'd live in Al's house and eat body-building meals with equal distribution among the food groups.

Flakes big as tarantulas on her sleeve, making sounds when they landed. Chicago. Keep walking things always get good. Footsteps behind her. Chicago Girls Rule: Never turn till you're sure, and when you're sure run like hell. Meantime, walk no big deal past Juniper Terrace to Evanston, where the streetlights are stylish and there are no signs. Mansions built from generations of quiet banking. Even in the winter Evanston had vegetation. And the vegetation was lush. And the lake came up and kissed everyone's backyard.

Joan walked till the suburb thinned and didn't know what to do with itself. A woman stared down from a picture. A man walked a German Shepard.

"Border patrol," the man said. The dog immediately pooped.

Go home get in your jammies open your arms. Maybe it'll work. She crossed the street and walked back where she came from. Rewind. White-brick mansions giving way to the lake, Howard Bowl, wobbly tavern men staring at her virginity, brain-smashing kids doing advanced math in their sleep. The footsteps were close. She ran, the footsteps ran. Okay. All right. She made fists inside her pocket and whipped around.

"You! God you scared me to death. Are you following me?"

"Ever notice the first snow and cars drive like they grew up in Florida? Even cabs do it."

"Why didn't you say something?" The Loomer was amazing. She was a pistol.

An air-clearing laugh. "See you picked up my bad habits."

"I needed to do something."

"Uh huh."

"I made it to Evanston."

"Nice coat."

"It's Mama's."

The woman brushed it off. "May I walk with you?"

"I don't care."

"I was married once."

"To a man?"

Sofia's breath cloud changed shapes. "Six foot five knew every song from *South Pacific* and liked drying dishes. Heart." She snapped her fingers. "Went like that."

"What was his name?"

"Buick. You wanted something back there."

"Hot cocoa, a family."

"I see. Perhaps I can assist."

She could not, a rat woman married to a Buick. Joan wished for that piece of shag rug they give you to nap on in kindergarten that smelled like rotten graham crackers and one look, you were out cold. Sofia Fitt was talking, but Joan was too tired to keep up. Mama was probably doing a window. She'd go by the shop, they'd walk home arm in arm.

"He'd pile ten books by the bed and by morning loved Bachelard. Bachelard, I think, said—"

Take me in your fat arms somebody and save me.

"—if you keep some dream in your memory and don't just piece together recollections, the house you lost in the mists of time will come out of shadow."

"What does that mean?"

"He had this book, hundreds of photos of people naked, 'course their faces were blacked out."

"Hmm."

"Each body type was matched to a particular animal type. Did you know every person has an animal?"

"Hmm."

"It's science."

"Which were you?"

She thought a minute. "California under-the-barn striped kitty."

The conversation made no sense, but it felt good having somebody walking near her. They passed a boarded-up refreshment stand, the Chicago Park District First Aid Trailer on a strip of Loyola Park known as the Jungle in summer because it had wall-to-wall teenager bodies.

"Imagine Buick coming on a night like this." She lifted a cigarette delicately from the pack with her teeth, lit a match with a flick of her thumbnail. "He was in the Polar Bear Club you know."

The heart attack.

The lake was black and the cold hardened everything to a shine. Apartments were lit amber, melting honey sheets.

"Let's eat something at Ka–Mars. It's freezing and I'm starved."
Joan blew through her mittens, no fingers seemed to respond.

"We'll go after."

"After?"

"Buick sat me down. Said, Sofia. Get your notebook I'm giving you five people you need to meet in this life. Damn if I didn't meet every one."

"Was it an accident?"

"No accidents."

"I need to go."

"Where?"

"Home."

"And where is that?"

"You know."

"No, tell me."

"I don't get what you're asking."

"You will."

"Why are we staring at the lake?" Joan said.

"Answers."

"I don't have any question."

"You're nothing but questions."

Ground, sky, lake, everything one blackboard. "Do you think maybe hot cocoa first?"

"Life isn't waiting Sofia, he'd say, life is motion. Ride it and everything stops. Then you can see."

"See what."

"What's there."

Joan looked around. Not a babushka on the street. Sofia was going on about time, how time was Jerry Lewis. Is that really what she said? Jerry Lewis?

"What if I ask you some questions and you get one right and I buy you hot chocolate and cinnamon buns and tuck you in."

"And if I'm wrong?"

"Same thing."

"Shoot."

"Will you remember this night?"

"That's the question?"

"That's it."

"I don't know. Sure. I guess. Yeah."

Sofia Fitt hesitated, touched Joan's face, then touched her own as if she was taking something in.

"I want to make you ready."

Everybody wanted to make her ready. The lake roared, she could hardly hear Sofia Fitt's words. They fell out of her mouth, froze, broke.

"Tell me something you remember about last Monday."

"Anything?"

"Anything."

"How many things?"

"One thing."

"That's not fair."

"Okay yesterday."

They were shouting at each other to be heard. Yesterday. Yesterday her brain was dead. Yesterday a large woman's arms, no that was an hour ago. That kindergarten rug. She wasn't sure what happened and what didn't. All she remembered was longing.

"This morning then. Tell me something from this morning."

Stinken' game. She had oatmeal.

"I had oatmeal." One of them made oatmeal every morning, and it was there at night, scummed and crusted. They dumped it in one piece.

"Oatmeal. Are you sure?"

She wasn't.

"An hour ago."

Easy. The blue apartment, Phil Silvers, woman in the window with the fat arms. Angora Al. Tavern sounds. Sofia watched her closely.

"The fat-armed woman, what was her name?"

"She—" Pain in her ribs and not from cold.

"She wasn't there, was she."

"No."

"Uh huh."

"I wanted her to be. Your teeth don't work."

"Let's see."

Joan produced the teeth on a string with half a dozen keys. Skate key, bike key, back door, front door, Auntie Bessie's, Auntie Rose's.

"Phew, they stink." Sofia Fitt untied the string, pulled the teeth off and tossed them into darkness. She was adding another key.

"This is to my door."

"I don't know where—"

The woman put her arms around Joan and pulled her close. So warm, so incredibly warm and furry, and the fur didn't smell so bad. "Tonight we're gonna clear the clutter."

"What clutter?"

"In your head."

Traffic swelled and faded with the waves. It would be better not to remember this night. Who would blame her?

"I'll show you how to mark time so you remember things."

She let the woman stroke her head, she was warming up, her insides were no longer shaking.

"Most people have five memories. I fell out of a swing, I fell in love, something about a river."

"Yeah. So."

"While they're busy with these five memories life is mooning them. Exposing it's red raw ass, and they don't even take a bite."

A memory. The shower stall at Edelman's, she was small between their sea and fur and Buddy was touching Mama and Mama was laughing. A memory. Buddy was driving the car, then he wasn't. He had a spell on Edens Expressway going north and wasn't driving, she was driving, a small girl driving a sack of bones, pushing his foot down on the pedal. Ordinary clouds, repeating highway lights, an Illinois day flat with nothing behind it. These were her two memories. She was living them and living them.

Sofia's face softened. She kissed the top of Joan's head.

"When we die they say we get the big show, must be a helluva minute, but what can you do with it? I mean you get it, you can't live it anymore. I'm asking you to mark this night. I'm asking you to remember me."

"Can't we do this inside?" Like normal people.

A hair of doubt over Sofia's face, a hair but Joan saw it. The woman took off her rat fur jacket, folded it like mink, shoved it against a fat oak trunk and pulled off her sweater.

"What are you doing?"

"Cheating the ass of time. How old are you? Twelve? You're making promises to yourself you'll spend the rest of your life keeping."

"Do you intend—"

"—to break your vows? Yes."

Her underpants were coming off. Big, unromantic underpants.

"God Sofia, what if somebody sees?"

"I guess they'll remember too."

She was naked as a native in a Sheck film, not many hairs down there, not like Mama. Seeing her naked was like seeing her in clothes except for the puffy places and lines like a cat clawed them, whiter than the rest.

A piece of waxed paper blew by, the kind they use to wrap kosher hot dogs. "I'll remember your old naked butt flapping around."

"That's good." Sofia wasn't shivering, her mouth was set on I'M DOING THIS INSANE THING.

"It's, you're not, the Polar Bear?"

She was walking to the water. "Better hurry. You're not gonna want to do this alone."

"Wait! Wait up! I have questions," Joan yelled.

"Here's your answer."

"If I don't?"

"I'm waiting ten seconds."

"And if I don't?"

"Nothing changes."

The waves were loud and white tipped. Her blood hurt from cold. If she got naked WAS SHE REALLY THINKING THIS? and went into the lake she'd die. Or get arrested.

Arrested wouldn't be bad. The police would find Buddy and Mama and sentence them to something. The old janitor from Saint Jerome's would be cleaning the station, he'd give her fried chicken and mashed potatoes, put his hand on her shoulder like he had a right and the cops, they'd take her serious. She lived in longing, longed to wear her hair right, crack story fucking farmer problems, be good enough to make them happy.

"Time's up!"

"Okay! Wait! I'm in!"

She laid Mama's coat down next to Sofia Fitt's, ripped her boots off, tights, stuffed everything in the coat, cop would see the neat clothes and go easy, kid around with her. Jumper, blouse, panties, Angel Grow Cup, folded everything like she'd never see it again. Look at her skinny body girl trunk running across the sand in one piece. What was her animal? Possum in daytime.

"Sofia? Sofia?"

"Right here Pony. Take my hand. Watch for trochoidals."

"Crocodiles?"

"Dangerous waves that look gentle. It'll feel like knives, don't think of it as pain."

"Oh fine, what am I supposed to?"

"It's sensation. We'll be in and out in three seconds, but you have to dunk."

Step in blackness instant ice stickle needles to the bone, nothing, numb. Her lungs hurt, she couldn't breathe. Sofia pulled her under then they were running to shore but with no limbs. She had no limbs.

"Scream it," Sofia said.

"I TAKE A STICK TO YOU! I COLD-WATER YOU!"

Bundled shaking running lung knife teeth tink no legs running to a house? Her house? A regular house on Chase set where the streetlights couldn't get it. Bone-breaking cold, nice house, fire in the fireplace, hot cocoa going down, blankets, blankets, more blankets, lots of books, piles of thought, wonder where the naked people book, more cocoa, shake slow, mind chlorinated detonated fizzed, soft chairs, old chairs, beaten up pillows, clock with no numbers but orange balls on the hands, Sofia Fitt's voice loving, kind.

"In Russia they'd call you *morzh*. Walrus. You did good. Oh, one more thing."

Oh.

"Hold out your hands."

Out of the blanket? Wait for me. Slow.

"Look at the back of these, remember them. As you grow, these hands will change and remind you you're changing. They'll help."

Then Sofia Fitt threw a fat quilt over the three blankets and waited until the shivering stopped.

Twenty-Six

ALL ACTIVITY ON MORSE Avenue was gathered in front of the Frock Shop window. From up the street it looked like a wooly mass of bees getting stung by their own kind, swelling, *zzz*ing, clumps breaking off, new parts sticking.

Sofia Fitt didn't notice, she was still excited about the polar bear thing, talking it up, walking Joan home to make sure there was no trouble. But trouble already found its form.

Joan saw three blazing gold mannequins, naked-ingot warrior mannequins lit from above and below, light making beauty of the people's faces, mothers shielding children's eyes—don't peek Arthur—Auntie Rose a Minnie Minoso with her broom cocked ready to swing, Buddy taking down a model, his arms a Heimlich around her ribs.

"What's he doing? Dang I thought it looked lovely," a woman said, "something different for a change around here."

"You call *traif* lovely?"

"Stunning. Absolutely."

"Idiots."

"Idols."

"Froikens open yet?"

"Behind you," Mr. Froikens said.

"Outdid herself."

"Came undone you mean," Froikens said.

"And with nudity," a man pointed out.

Kids pulled moms' hands off.

"What's happening here?" Sofia Fitt said.

"Nobody had a chat with the guy lady."

"Aw he's gonna ruin it."

"Where's the wife? Does anybody know?"

"Look for yourself lady, we're spectating."

"Expectorating?"

"Meshugie."

"That's one down, two to go."

"You sound like Jack Brickhouse."

"Back, back, back, way back, hey hey hey!"

"We need to call somebody?"

"No law against dummies."

"Which one's the dummy?"

"Do you understand this?" Sofia asked Joan.

She did.

Mama made a window that could not be undone.

They could dress the models in dead leaves but those gold faces and arms and legs would shout a different story. They would never be shut up. Buddy'd have to take it apart and start from nothing.

Water at the bottom of the window was frozen into waves. People were bumping Joan trying to get a look.

"Give himself a stroke."

He was lifting a second model out of the window, not noticing the crowd, not caring, then he saw his daughter—

"Careful," Sofia Fitt said.

—and smiled at her. The crowd shifted their gaze. He put his arms around Celia and whispered to her and went back to his corner. The middleweight champ of— No, Dad. Come on no, Dad.

Rose handed him something. A hammer.

He smiled to the crowd and raised it high.

Celia was alone, her arms bent like she'd never stop asking, Why this?

Joan tried the door. Locked. His face, she'd never forget his face, eyes blank, almost forgiving. She felt around her neck for the key.

"You don't go in there," Sofia Fitt said. "I'm not letting you go."

And she wouldn't have, if she'd thought about it. But ice water cools the brain, makes soldiers out of the senses.

"Leave her," Mr. Froikens said, "this needs stopping."

"A child?"

"I think, I bet the guy's part of the display."

He lifted up that hammer, swung it over his head, and when he got through moving, ten thousand were dead.

He swung at Celia, the crowd groaned.

"Swing and a miss."

He played them, the coffee-slurping bored angry lonely cheering for one side or the other.

Joan locked the door behind. Rose dusted the air; Joan saw dust balls leave the tip of the broom and float gently to the ground. Rose never touched her. Joan was in the window, people condensing into one sound through glass, banging, banging till Joan thought it would burst.

"Smile kid," Buddy said.

"Not Celia, come on she didn't do anything."

Through his smile. "Don't ever say don't."

He tapped the hammer against Celia's porcelain arm, it broke at the elbow and smashed to the floor. He scooped shards with both hands and held them over his head. Victory!

"Keep smiling Rose," he said.

"They're leaving, they don't like this," she said.

"What? Don't tell me. I'm makin' 'em think it's on purpose."

He must have cut himself; there was blood. Mothers were leaving with children. "RE-MODELING," he shouted. "RE-MO-DEL Rose, write it down." He taped the paper to the window. "Again."

Rose wrote till the window was half covered and hardly anybody was standing. Joan could see the bottom of Sofia's jacket.

"So. The kid returns. Get down from this window, your ma left me a helluva mess."

"Go home child." Rose was at the velvet curtains when she said this.

"You go on Rose, go home."

Sofia Fitt was knocking at the door with her fists.

"That where you were? Her? That why you left the old man at shul? Rat bitch got no business here."

He pulled down the shade. Gone. So easy.

"Leave the child." Rose's head between the velvet.

"Go!"

Another one gone.

Joan tried lifting Celia. She weighed a ton.

"Show's over I think." He picked up the hammer.

"You can't!"

"No? A father's duty, honey baby? You want Celia? You keep her. Sure. I got a place till Mama comes, then we, aw shit," he held up his hands like the M & M commercial, "I'm bleedin' Joanie."

"Dad."

"Only forgiveness matters. Monkey, help me out here, take her feet, we can do this together me and you."

And her father was showing her cuts, so many and deep and needing her Bactine.

Twenty-Seven

- -

IT WAS BUDDY'S VERSION of happiness. Maybe *happiness* wasn't the right word. An urgent generosity protruding from his core as he helped his daughter carry Celia down the basement steps, walking backward, carrying most of the weight himself.

"Careful going down. Here. Let the old man shoulder the burden."

He set the model's feet down gently on the damp basement floor, washing machines going, dryers going, clothes on the line, Dubrow's camouflage pants from his old army days, the guy wore them to clean his car and took a long time doing it so everybody'd see him in that uniform. Thought he was a four star, poor shit.

For once Buddy knew exactly what to do with himself, remembered as though a lesson from some admired teacher kicked in. His Italian teacher, for example, the miniature Mrs. Berardi perched on her miniature heels. There was anger and it was over and he was alive. He'd keep the kid safe make her a real breakfast teach her a lesson bring it home with woven placemats and coffee. He'd fill the creamer too, fill the sugar bowl the wife left empty, lay 'em side by side, the Midwestern centerpiece. Find where she kept the cloth napkins, utility closet probably. He'd never seen in her utility closet, which set him back a minute, the possibility of folded linens hiding from him. Never mind. Full silver and saucers under the cups—the way she'd do it. The kid would need him today, and today he would be here. He'd give her what he wanted from a wife, what they both wanted. And she'd say thanks, Dad. He had friends in high places in the good seats, and now he was with them.

"Does anything ever get dry in this basement?" Joan said.

"What?" Buddy was confused. She pointed to the pants, a splotched forest and sand dunes waving at him. He nodded.

"Mama doesn't like me down here."

"Likes being by herself, does the laundry to get away from us. Oh you didn't know that?" He ran his hand over the rough end of Celia's broken arm. "I can probably fix this. Takes a book with her and baby-sits the damn load don't come up till she cooked every sheet."

It was true. It didn't matter. The day had resumed its absent-minded humming, and Buddy floated in the silence above it. Soon the kid would understand. A wonderful breakfast, a textbook breakfast. Question was, eggs and bacon? Or oatmeal. White toast, he thought, in either case. How'd she like it? Did she even like toast? He took a breath and held it. That smell. The basement was a foreign land of women doing things to towels.

"Who does that?" He unlocked the shed door.

"Does what?"

"Laundry like she can't leave it. I get her a Maytag with a timer but you can't tell your ma, here, look for something to throw around this thing so she don't dirty herself."

"Good idea."

She was a good kid.

The shed was darker than he remembered, he turned on the miner's light he'd worn around his head so wherever he looked she'd see slices of things. Lots of crap down here, cartons with ?, MISC. SWEATERS, old toy box, wicker hamper the wife painted so many times she finally screwed it royal trying for chartreuse. He stepped on a hail of mothballs and almost slipped.

"Careful in here she got it boobied."

The electric fan was in its original box. They'd argued over it. Buddy said it looked like work and it never got installed, but with a few tools . . . kid was going through boxes. Where'd she keep things? No idea. It'd come to him, that's the thing see. You wait, things come. That train station in Milan where they didn't even make an effort to speak English, long lines of people and the train's comin' and he who studied at night school for years with the tiny Mrs. Berardi could not remember the word for train. Traino? Trainee? Gli trainini? And just when the guy was gonna shove him to the back of the line he remembered his teacher's vanilla perfume and her surprisingly low laugh and that tight little rump in a black skirt and it comes perfect. No need to mention trains. *Un bigletto per Firenze, per favori.*

"Joan? I'm gonna tell you something and never forget it. You're the captain of your own ship's destiny."

"Gee Dad, isn't there a light in here? This box, I think there's something in this box."

He was sweating. He shoulda changed his bloody shirt so nobody got the wrong idea. Shirt made him woozy but first things first and he wouldn't let her touch his cuts either. She was his one and only. She liked her toast burned black swaddled in butter sliced on the diagonal, same as him. You do the best you can, it's all borrowed time.

Kid took the corners of yellowed chenille that used to be white, used to cover the marriage bed, they shook it out together and draped it over Celia. He asked her to fix the folds and "get it just right." Metal sounds. He shoved in the padlock.

"Dad?"

"I don't want to hurt you, 'member that's the last thing I want."

"OPEN THIS DOOR!"

"I never wanted to hurt you so you gotta understand—"

"What? WHAT? OPEN THE DOOR! What are you doing? Dad? This hurts. THIS REALLY REALLY REALLY HURTS."

"It'll take time baby and Daddy's giving you time sweetheart. Hocus pocus?"

Screaming. He hadn't counted on screaming. Lay out the lessons they piss on 'em. His own mother. Half hour, hour, it'd all
be over. "You stop, somebody's gonna hear you like that."

The dark must be thick, she was bumping stuff, knocking stuff
over. "Stay still monkey." He put his cheek against the door. She
was crying. This shook him, his kid who never made with the tears.

"YOU'RE SCARING ME! THIS IS CRAZY! DADDY
OPEN THE DOOR!"

"Don't shout at me Joan. You know I don't respond to shouts."

"Please."

"It's not forever."

"How long? Is this long enough?"

"Honey, it's a father's duty to—"

"I UNDERSTAND!"

"Nobody understands nothin'."

"How long?" She was sobbing.

"I can't hold things no more, wife leaves, child leaves, a man's
gotta do something. CAN YOU UNDERSTAND? Who needed
New York? Did I need New York? Was New York a necessity?
There's reasons behind things and I gotta get to them see, that's
the only way you get peace. You air things so they don't fester."

"Mom went I didn't go it wasn't me."

"No. No. You leave me standing like some jerk at shul you go
out all night like a tramp would, that's right, no calls, nobody tells
me, I find that gold-plated window crap, and she was telling me
somthin' with that, oh yeah, there was a message in there."

Crying.

He blew his nose.

It seemed to her like a long time, but darkness took her sense of
time.

She talked to herself as the older sister of herself. It's not forever, people need their stupid clothes and they'd miss her, somebody would miss her. Sofia Fitt. She'd gone naked in that lake to make life—what was life supposed to do?

She tried to remember each thing she'd seen in the shed so it didn't become a box of spiders. Aluminum beach chairs hanging on nails. Old plastic shower curtains and the hamper. Her lilac autograph hound. If she'd danced with Mama. If. If. If. If. If. If.

Cold.

She felt for the bedspread, wrapped it around.

Imagine a house with no clocks, no watches, just a continuous TV show with two guys talking about time and you have to figure time out from these two guys. Could be three days from now, one guy says, could be a minute, the other guy says.

She remembered a box labeled BEACH THINGS and tried to picture a beach.

Don't move. Moving will make this real.

Small skittering sounds. A washing machine changed to the spin cycle.

Didn't anybody ever fucking come down here? Didn't they need their stupid fucking clothes?

Kids playing in the cement courtyard. The landlord's son, Cal, his sister, Darlene, and Nancy Notarius, who walked in her sleep, walked outside and had conversations and even laughed in the right spots. Her parents, Roy and Adrienne, double-bolted the door from the inside, but in sleep Nancy was invincible. Shimmied down porches, climbed drain pipes, walked to the Black Cat in her nightgown, ate peanuts, climbed back in bed. They called her the Houdini of Posturpedics. Joan yelled Hey! Hey! Useless. Awake Sherry was not all that bright.

She let her thumb find her mouth.

She must have slept. A ruler of light under the door woke her.
    "HEY! IN HERE!"
    "Hello?" It was Jim Dubrow.
    "Open up! I'm stuck in the shed. I got locked." She banged the door. "Over here."
    "What's this? Somebody in there?"
    "Yes! No. It's an accident."
    "You had an accident? I'll get the police. Stay still don't move. Will you need a doctor? I'm trained in survival techniques."
    "GO GET THE JANITOR HE'S GOT KEYS."
    "What?"

"GET THE JANITOR."

"The janitor."

"YES."

"You say you want a janitor."

"Yes."

"I know you, you're that Trout girl aren't you. Yeah. I'll get your dad."

"Not my dad."

"You say you don't want your dad?"

"He put me here."

"What? You crying? Oh now don't girlie, don't cry like that."

Jim Dubrow got Mrs. Dubrow who called Bessie who came with the huge Polish janitor whose wife kept cats. Nobody called the janitor unless they were freezing or the toilet plunger didn't work. The janitor said he did not have any keys to any sheds and swore and left to get certain implements.

Bessie wanted to know if Buddy did this.

"Will you tell?"

"You have to say so I can fix it."

"Nobody can. Fix it."

"Did he do this to you?"

"I don't want Mama to know."

"Can I tell Uncle Joe?"

They'd gotten used to Bessie talking to Joe inside her purse. That pearlized clutch bag was the last thing he bought her. "*Mamalah shaynalah zeesalah* why people do things we can't know. You warm in there? *Boobalah* I'll make you I'll . . . just a minute I got business."

"Don't leave!"

"I am not."

"Stay by the door."

"I'm staying right here by the door, see?" Bessie knocked. "They couldn't move me with a steam shovel. Wait. You got anything to sit? Sit. I'm not moving from you."

Joan heard the click of her purse.

"Joe you made me promise but we got troubles and you're not here and I gotta do something Joe because Winna's gone and Buddy's, well, Buddy's like you said he was, and Joe? You shoulda seen where he put the kid and what Rosie did to the shop. Ach ach. Made it a hospital where nobody gets better so then Winna paints the dummies like they're Academy Award Oscars and naked Joe, naked. So Buddy goes *mishugie* and Rose thinks he's gonna fire her and she'll have to do phone work for Sears and Roebucks again so Joe? Forgive me. I'm interfering. I know you'd do like me. Love, Bess."

Dead flies in the shop window let 'em alone, stay empty give a man some peace.

Hell, he told the wife to leave, but what kind of wife leaves? Witz's wife don't leave. Hasn't seen anything but a cleaners and his left side for thirty years. Pauvich's wife don't leave. A little brassed up for his taste and couldn't have kids, something twisted with the plumbing but she could cook. Pauvich got whole birds stuffed with fish and Viking portions of beef stuffed with pork. Pauvich's wife cooked, whole goddamned animal kingdom went into mourning.

He counted the register, not a penny off. Rose. But she was starting to bug him. It wasn't so much fun watching Rose knot up plastic bags. Woman don't make love fifteen years the plastic starts to stink. He would make things right let the wife come home to— Phone. Okay take it calm. Tell her you love her and she's beautiful and all the stuff.

"Who?"

Some creditor predator and Buddy tried to get the guy off the line get back to the cool silence of the basement but the guy wasn't buyin'.

"The wife was taking care of it and she's outta town, yeah, yeah, yeah I couldn't tell you, uh-huh look. You're not listening.

I'm saying I don't handle that end, okay? No. No. No she said she— That's not how you talk to a guy who— Yeah right, but we got history! We got— Hello?"

Over a lousy 342 bucks he could pay from the till, it was the point of the thing.

He wanted the wife home, wanted her against his skin. Wanted the old shop back Winna bustling getting a kick outta things. He'd let her order new dummies, taller dummies from bigger dummy catalogues and they'd put his crap on sale and make sense of things. Together.

He pulled cheap dresses off cheap hangers, wire hangers Rose got from Witz, and kicked them on the floor.

Classics doll, and the wife'd light up. Then he'd sit the kid down put his arms around her, it would feel good.

Buddy attacked a dressing room. Dresses inside out on the floor like kids tried 'em on, mirror printed up, why'd they have to touch it? Wasn't looking enough? He Windexed every inch, ran a carpet sweeper, dumped the old flowers, pictured their Formica kitchen table with the crumbs and rust between the drop leaf, African violets in the window, three of them at the table, and he'd make eggs to order and listen to the kid's gripes let her get it all the hell outta her system and he wouldn't get angry. No. He might feel something but he wouldn't let it out.

The second dressing room was even worse. Lipstick prints, something sticky attached to the bench he had to pry off with a scissors but he could do it, he was up to the task.

People make mistakes. All right?

He could admit it, see, that was the difference, to know you were wrong and say it. That was freedom.

He'd put red onions in the eggs, make one of those breakfast dinners maybe they'd all eat in pajamas. Then the kid does homework and he takes the wife, gently, gently takes her hand, takes her to the bedroom lets her cry it out because there'd be tears, sure, tears were needed and he'd say Honey baby doll, where'd we lose the gist?

Rose, she'd say. And he'd say Fired! just like that. Or take her to
the rib joint get a napkin let her make a fresh plan, that was the
idea see, give her the pen, see what she'd do. Or stay home and
make hash browns with the eggs and while he's cutting onions tell
'em the story of the people with all their troubles and the rabbi
got so sick of their whining he made 'em dump the problems in a
pile and pick somebody else's. Then he'd pause, the onions would
sting. Winna would guess the ending, she was smart like that. Hell
let her finish the story, tell the kid how bad off the people were
with somebody else's troubles. How they begged for their own
back. Then he'd say something like Forgiveness is the fuel of life.

Or less formal. I forgive you.

His anger? Gone. Just thinking about all that food and forgiveness made him full. He got the sticky thing off, rinsed his hands,
finished the mirror, picked up carpet lint with his hands.

Ma didn't want to be in the Home, but that's what they did in
those days. Nobody had room. Natey had room, but Ma didn't
believe in airplanes. He visited every Sunday faithful, took the
kid to that solarium had her sing a few for the *alta cockers,* she
don't remember "Thank Heaven for Little Girls," "Honey Bun,"
the little curtseys and he looks for his mother but she's not in that
sunroom. She's never in that sunroom. Checks into the home
don't get outta bed, don't eat, a few months she's gone.

He filled the steamer with distilled water.

See Winna? No iron deposits. I'm paying attention, doll, protecting the investment.

He waited for the familiar warmth and moved the hose up and
down loosening a few creases, but those dresses puffed up like
they had women inside. And now he was hearing sounds coming
from the back alley.

Nah. These walls were full a sounds. Anyways if it was Sofia
Fitt the porch women'd catch her. They got nothin' to do but sit
on their ash cans, asses and cans, he heard it again. Sofia Fitt sniffing around for access. Enough to slide an arm through.

Nah she'd never make it.

But what if she did, the Rat Bitch, wood pulling tiny strips off her knuckles, the opening flattening her breasts. Maybe knew about the kid, got the wrong idea.

"Who's that? What the hell you want? I got a gun don't fool with me."

He had in his hand, of all things, a Swiss Army knife. He stared at the tiny cross, pulled out the largest blade. Ridiculous. No better than grass. He walked around with the foolish blade. Hello? Hello? Then some vague woodsy lesson came to him and he made himself bigger than he was. HELLO? She'd see his blade and laugh. How'd she get so familiar with his life anyway?

He searched everything. The best he could find was a volunteer elm brushing the alley window, skinny and with half the leaves laced away by insects. And then he thought, what if she doesn't come home. Irwina. What if she gets on a train and keeps goin'?

And he had to throw cold water on his face, run some through his hair to stop the whip whip of buildings lashing by, electrically tangled wires shooting city juice, towers of water, vats of water, vast storehouses of water pa-pumping through rural fields. A country kid making a day of sticks.

Winna go find the conductor. HAS ANYBODY SEEN THE CONDUCTOR?

Why? What's wrong?

Tell him to stop the train.

I can't.

You gotta.

Where is he?

I hafta tell you everything? In the dining car. They're always in the dining car. Go! Tell him you got family!

STOP THIS CAR!

It's a train lady, the conductor says, it don't stop til Rattoon.

Winna you never get it right.

I'm sorry.

You are?

Yes really.

She'd have to throw a fit to stop an Amtrak, how many men to hold her down? Shut her up with a free pork chop? Kick her off to Greyhound? Those guys were trained, they could handle the cases. She's stepping off the platform in some backroad town of casseroles and horseshoes and Lilt perms belted together under the sanctity of corn.

"Aw doll, we got so much to say! Come home! First off, the nighty thing? You were beautiful. You were! Gorgeous! I don't know why I didn't bite. Come to me, we got talking."

Twenty-Eight

I RWINA TOOK A CAB from O'Hare and got a driver who didn't speak English. She found a crumpled paper in her purse and wrote out her address. He smoothed the paper with exaggerated, treasure-map gestures and looked at her in the rearview like she soiled on something holy.

"1-6-2-3 Lunt?" he said.

"Yes. You can take the drive straight to Sheridan then—"

"Sherry Dun?"

"Yes. Then I'd go with Touhy or Pratt."

"Ptooey." He laughed to the photograph tied around his sun visor with purple yarn. Three dark-eyed boys and a woman, a wife probably. The boys looked like the wife and they all looked they'd spent a lifetime staring at fire.

"Do *not* take Morse Avenue," but he was driving, a plan set in his head. She took off her shoes, rubbed her feet, and tried to think how she'd explain spending all this money and bringing back undergarments she could have ordered with one phone call. The driver took Morse. Well fine. She'd tell Buddy she couldn't pull off a miracle every time and that New York had been glorious. New York was filled with ideas. That's it, ideas. Let him roll his eyes. They passed the Frock Shop. The empty window, the CLOSED sign.

"Stop!"

His brake was so immediate her cheek slammed into the back of his seat.

"This?" He pointed at the shop.

"Yes. I need my suitcase." She made a square sign with her hands.

"This?" He pointed again, incredulous.

"Yes."

He pulled out the crumpled paper. "This not this."

She pushed the last of her money into his hand. He glanced at the photo of his wife and children. Take it, the wife said, they are foolish in this country, heads of air and fishtails.

Irwina could hear him muttering from the trunk. Her feet had swollen and she couldn't get her shoes back on. There was a sugar dust of snow. The driver opened her door and looked at her feet as if he wanted to help them. He insisted on carrying the suitcase.

"Shopping?" They both looked at the dark store window.

"No this is fine, thank you." She had nothing more to give.

He set down her luggage and banged on the door.

"Nobody."

"No I know, it's okay."

Fifteen years and never once had they closed on a workday. They'd outlived sickness, competitors, private battles, zero cash flow, low inventory, slander, school-closing snowstorms, lack of faith, disappearing customers and the monotony that flared from watching oneself perform the same tasks day after day but always, always, one of them opened the shop. There was a box outside the door. Enormous, heavy looking, smothered in three-cent stamps, return address, Sufi Sid.

The driver refused to leave until he understood this was actually her store, that she had a key, this barefooted woman who overpaid him. He put her suitcase inside, carried in the box, nodded to her with something like respect.

Dead flies in the window and that's all.

No, flecks of gold.

Piles of clothes on the floor, clothes off hangers, sweaters flung like thieves on horses had left them for dead. But there was money in the register. Didn't make sense. And where were her models? Where was everybody? She looked for the cab driver, gone, took the cash, folded it into her coin purse. The steamer was still warm.

Inside the box no note and lots of gauzy material. She pulled and kept pulling, enough material to carpet the shop. Small flowers were stitched here and there. She ran her fingers over the leaves. Hand work. Delicate work, vivid colors that must have taken somebody forever. The flowers made her sad. She felt something underneath. Poles? Stakes? This was a tent. My god the turban sent her a tent the size of Highland Park and for an instant she saw herself inside the thing, sun pushing color through blowsy walls. What would she do in a tent? Lay on her belly see the city through insect eyes? The peace, the quiet. Would her senses get keen? Her body function like a dog whose master was in trouble? She wanted to dump it, but the hand stitching . . . She called Bessie.

A rush of emotion made her dizzy without understanding.

She held the receiver out from her ear. Bessie was wet with information.

"What? What?"

Phone goo. Irwina forced her mind to step in it, make order. She picked up the blue receipt pad and wrote 1-2-3-4-5 down the left side.

"Bess I can't understand you when you talk so fast."

She was crying, swearing, invoking dead relatives, but events were emerging. Irwina wrote:

1. Well Shaken

Joan was at Bessie's, she was okay, well but shaken. Okay? Okay from what? A flash of her child as a martini in blackness. She put the pen down.

"I didn't mean to get in no middle but she's somethin' that

kid, sitting here by me like nothin' happened, but I saw it and it was filth—"

"How long?"

"I don't know."

"Hours? Days?"

"A couple hours not even. Jim Dubrow got the janitor, and the janitor he didn't have a key so they had to—"

"Say what you said again. Who told you? Did she tell you?"

"She don't want you to know. I heard her cryin'. We got that Pollack galumph—"

"The janitor."

"—found her with that thing in there."

"Thing? What thing?"

"One of those dummies you ritzed up. Somebody locked me in the dark I'd be a basket."

"And Buddy?"

"Buddy I don't know, home I guess. You gonna get the kid?"

Of course she'd come, what did Bessie think? Of course she'd get the child. Irwina tore off what she'd written and put it in her purse.

Snow. She had no shoes.

She went back in the shop and remembered to call a cab. Ten minutes? Fine. She'd be the woman in the black coat walking east on Morse. No, really, she couldn't wait in the store. (Don't yell, it's not Yellow Cab's fault.) The child could rest in a cab and she'd get her to talk, hold her, see her eyes. Buddy. The window. The child took the rage meant for her. With Hush Puppies she could run against the wind. She'd undo everything. She'd do something. Do what? The shop and the child had been their only language for fifteen years. She had everything to say and nothing to say it with.

Twenty-Nine

"ARE WE LEAVING HIM?" Joan said.

"Don't make this harder." Mama had her hands over her stomach. "Those magic games of his you know they were for you. Dangerous exploding things you had to ignite. I want you to know, I did not approve of his tricks. He did it anyway. He did it from love."

"What time's he getting home?"

"Six-thirty. Or so. He made a pit stop. He sounded okay."

"Did he say—"

"He sounded sorry."

"He said he was sorry?"

Mama held a match to the bottom of white candles, enough warmth to set them firmly in silver holders. She spit on her fingers and pressed the flame out. "I could tell by his tone, you think this is silly don't you, this is stupid but it's not the dinner per se, it's the sitting down and getting him off his track. I shout he shouts louder, I leave he finds me. Do you see where I'm going?"

A mother's logic. It made sense if you stood by a stove, but outside it wouldn't hold shit.

"You don't know."

"For three hours I've been knowing and honestly, Pie? I'm not sure how much more I can know. All right look. We're not losing our minds over this. We are not. I know the shed was an awful, terrible awful horrible thing. I know this. Believe me. I know."

"You don't."

"What you must have gone through."

And other things Mom. Blurry, sea-salted things. My diary smells like his fingers. He takes us in pieces so nobody can see.

"Who knows him like a wife? He'll come home sorry, he'll be tired, he'll eat, he'll sleep. When did you get tall? Look at you, you're taller than me. You take after his side but you've got my forehead." She took Joan's hands. "If I could make it go away." Brought the hands to her lips and kissed each one, slow, with her eyes closed. It looked like the face girls made practice kissing their own fists, giving each other romance grades.

"It's okay. Mom. It's okay."

"I'm telling you something don't walk away. He locked you up because you scare him. No, that's right. Nobody scares him like you."

"Sofia Fitt does."

"Well she scares everyone."

Mama chopped carrots, the butter slow melting. She poured honey from the jar, catching the drip with her finger, licking it. *Tzimis.* She'd add raisins and almond slivers. The sweetness of carrots and she was naming the good things Buddy did. The Schwinn, skating at Rainbow, a typewriter when other kids . . . she talked like he was a decent man and far away. "And when you had your tonsils out—"

"Don't."

"It's never one way."

"This was."

"You find the bad in things."

"Where's the good?"

"I understand the components of your father's temper."

"Components."

"That's right."

"Let's go, let's grab stuff and get outta here now before he comes home."

"And what. And go where. With what money. You have no idea how the world operates."

And you do.

Flipping carrots, circles of black around the edges, soft in the middle. The apartment had good smells. It needed a good family to eat them. A family who fought over doing dishes like Mr. Slater who said the cook never cleans and squeezed his big hands into living gloves. It needed the grease of Lil's *gribinis* and Mrs. Dubrow's pig's foot soup to keep things moving.

"But I want you in your room when he gets here and I'll get you. What. What's with that face? Look I am not a miracle worker! I am not Gunga Dinn!"

"We can leave later, when he's sleeping."

"Tonight, later, I can't run on the street demanding a new life. Think Joan. Think. And I have you."

"Don't Mom."

"What."

"Fight him."

She was counting things on her fingers. "Food, shelter, car, money, work, and there will be mornings and there will be nights, you don't realize, I've never been alone in my life. Not for one day. I went straight from Ma to your dad. So." She opened the cabinet, stared at cans, shut it. "And then I've got you."

"You said that."

"God I need a nap."

"What?"

She took the potato bowl from the fridge, covered it with Saran Wrap, put it back. "What was I saying?"

"Sleep is not a good idea."

"Oh. I remember. Try not to be afraid. I'm putting the meatloaf in at 375, the buzzer goes off you're to take it out and let it settle for at least ten minutes."

"How long do you have to sleep? I don't think—"

"This is extremely important. Meat cuts better when it's had a chance to settle." She shut off the carrots and covered them.

"You shouldn't sleep."

"If I'm going to have an effect. And I'm exhausted from the trip, don't forget."

Joan followed her mother to the bedroom.

She was already in bed, turning to the wall, telling the wall "I'll wake one of those mornings you poke out your head and nothing pokes back. You know? You don't know."

"It's night."

"A soundless Dave Garroway morning oh I love those men behind that desk with those big clocks. New York, London, Tokyo, Paris. Dave raises his right hand, you know every morning I put my hand over his, I do Pie, when you're at school I feel Dave's PEACE through the screen."

She was drifting.

Maybe Bessie gave her a relax-a-pill, maybe that's what she handed Mama when they left. Bessie had wanted Joan to stay. They argued, they hugged her, the sisters were extremely upset and Rose kept calling but nobody had time for Rose. They kept asking Joan what happened then wouldn't let her say. Bessie put out herring in cream sauce and sat at the table scratching her belly. The world was Bessie's bathroom. Joan couldn't eat. Maybe a Hostess Snowball, something where the skin could be coaxed off whole. Celia was beat up down there she told them, and it was so dark. But it was impossible to explain a dark like that. They started talking in Yiddish and she drank more water and they wanted to know if he hit her, hurt her in any way and kept looking for marks and seemed disappointed not to find any. Bessie put out a plate of rye toast. Half a piece, try. Joan asked for thirds on the water so they wouldn't take her with a grain, but they were mouthing off in Yiddish again.

She sat on her cousin Donnie's old bed under a bulletin board with his pennants and clippings.

Donnie in his basketball uniform, taller than the coach. She ran her fingers up and down the orange corduroy bedspread, its rows predictable and constant. Cynthia was divorcing Donnie and he was giving up law for a deep-dish pizza business, dating a series of *Playboy* bunnies whose photos Joan had found covered with X's and O's in the back of his Corvette. Bessie never changed Donnie's room, never sent Joe's suits to B'nai Brith.

"Hugh and Dave are Rogers Park boys, I could find them in my sleep," Mama was saying.

Buddy would be home soon. Joan sang a TV kid song in her head: *Yoo hoo, it's me, my name is Pinky Lee. With my checkered hat and my checkered coat and my silly laugh like a Billy Goat* . . . Are you sleeping Ma?"

"Mmmm."

"Can I get in?"

"Mmmm."

The bed still had a cool side. Joan found her mother's body, put her feet beneath hers and, because she was sleeping, threw an arm around her waist and pulled her in closer. So light, so nothing to her. She comforted herself with what they'd take. Simple clothes that could be washed in a sink with foil packets of Woolite. Travel toothbrushes. Her mother's bottom inched back till it found her belly. There was some old friend in Cape May with a house by the sea. Maybe go there. What was her name? Gazeena. Gazeena by the sea.

Thirty

THINGS IN THE BED where Mama had been. A coin purse with a gold shard and a hundred-dollar bill inside, a large box with stamps nearly covering her mother's name. The dribs of evening clung to gold flecks in the wallpaper, and the room seemed lit by tiny fires. She heard Buddy, shoved the box in the closet, the purse in her underpants and pretended to be sleeping. His weight tipped the bed.

"I seen this comin' so don't go crying what happened Daddy? Where'd she go Daddy? Why didn't you stop her Daddy 'cause I seen and I'm tellin' you— You gonna cry on me? Good. Don't."

Joan bit the pillowcase. He lay down beside her.

"Made some calls to the downtown boys so she's around they're gonna find her."

No. They won't.

He had Mama's lipstick and compact in his fist, her familiars, and Joan wanted them. The coin purse dug into her side. She wanted to cry, was crying somewhere squeezed down because to cry in front of Buddy was to lose. And she couldn't lose anymore. She would wait. Like she waited on the hall steps for Mama to come home, waited when she swam past lifeguards, past that raft of guys sunning in Speedos. Waited when she pulled all-nighters like a college kid but only studied the window. Wait, he will sleep.

IFT the compact said and it was open, she could see the metal center where the powder had worn to a smile, mistakes in the etching like the engraver's hand shook.

What happened next would become one motion in memory. Reaching for Mama's familiars, Buddy shooting off the bed, throwing them out the window, Mr. Slater across the courtyard in his undershirt holding something close to his chest, streetlights going on at once, Lil at the table, Leon, her father's face.

Wait and he will sleep. And when he did, Joan took nothing but the box because she could think of nothing else to take. In the snow she found the broken compact, the lipstick and applied these without looking, pressing her lips together, applying again, taking herself out of the neighborhood.

At the corner of Jarvis and the lake, Joan opened the box with the edge of a key, pulling out poles and wads of what she finally identified as shelter. A tent. A tent was simple. It breathed. This one had flowers she didn't recognize embroidered here and there to save her from whiteness. She knew where she'd sleep that night.

Joan pitched it in the sand of Jarvis Beach clearing rocks, smoothing down the cotton floor, paying no attention to strangers asking, offering, laughing. Her arms and legs could touch a ceiling and walls. No door, no key to open it. No windows to see and be seen. One stake missing. A corner blew up and down all night and alley cats sang songs from Jupiter.

Joan woke freezing. Make it summer, early and hot. Today would be a scorcher. The Cubs would play a double-header against the Giants, and they'd sell out of cold beer. A dog walker passed, her face swathed like an Arab. Make her part of the plan.

She knew the lifeguard who came every summer. Pete. He'd ignore her, looking instead at his fine brown arms, his suit to make sure of something. He went to Mather. She knew how he'd arrange himself on the perch and follow girls under his sunglasses without moving his head. Knew how fast he'd enter the lake in case of emergency, blowing his whistle and yelling, as if that ever saved anyone.

She had more keys than a janitor: bike key, skate key, Sofia Fitt's, Bessie's. She would not go back to Buddy. She knew how to wait, knew what time hot-dog vendor Harry would show up with his metal cart, slicing tomatoes thin as rose webs. And she knew the lake, had touched its map of dips and sandbars, had lived through the moods of its waves.